LADY CATHERINE'S DEMANDS

ELIZA AUSTIN

Boldwood

First published in 2013 as *Colonel Fitzwilliam's Dilemma*. This edition published in Great Britain in 2024 by Boldwood Books Ltd.

Cover Design by Colin Thomas

Cover Photography: Colin Thomas

A CIP catalogue record for this book is available from the British Library.

Paperback ISBN 978-1-83603-200-7

Large Print ISBN 978-1-83603-199-4

Hardback ISBN 978-1-83603-198-7

Ebook ISBN 978-1-83603-201-4

Kindle ISBN 978-1-83603-202-1

Audio CD ISBN 978-1-83603-193-2

MP3 CD ISBN 978-1-83603-194-9

Digital audio download ISBN 978-1-83603-196-3

Boldwood Books Ltd
23 Bowerdean Street
London SW6 3TN
www.boldwoodbooks.com

1

'We have cause for celebration.' Fitzwilliam Darcy looked up from the letter he was reading and smiled across the breakfast table at his wife.

'We do?' Lizzy returned his smile.

'Absolutely. We are restored to favour.'

'I was unaware we were out of favour.'

'Lady Catherine is to pay us a visit.'

'Ah, I see.' Lizzy arched a brow. 'And to what do we owe this sudden change of heart? I was of the opinion that I am disobliging and selfish, unworthy of her notice.'

'No!' Georgiana and Kitty were seated together on the opposite side of the table. They shared a glance, but it was Fitzwilliam's sister Georgiana who cried out in passionate defence of Lizzy's character. 'Never. Not you, Lizzy.'

'Thank you, Georgie, but your aunt doesn't share your good opinion of me, and nor will she. Not ever. In agreeing to become your brother's wife I apparently demeaned the Darcy name beyond redemption.'

'Lady Catherine wanted Fitzwilliam for her daughter and isn't used to being gainsaid. It was the silliest notion in the world, of course. Anyone with eyes in their head could see the union would never have worked.' Georgiana wrinkled her nose. 'Anyone except Lady Catherine, that is. She has always been blinded by her determination to have her own way.'

'Well, it sounds as though Lady Catherine has come to her senses,' Kitty Bennet, Lizzy's younger sister, said.

'I doubt that. She was quite adamant that I placed a permanent blight upon the estate the moment I became Pemberley's mistress.'

'She has clearly realised her mistake,' Will replied. 'And wishes to tell us so in person.'

'Surely that is unnecessary?' Georgiana looked crestfallen. 'She terrifies me.'

'I have never met her.' Kitty flashed a wary smile as she buttered a second slice of toast. 'But from what I have heard about her, I am sure she will disapprove of everything I do.'

'Does she give a reason for her visit?' Lizzy asked. 'Although I can probably guess.'

'She is in raptures over your condition.' Will fixed Lizzy with an intimate smile. 'And wishes to heal the breach between us.'

Lizzy tossed her head. 'That is very generous of her, considering it was she who created the breach in the first place.'

'Be that as it may, I cannot refuse to let her come.'

'No, of course not, and I would not have you do so.' Lizzy paused. 'She heard about the forthcoming addition to our family from Charlotte Collins, presumably.'

'No, I wrote to inform her of it myself.'

'Oh, you didn't mention it.' And Lizzy knew why her husband had remained silent on the point. If Lady Catherine had continued to cut Lizzy, Will would have preferred her not to know his olive branch had been ignored. Will, much as he would deny it if quizzed upon the subject, was more disturbed by the rift with his aunt than he would ever admit. 'When can we expect her?'

'In about a week. They plan to make the journey in easy stages.'

'My cousin Anne will accompany her?' Georgiana asked. 'And Mrs Jenkinson too, I presume? Anne can never go anywhere without her faithful companion to fuss over her.'

'Georgie! That was almost a discourteous remark. I am sure Lady Catherine will say my bad influence is rubbing off on you if she hears you speak so flippantly.' Lizzy sent the younger woman a warm smile. 'I, on the other hand, am very pleased with you. It proves you have already learned not to take everything you see at face value.'

'Oh, Lizzy, you know I didn't mean anything by it. It is just that I sometimes think Anne is stifled by the constant attention she receives from Lady Catherine and Mrs Jenkinson. She is so busy trying to live up to people's expectations that she has no time to be herself.' Georgiana sighed. 'Poor Anne. As if being heiress to such an extensive estate as Rosings isn't enough of a burden. I should have hated to find myself in that position at Pemberley.'

Lizzy, who had thought much the same thing during her infamous visit to Rosings, was surprised by Georgiana's perspicacity.

'Mrs Jenkinson will not form part of their party.' Will waved Lady Catherine's letter across the table. 'My aunt dedicates a considerable part of her missive to complaining about her ill-usage at that particular lady's hands.'

'Good heavens,' Lizzy said. 'Has there been a falling out? I thought Lady Catherine and Mrs Jenkinson were of one mind on all matters.'

'It seems blood is thicker than water. One of Mrs Jenkinson's nieces has married rather well and required a governess for her growing family. Mrs Jenkinson felt unable to turn the position down.'

'From which one must surmise the niece didn't marry *that* well and played upon her aunt's strong family values to acquire a good governess at no cost.'

'Oh dear.' Georgiana's eyes danced with mirth. 'I still have a lot to learn from you, Lizzy. That idea would not have occurred to me.'

'I can assure you it has occurred to our aunt,' Will replied, 'and she had a very great deal to say about undutiful servants who have no sense of loyalty.'

'Shall Lady Catherine and her daughter travel alone, Mr Darcy?' Kitty asked.

'No, they are to be accompanied by a gentleman.'

Lizzy groaned. 'Not Mr Collins, please.'

'No, my dear, not Mr Collins but a Mr Asquith.'

'Asquith?' Lizzy wrinkled her brow. 'I have heard that name before. It came up in my correspondence with Charlotte Collins but I cannot think—'

'According to Lady Catherine, he is a gentleman in straitened circumstances. He applied to Mr Collins for a position at the church school. Collins sought Lady Catherine's advice on the matter naturally—'

'Oh, naturally,' Lizzy replied, sharing a smile with Kitty.

'Lady Catherine insisted upon meeting the young man for herself, since she likes to concern herself with all the details of life in her part of Kent,' Will said. 'He had been recommended to her as well apparently, although she does not say by whom.'

'It must have been someone whose opinion she respected,' Lizzy mused. 'Or there again, perhaps she simply wanted to have the final say.'

'Which she did. She was so taken with Asquith that she engaged him as Mrs Jenkinson's replacement.'

'Anne de Bourgh has a male tutor.' Lizzy was shocked. 'I can scarce believe it, although I am sure it will do her the world of good.'

'I dare say there is a maid present at all their tutorials,' Will replied, 'but it seems Asquith is well-educated, well-travelled, sensible, and deferential. He will travel with them and make all the necessary arrangements for their comfort at the various posting inns on their route.'

'And Lady Catherine's coachman could not have done that for her?' Lizzy lifted her shoulders. 'Still, I confess to a great curiosity about the young man and look forward to making Mr Asquith's acquaintance. Although any man who meets with Lady Catherine's approval will, of course, be meek and obsequious. Anne will be in no danger of corruption from contact with him, I am absolutely sure of at least that much.'

'Do you not find this departure on Lady Catherine's part intriguing?' Will asked. 'I, for one, would never have predicted it.'

'Nor I,' Lizzy agreed. 'And I anticipate being entertained by it, especially since I recall now that Charlotte told me Mr Collins was quite put out by Mr Asquith's elevation to Lady Catherine's inner circle.'

'Ah, now this starts to make more sense.' Will frowned as he continued to read. 'It seems Colonel Fitzwilliam can be spared from his duties, and Lady Catherine has asked us to invite him to stay also.' He looked up from his letter, caught Lizzy's eye, and his frown gave way to a smile. 'Clearly he is now the favoured candidate for Anne's hand, and she needs our help to persuade Fitzwilliam to see the advantages in such a match, although she would never admit to it of course.'

'She thinks you will encourage the colonel, I suppose,' Lizzy said.

'Then she is in for a disappointment. Fitzwilliam is his own man, and I wouldn't seek to influence him, even if I thought it would do any good.'

'Are we expected to promote the romance during their stay at Pemberley, regardless of the feelings of those involved?' Lizzy exhaled. 'In any case, invite the colonel by all means. I enjoy his society, even though I cannot help feeling sorry for his situation.'

'Save your sympathy, Lizzy. As I say, Fitzwilliam will not be coerced into a situation that doesn't suit him, no matter how desperate his circumstances.'

'Well, in that case I shall not interfere and will allow true love to take its course. Speaking of which...' She turned towards Georgiana and Kitty with a mischievous smile. 'If Colonel Fitzwilliam can be spared, I dare say Major Halstead and Captain Turner are due for a furlough as well.'

Both girls brightened and then blushed at the mention of those gentlemen's names. They had been guests at Lizzy's first house party as mistress of Pemberley, six weeks previously, and had found great favour with Georgiana and Kitty. Will was still dubious about the major's suitability for his sister, but Lizzy reasoned no man who took an interest in Georgiana would ever pass muster in her brother's eyes.

'Do you think so?' Georgiana asked with such feigned casualness, Lizzy burst out laughing.

'I am sure there is every possibility. I shall write and invite Colonel Fitzwilliam and extend the invitation to include his two friends. It will be so much easier to entertain Lady Catherine if others are present.'

'I will not have you over-exerting yourself,' Will replied, fixing Lizzy with a stern look.

'Oh, nonsense. I am as strong as an ox. Besides, since we are not going to London for the season, it seems only fair the girls should have their share of entertainments.'

'And Jane and Mr Bingley are now close by,' Kitty reminded them all. 'I dare say they will not wish to leave Campton Park for very long, having only just moved into their new estate. But since it is only ten miles away, the journey will not be much of an inconvenience.'

'Jane's condition is more advanced than mine, Kitty. We cannot expect her to gallivant all over the place just to oblige us.'

'No, of course not, but when she hears of your plans, I am sure she will wish to come.'

'Have you left your card with our new neighbours yet?' Will asked Lizzy.

'Actually, Georgie and I planned to call this morning.'

'I know Lord Briar and think well of him. I am glad he will be living so close. By all means, include him in our entertainments if you find their society congenial.'

'Thank you. I am sure I shall, and Lady Catherine can hardly object to such eminent company.'

Will stood up, leaned over Lizzy, and kissed her brow. 'Excuse me, my dear. I have business with my steward.'

Georgiana sighed as she watched her brother leave the room. 'I still can't get over the way Fitzwilliam now displays so much affection towards you in public,' she said. 'I never would have imagined him to be so openly demonstrative. He always seemed so severe before his marriage, but now I see a very different side of him.'

Lizzy wanted to say that if Will had shown even half as much affection for her in company as he did in private before their previous house party, then a very great deal of mischief on the part of Miss Bingley and Mr Wickham could have been avoided. Instead, she smiled and made no reply.

'You won't let Lady Catherine interfere in my affairs, will you, Lizzy?' Georgiana seemed suddenly anxious. 'She will insist upon knowing what is best for me, and I don't have the courage to stand up to her.'

Lizzy patted her hand. 'Fear not. She already thinks so ill of me that the blame for anything you do to displease her will be lodged at my door.'

'Oh, but that would not be fair.'

'No, perhaps not, but Lady Catherine's censure cannot harm me.'

'I too received a letter this morning from Mama,' Kitty said. 'She feels very left out of things now Jane and Mr Bingley have moved to Derbyshire, and I am here as well. She seems to think you and Jane will need her support when your confinements get closer.'

Lizzy suppressed a shudder. That was the very last thing she required, and she had already told her mother so, in very direct terms. She now appeared to be trying less direct means of eliciting an invitation. Georgiana had spoken the truth when she said Will was now a far less severe, more tolerant person, but she was absolutely certain that new latitude would not extend to Lizzy's mother if she came for a protracted stay. She would speak with Jane about it. Between them they would devise a means of keeping her away from Derbyshire, even if it meant applying to their father for his intervention.

It seemed cruel, but Lizzy didn't feel equal to subjecting her husband to her mother's inane chatter at such a happy time in their marriage. If Mama arrived, there would be no getting rid of her for weeks, and God help her, the prospect appalled Lizzy almost as much as it would horrify Will. She had never been her mother's favourite daughter, and her refusal to accept Mr Collins's offer of marriage had caused a serious rift between them. Now that she was married to Mr Darcy, she could do no wrong in her mother's eyes, and Lizzy found it hard to forgive such transparency.

'Come, Georgie,' she said, sighing. 'If we are to call on Lady Briar, we ought to get ourselves ready.'

'I shall be but a moment,' Georgiana replied, putting aside her napkin and standing up.

'Are you sure you don't want to come too, Kitty?' Lizzy asked.

'Quite sure, thank you. I have a letter to write and a sketch of the lake I particularly want to finish while the light is right this morning.'

2

Anne de Bourgh barely noticed the discomfort when their carriage passed over a rough piece of road and the wheels caught in a deep rut, rocking the conveyance on its springs and jolting its occupants. She was completely taken up by the melodic timbre of Mr Asquith's voice as he related tales about his adventures in the Indies. He had travelled to so many exciting places, seen so many things, and met so many interesting people. She, on the other hand, had been nowhere. In fact, she hadn't very often left Kent. Her health was too frail for any unnecessary risks to be taken with it. As Mama was so fond of reminding her, considerable responsibilities would one day fall to her lot.

As if she could forget!

'Those people sound like savages, Mr Asquith,' she said, gasping. 'Were you not afraid for your life?'

Mr Asquith smiled his beautiful, gentle smile and Anne felt her face flood with colour. He was such a handsome man, so charming, so well informed, so non-judgemental, and so tolerant of her many weaknesses. It would be so very easy to fall in love with him, and what a commotion that would cause.

'Not in the least. I was accompanying Master Harry back to his father's plantation. Sir Marius looks after his slaves well, and they have no reason to complain. I have always found if you treat people fairly, they react in like fashion, Miss de Bourgh. It is my opinion people are not born evil or deceitful, usually they become so out of severe necessity.'

'Do you really think so?' Anne sat forward, feeling none of the breathlessness this simple exertion would once have caused her. 'How extraordinary. I do not have your worldly experience, of course, but have often thought the same thing. I don't suppose all poor people are thieves or malingerers, and they would much prefer to find honest work in order to provide for their families if they possibly could.'

'Quite so.' Mr Asquith nodded as though she had made some remarkably deep, insightful statement and he concurred with her opinion. Earning his approval, even if she wasn't sure she deserved it, gave Anne a ridiculous amount of pleasure. 'Since talk of slavery being abolished has become so widespread, many informed people believe it will eventually happen, despite so much opposition to the move. I know Sir Marius hopes to persuade his slaves to remain with him in paid positions when the time comes, and I dare say they will wish to do so.'

'Because they know they are well off and have no cause for complaint,' Mama said briskly.

'Quite so, Lady Catherine. That is certainly true in the case of Sir Marius's plantation. Almost all of his slaves seem rather content with their lot.'

'Then perhaps he is too tolerant and ought to work them harder.'

Anne tried not to feel jealous when Mr Asquith bestowed one of his dazzling smiles upon her mama. 'I believe a willing worker will always be more productive. I saw that for myself while on Sir

Marius's property. Some of the wretched creatures on adjoining plantations were not treated nearly so well and were unable to work so hard as a consequence.'

'Hmm, perhaps.'

As the carriage rattled along, Anne glanced out of the window. She was unsurprised that Mr Asquith had the last word in this exchange with her mama, as he so often seemed to. It was rather extraordinary when one thought about it. Mama was nothing if not forthright in the expression of her opinions, but Mr Asquith made his point with such charm and deference, even Mama couldn't find fault with his manner. He wasn't afraid of Mama. She appeared to respect his courage and intellect, just as Anne had always thought Mama privately respected Eliza Bennet, now Mrs Darcy, for standing up to her during her visit to Rosings last year. So few people challenged her opinions that Mama didn't always know how to react when it actually happened.

Mrs Darcy. Anne briefly closed her eyes, revelling in her narrow escape. For years, she had known Mama intended that title for her. She had dreaded the day when it would come to pass, as she was sure it would, because everyone always did what Mama required of them. Frankly, Mr Darcy frightened her. He was so severe, so... well, so everything she was not. He did not love her, but she had always supposed he wouldn't be able to resist having Rosings as well as Pemberley beneath his stewardship. The very thought of sharing her life with such an aloof person had made her perpetually unwell, and she was heartily grateful to Mrs Darcy for saving her from a situation that would have made her even more invisible than she already was.

But her relief had been short-lived. This visit to Pemberley, ostensibly to heal the rift between Mama and the Darcys, had actually been arranged so that Colonel Fitzwilliam could admire her.

Admire? Humiliation washed through Anne. She would be the first to admit she was no beauty. She possessed few talents and even less conversation. People made her so nervous, and she never knew quite what to say to them. Besides, her mother seldom left her with an opportunity to speak for herself. Even so, all and sundry plied her with compliments, simply because of who she was. It was all so shallow, so pointless. Anne abhorred being the centre of attention. She abhorred false flattery even more.

She wasn't supposed to be aware of her mother's efforts to bring her and the colonel together, but she had overheard Mama discussing it with Mrs Collins. The colonel frightened her almost as much as Mr Darcy did, but she knew he could not afford to turn his back on her any more than Anne could refuse to do her duty. Dear God, why could she not have been born a farmer's daughter, where she would at least have had some say in her own future?

Anne glanced across at Mr Asquith, seated with his limbs elegantly arranged and his back to the horses, smiling at something her mother had just said. Oh, how she wished things were different. She knew nothing of Mr Asquith's family. He was very reticent on the subject, and strangely, to Anne's precise knowledge, Mama had not made too many enquiries in that respect. Not that any were necessary. It was obvious to anyone with eyes in their head that he was a gentleman without means. His education, his manners, his refined tone, and his elegant way of conducting himself all attested to that fact. If only Anne was free to please herself… Of course, she never would be and so there was little point in having regrets.

'Are you warm enough, Anne?'

Her mother's voice jolted Anne out of her reverie. It was amusing; until recently, she was constantly being asked that question, but hadn't noticed it was being posed far less regularly since Mrs

Jenkinson had left. When Mr Asquith had first arrived at Rosings, she heard her mother explain to him about her frail state of health, informing him that under no circumstances was she to be over-exerted. Anne gleaned a lot of information by listening to her mother's conversations. Mama had a lot to say on every conceivable subject, whereas Anne was so quiet people often forgot she was in the room. That had proven very useful on more than one occasion. Mr Asquith had merely raised a brow. He said he was sure that was a temporary situation and, as Miss de Bourgh grew older, her health would most likely improve. No one had ever suggested she would outgrow her maladies. They usually rushed to agree with her mother's assessment of Anne's situation, sympathised, and then pampered her.

Mr Asquith did not do any of those things, and it was a liberating experience.

'How many more days shall we have on the road, Mr Asquith?' she asked.

Anne had always found travelling exceedingly tiring, but then she had never travelled with such a compelling companion before. Enclosed in a comfortable carriage, with just her Mama and Mr Asquith for company, put a very different light on matters, and she wished the journey could go on indefinitely. Better yet, she dared to pretend, at least in her own head, that it was just her and Mr Asquith making the journey and that his glamorous smiles were all for her. She absolutely did not wish to face what awaited her at the end of this particular road, so she put it out of her mind.

'Two more nights should see us in Derbyshire, Miss de Bourgh.'

Only two nights? Anne sighed. It hardly seemed fair.

* * *

Joshua Fitzwilliam received Eliza Darcy's letter of invitation with a mixture of pleasure and a sigh of inevitability. He had used regimental manoeuvres as a legitimate reason to decline an invitation from Lady Catherine to visit Rosings the previous month, knowing full well why his presence was required there. Darcy had had the temerity to scupper Lady Catherine's carefully laid plans by marrying Eliza instead of their cousin Anne, and now Joshua was expected to take up the role of heir apparent.

He moved to the sideboard, poured himself a substantial measure of brandy, and indulged in a second sigh. Part of him wondered what the devil was the matter with him. Marriage to Anne, procuring stewardship of a grand estate such as Rosings, would see an end to his financial problems. It would be a solution the majority of men would snatch up with both hands.

Unfortunately, Joshua had an annoying penchant for not following the majority.

He didn't have feelings for Anne, but how many people in his situation could afford the luxury of marrying for love? Darcy had done so, and Joshua tried not to envy him his good fortune. With her flashing eyes and irreverent attitude, Eliza was one of the few women in England with the fortitude and will to induce his cousin to unbend as he embraced married life. Indeed, he had seen remarkable changes in Darcy when attending his house party just a few short weeks ago. And now their union was to be blessed with a child.

Don't think about Darcy, he told himself, *or Eliza, either*. If he thought about the woman he had been so attracted to the first time he met her, it would get him nowhere. That was his secret; his cross to bear in solitude.

And so he returned his thoughts to Lady Catherine and her stark determination to see him wed to her daughter. It would indeed mean he would be set for life, but not on his own terms. Lady Catherine might live for many more years yet and was not the sort of person who would give up the reins of management until she was in her dotage. Worse, she would assume she could interfere in his marriage and tell Joshua how to behave. That was as unacceptable as resigning his commission would be, but both situations would have to be confronted if he decided to oblige his aunt.

Not all love matches endured, he reminded himself. His own brother had married a woman he was besotted with, assuming his regard was returned. She had married him, it transpired, for his title and position, thinking he was well set-up. Nothing could have been further from the truth, but Joshua's sister-in-law had still run through what blunt his brother did possess in less than no time. Tobias did nothing to prevent her for fear of losing her non-existent regard. Joshua had lost all respect for his sibling when he saw the manner in which he allowed his wife to rule the roost, bringing the noble Fitzwilliam clan close to dun territory in the process.

Joshua took a long sip of brandy, thinking that marrying for financial security rather than personal fidelity might be the wiser course to take, after all. Not many couples found the happiness the Darcys and the Bingleys enjoyed. If his aunt was so anxious to bring the union about, he would lay down his own terms before agreeing to it. Only if Lady Catherine gave her solemn word to stand aside and let him manage the estate would Joshua be persuaded. He would make her understand that he would be the master of Rosings in reality as well as through marriage to her daughter, and that everyone would answer to him. In short, he would brook no interference from Lady Catherine.

Yes, that was what he would do. He stared at himself in the mirror above the fireplace and raised his glass in a mock salute, determined to start as he meant to go on. Perhaps it would not be so very bad. Joshua would go to Pemberley, face his aunt and cousin, and see how matters progressed. He would spend time talking to Anne, and try to discover what she required from her life. He realised with a jolt that he had never spoken to her in private before and really knew very little about her own aspirations. He was not even sure if she actually had any.

Eliza had invited Halstead and Turner to accompany him, which would give his friends great joy. Joshua was still unsure how he felt about Halstead pursuing Georgiana, custodianship of whom Joshua shared with Darcy. He would watch them together, speak with Darcy about the matter, and get a better understanding of Georgiana's feelings for his friend. Joshua chuckled. He was already well aware of Halstead's, since he never lost an opportunity to sing Georgiana's praises when in Joshua's company.

Joshua rang for his batman. When he appeared, he told him to summon Halstead and Turner. After the recent manoeuvres, in which all three men had taken an active part, they were due for some leave. Joshua might as well tell them the good news before he had a chance to change his mind and find an excuse to decline the invitation.

* * *

'How did you find the Briars?'

Lizzy lay on a settee in her private sitting room, her head resting in her husband's lap. 'I liked them very much.'

'I thought you would. Do they plan to stay in Derbyshire until after Christmas?'

'They look upon themselves as quite settled here. They have no plans to go to town for the season. Their two sons are otherwise occupied. One is in his final year at Cambridge, and the other is in Europe doing whatever young men do when they have finished their tenure at university and need to let off steam.' Lizzy glanced up at Will. 'Presumably you had a Grand Tour.'

'I did.'

'Ah, so you will be able to satisfy my curiosity on the point. I have often wondered what young men of fortune and privilege do with themselves in Italy, and Greece, and all those other places that are considered *de rigeur*.'

Will chuckled. 'You would be too shocked. I am sure it's not good for you to be shocked, not in your condition. Suffice it to say that idle young men do need, as you so charmingly put it, to let off steam away from their own doorsteps.'

Lizzy sent him a speaking look. 'Your son needs to be informed.'

Will rested a warm hand possessively on her belly. 'What makes you so sure you are carrying a boy?'

'I certainly hope I am.'

'Good heavens.' Will flexed a brow. 'Why?'

'You need to ask me that?' Lizzy lifted her head from its comfortable resting place, genuinely surprised. 'Of course you want a son to inherit and carry on the Darcy name. I know the anguish my mother suffered each time she produced a girl. She told me recently, as each confinement approached, she was convinced she would have a boy at last, cutting off the Longbourn entail. But she never did. I would prefer to know at the earliest opportunity that I have not inherited her inability to bear sons.'

'Lizzy, as far as I am aware, it is impossible to inherit such traits.' He pulled her onto his lap and kissed her brow. 'Besides, I have nothing against daughters, so please don't spare the matter another thought. Pemberley isn't entailed, nor will it ever be. If we have no sons, then our eldest daughter will inherit.'

'Thank you.' Lizzy felt a welling of deep love for her husband's consideration. She knew he couldn't possibly be telling the truth.

All men secretly desired at least one son, did they not? He sought only to put her mind at rest. 'It is silly to worry about such things, I know, but I feel rather sorry for your cousin Anne, having the future responsibility for Rosings resting upon her shoulders. I am not suggesting that management of a large estate is beyond a woman, but it would be harder for her than for a man. Any woman in that position would be viewed as an easy target and taken advantage of.'

Will laughed. 'In Anne's case, not while there is still breath in Lady Catherine's body. It would be a brave man who tried to take advantage of my aunt.'

'Quite, but Anne is not cut from the same cloth.'

'Which is why my aunt wishes to see her married. If not to Fitzwilliam then to someone equally suitable.'

'Of Lady Catherine's choosing?'

'Very likely, but we cannot interfere.'

'No, I suppose not, but... oh, I don't know, it all seems so clinical somehow.'

'Lady Catherine has many faults, I will be the first to admit that, but she does love her daughter and wants the very best for her. She understands Anne's limitations and wants to ensure she, as well as the Rosings estate, prospers after she is gone.'

'If you are trying to tell me not to get involved, then you need not waste your breath. It is not my concern.'

'And we seem to have drifted a long way from the subject of the Briars.'

'That's because you very cleverly turned our conversation away from the subject of your infamous Grand Tour.'

Will sent her a smouldering smile. 'What makes you suppose it was infamous?'

'If it was not, you wouldn't be so keen to avoid talking about it.' Lizzy reached up a hand and gently traced the line of her husband's face. 'However, I will not press you. And, as to the Briars, I saw Lord Briar only briefly but he seemed like an agreeable gentleman, very affable. He sent you his compliments, by the way. As to Lady Briar, I thought her quite charming, although she is delicate and suffers with her nerves. I spent half an hour with her and her sister.'

'She has a sister residing with her?'

'Mrs Sheffield is a lot younger than Lady Briar, but very interesting, and quite charming. She cannot be more than five-and-twenty but is already a widow. Her husband died of a fever over a year ago, somewhere abroad. She did not say where. Anyway, she has just returned to England and at the moment her home is with her sister.'

'What is she like?'

'Educated, well-bred, and very beautiful. She and Lady Briar appear very close. Although Mrs Sheffield is considerably younger, she seems to take care of her sister, rather than the other way around.' Lizzy canted her head, thinking the matter through. 'But she was nervous and on edge the entire time. Mrs Sheffield, that is. Oh, she hid it well, but there is more to that lady than meets the eye. You just mark my words.'

'Well then, we shall invite them to dinner, and I dare say Mrs Sheffield will have told you all her secrets by the time the first covers are removed.'

Lizzy punched her husband's arm. 'You make me sound like a busybody.'

'Not at all. It is just that people tend to confide in you because they trust you to be discreet.'

'Hmm, perhaps.' Lizzy felt her eyelids drooping, and she stifled a yawn with the back of her hand. She seemed to be tired all the time nowadays.

'Come, you need to rest before dinner.'

She felt herself being lifted by a strong pair of arms, and the next thing she knew, she was nestled between crisp cotton sheets. She had so much to do, so many arrangements to make, but they could wait. She would sleep, just for an hour, and then dress for dinner.

3

'Let battle commence,' Lizzy muttered under her breath as she stood with Will, Georgiana and Kitty beneath the entrance portico at Pemberley, watching Lady Catherine's barouche make its way up the long driveway.

'Did you say something, my dear?' Will asked.

Nothing that bears repeating. 'I was just remarking that your relations have made good time. I had not expected seeing them until tomorrow at the earliest.'

Will sent her a droll look before returning his attention to the approaching conveyance. 'Ah, is that what you said?' His lips twitched and she felt the muscles in his forearm strengthen beneath her fingers resting upon it. 'I must have misheard you.'

'Stop making fun of me,' she hissed, so Georgiana and Kitty, chatting together a short distance apart from them, could not overhear. 'You know how nervous I am about making a good impression.'

This time, Will definitely smiled. 'It is Lady Catherine who ought to feel nervous if she plans to cross swords with you.'

Lizzy quirked a brow. 'Really? Am I so very ferocious? I am unsure what that says about your opinion of me.'

'Merely that if my aunt wishes to heal the rift between us then she would be wise to show the deference due to you as my wife.'

'Why do you always know exactly the right thing to say, especially when I think I have just cause to be vexed with you?'

He patted the hand still resting on his sleeve. 'Because you are my life and the only thing that is truly important to me.' He paused, sending her a playful look. 'Apart from my estate, my sister, and my new horse, naturally.'

Lizzy bit her lip to prevent herself from laughing and did her very best to look severe. 'You will pay for that comment later.'

'Oh, I do hope so. I rather enjoy your chastisements.'

'Behave yourself, Mr Darcy!'

'If I must, Mrs Darcy.'

The carriage came to a smooth halt directly by the portico. Will's footman ran forward to let the steps down and help its occupants to alight. Unsurprisingly, Lady Catherine was the first to emerge. Lizzy studied her, seeing few outward changes in her haughty visage. She looked up at Pemberley's façade and frowned, as though looking for imperfections, expecting to see signs of it crumbling in protest at having Lizzy foisted upon it. She was slow to return her attention to those waiting to greet her, and when she did so, her gaze merely glanced off Lizzy before settling upon Will.

'Welcome, Lady Catherine,' he said, stepping forward and taking her hand. 'I trust the journey was not too tedious.'

'A decent carriage made it bearable.'

When she could no longer avoid doing so, Lady Catherine turned her attention to Lizzy. 'Mrs Darcy,' she said, her tone bordering on the uncivil.

'Lady Catherine,' Lizzy replied with equal verbal economy,

bobbing the merest suggestion of a curtsey. 'Welcome to Pemberley.'

Lady Catherine wrinkled her nose, as though offended by a noxious smell. Without responding to Lizzy, she turned to Georgiana and her severe expression softened, just fractionally.

'Georgiana, you have grown since we last met.'

'Lady Catherine.' Georgiana curtsied. 'We are very pleased you have come.'

'And I am most anxious to learn of your progress on the pianoforte. You must not, under any circumstances, neglect your practice.'

'I can assure you, I do not do so.'

Lizzy interceded. 'May I bring my sister, Catherine Bennet, to your ladyship's attention?'

Kitty nervously curtsied, while Lady Catherine viewed her with a disinterested air. 'Miss Bennet,' she said distantly. 'I was unaware your sister resided at Pemberley, Mrs Darcy.'

'Kitty divides her time between Pemberley and my sister, Mrs Bingley, who now lives just ten miles from here. Kitty and Georgiana are the greatest friends.'

'Are they indeed.' Lady Catherine seemed most dissatisfied to hear it.

Lizzy felt her temper rising. Given that they had not even entered the house yet, this was a sorry start indeed. She quelled the riposte that sprang to her lips and turned her attention to Anne de Bourgh, who had now also removed herself from the carriage and joined the party at the portico on the arm of a gentleman. Lizzy was surprised at the immediate differences she noticed in the young lady. There was some colour and the hint of animation in her usually wan countenance.

'Miss de Bourgh,' Lizzy said, offering her hand. 'You are very welcome.'

'Mrs Darcy. It is very pleasant to be here again. Of all seasons, I think I enjoy autumn the most. The colours of the leaves, you understand.'

'Quite so, and Pemberley has no shortage of trees to admire.'

Lizzy was too stunned to say anything more. Anne de Bourgh had just spoken more words to her in one sentence than she had the entire time Lizzy had been in Kent the previous year. Anne turned her attention to Will and the rest of the party, but Lady Catherine didn't allow her daughter to speak two words before interrupting her.

'This is Mr Asquith,' she said, offering no further particulars regarding that gentleman's reasons for being with them.

Lizzy appraised him while he exchanged a few civil words with Will. Tall and lean, dressed in sombre yet elegant clothing that wasn't the first word in fashion, the man had an engaging air and exquisite manners. His disarming personality had survived several days in the close confines of a carriage with Lady Catherine, which said much for his disposition – or desperation. Lizzy was already starting to understand the cause of the differences in Anne de Bourgh and wondered why Lady Catherine had seen fit to expose her daughter to such a vital man. That Anne was taken with him could not have escaped her all-seeing eyes. Georgiana and Kitty, who supposed themselves enamoured of other gentlemen, were eyeing him with interest also. Lizzy could think of few young ladies who would not, and she decided he would make an entertaining addition to their party.

Lizzy wondered if Lady Catherine meant to show Anne a little more of the ways of the world through contact with a man who had clearly seen much of it. If so, it was a risky strategy that did not allow for the romantic nature of even the most sensible of girls. Lady Catherine's reasons made for an interesting conundrum, and one Lizzy would store away for future examination.

'Mrs Darcy.' Mr Asquith bowed over her hand with a charming smile. 'It is most gracious of you to welcome me into your house.'

'You are very welcome, sir,' Lizzy replied, meaning it. 'Shall we?'

She turned towards the entrance vestibule. Lady Catherine claimed Will's arm and he proceeded her into the house. With a wry lift of one brow in Kitty's direction, Lizzy fell in alongside her sister, while Georgiana lingered behind with Anne and Mr Asquith.

Lady Catherine sailed into the drawing room on Will's arm and regally placed herself in a chair beside the fire. She narrowed her eyes as she glanced around her.

'This room has been redecorated,' she said, clearly not approving of the changes Lizzy had made.

'Certainly it has, Lady Catherine,' Lizzy said evenly. 'It was long overdue.'

'My sister made a point of leaving it precisely as it was. It became something of a tradition with her. And the bronze figurine that was always on the mantelpiece is gone.'

'It has been sent away to be cleaned,' Lizzy replied, looking towards her husband and willing him to intercede, or at the very least, smile at her.

'The room is vastly improved,' Will said, as though sensing her silent entreaty. 'It was far too gloomy the way it was.'

Lady Catherine sniffed. 'What are you two girls giggling about?' she demanded, looking towards Georgiana and Kitty, seated together a little way apart from her.

'We were discussing sketching, Lady Catherine,' Georgiana replied. 'Kitty and I share an instructor.'

'Really, you do surprise me. I was of the opinion you Bennet girls had no particular skills other than a fortunate penchant for finding rich husbands.' A sharp, audible intake of breath on Kitty's part failed to quiet Lady Catherine. 'Is that not what you implied when you visited Kent last year, Mrs Darcy?'

Lizzy silently counted to ten before responding. She glanced at Will. His expression had darkened, and she could see he was about to spring to her defence. Perversely, she didn't wish him to. Lady Catherine had been unpardonably rude, as she so often was because no one ever contradicted her. She had deliberately thrown down a gauntlet Lizzy was more than prepared to pick up. She had anticipated being on the receiving end of Lady Catherine's barbed tongue and was willing to put up with her spite if it meant Will would be reconciled with his difficult relation, but she absolutely would not be bullied or have her family insulted. She sent Will a reassuring smile and turned to Lady Catherine with that smile still firmly in place.

'Then let me hasten to reassure you on both counts, ma'am. My sisters and I possess many talents, and Kitty is the perfect example of that. Her sketching is on a par with Georgiana's. I am sure she will be happy to show you examples of her work, should your ladyship be interested.' Lizzy paused. 'As to our attracting rich husbands, I am unsure if that can be described as a talent. Whether or not we are worthy of them is a question for the husbands themselves to answer.'

'And for my part,' Will said, not only sending Lizzy a smile, but also stepping forward to rest a proprietary hand on her shoulder, 'I must insist upon being the fortunate one.'

'Unquestionably,' Mr Asquith replied with a polite smile.

Now that was interesting. Mr Asquith did not toady to his employer. Lizzy wondered, in that case, how long he would remain beneath Rosings' roof.

'It just so happens that Mr Asquith is a talented artist and has been instructing Anne in the art of sketching.'

'Is that so, Mr Asquith?' Lizzy turned to him with a smile. Lady

Catherine had conceded defeat by changing the subject back to sketching, and Lizzy was willing to keep the peace by following her example. 'In that case, perhaps Miss de Bourgh would care to join Georgie and Kitty in the morning. I know they plan to capture the changing colours of the Pemberley woods mid-morning, and I am sure they would appreciate your company, to say nothing of the benefit of your advice.'

'Thank you, Mrs Darcy. I should be delighted.'

'Georgie? Georgie, Mrs Darcy? You cannot shorten my niece's name in such a manner.'

'Oh, but I like it, Lady Catherine,' Georgiana said, her desire to support Lizzy clearly overcoming her fear of her aunt.

'Hmm, well I do not understand this modern obsession with shortening perfectly acceptable names.' Lady Catherine frowned at Lizzy. 'However, I am unsurprised to discover Anne has a natural talent for sketching, now that her health permits her to indulge.'

'I am glad you have found an occupation to which you are so well suited,' Lizzy said in a quiet aside to Anne de Bourgh.

'Suited, perhaps. I certainly enjoy it. Talented... well, I am unsure about that.'

'Nonsense, child.' Lady Catherine had clearly overheard Lizzy's conversation with her daughter and immediately interceded. 'I hope I am not the sort of parent who is blind to her child's faults. Indeed, I am not, and if I say you have talent, then talent is what you have. You merely need to apply yourself and others will see it too.'

'With Georgiana and Miss Bennet to encourage me, Mama, I think I can safely promise you I will do so.'

Servants bearing refreshments brought all discourse to a temporary end, but Lizzy was satisfied with the way she had defended herself. When Lady Catherine lifted a delicate cup to her lips, replaced it in its saucer and grudgingly offered her and

Will her congratulations on the forthcoming addition to their family, Lizzy knew she had won this initial skirmish. Lady Catherine would be well advised not to challenge her for a second time though, since Lizzy would not be so lenient with her again.

'I hope you left Mr and Mrs Collins in good health, Lady Catherine,' Lizzy said.

'Indeed. Mrs Collins is much occupied with her baby daughter. Too much so in my opinion. No good will come from mollycoddling the child, and so I told them both in the strongest terms before we left. You will do well to remember that, Mrs Darcy.'

'Thank you, ma'am. I certainly shall.'

'Who else is to join us, Darcy?' Lady Catherine asked.

'Colonel Forster and two other officers from his regiment will be with us tomorrow.'

'Two others?' Lady Catherine frowned. 'What others?'

'Major Halstead and Captain Turner. They are particular friends of Fitzwilliam's and were here with us a little over a month ago. We enjoyed their society. We also have new neighbours, Lord and Lady Briar. And, of course, Mr and Mrs Bingley are now close enough to be intimate with us.'

'Briar? I believe I knew a Lord Briar when I was much younger. Did they not reside in Sloane Street?'

'That would be the present Lord Briar's father,' Lizzy replied. 'The current Lord Briar purchased an estate close to Pemberley a few months past and plans to reside mostly in the country. They have Lady Briar's sister, a young widowed lady, living with them.'

'If she is a widow, she will not be seen in society.'

'She is out of mourning, ma'am.'

'Hmm, even so.' Lady Catherine accepted a cake as she considered the matter. 'Has this widowed sister been left well provided for?'

'I believe Mrs Sheffield inherited the bulk of her late husband's estate.'

'They why does she not live on her estate?'

'That is a question you must address to Mrs Sheffield,' Lizzy replied. 'It is hardly one I could ask a lady whose acquaintance I had only just made.'

'If estates are left unattended, workers take advantage.' Lady Catherine straightened her spine. 'That is why I never leave Rosings for long. I can assure you, no one takes advantage of my good nature.'

It was all Lizzy could do not to choke on her tea. To her precise knowledge, Lady Catherine did not possess a vestige of good nature. 'I am sure they do not,' she managed to say.

The visitors revived themselves with the array of refreshments offered. Even Miss de Bourgh ate something, as well as drinking two cups of tea. Lady Catherine held court, as though she was the hostess rather than Lizzy, firing random questions at one and all. Lizzy, having already won a battle of wills with her, was content to allow Will's aunt to administer advice and opinions as she saw fit, and took little part in the conversation herself.

Even so, by the time the new arrivals took themselves off to their chambers to rest before dinner, Lizzy was already feeling the strain.

'Did Lady Catherine happen to mention how long she plans to stay?' she asked Will, leaning heavily on his arm as they went up together.

Will patted her hand. 'You did well to tolerate her unpardonable rudeness so calmly.'

'What you mean is, you expected me to be blunter.'

Will chuckled. 'Not at all. You got it exactly right.'

'Thank you, but I shall be glad when the other gentlemen

arrive tomorrow. It will make things much easier.' Lizzy grinned. 'Safety in numbers.'

'Lady Catherine will not test you again. You have nothing to fear from her.'

'What did you make of Mr Asquith? Speaking for myself, I rather liked him.'

Will quirked a brow. 'Every lady in the room appeared to, including my aunt.'

'Ah, so you noticed that too. Your cousin has improved considerably, no doubt due to his influence. The changes in her appearance and willingness to speak up for herself are quite remarkable.'

'So I observed.'

'I can't believe how much latitude Lady Catherine affords him. I never would have thought it of her. What do we know about him?'

'Absolutely nothing. He is clearly a gentleman, or has at least received a gentleman's education. I shall quiz him on his background at the first opportunity, just to please you.'

Lizzy sent her husband a playful smile. 'Are you trying to pretend you would do so for me and are not curious yourself?'

'Well, he does seem to have got the measure of Lady Catherine and knows precisely how to behave towards her. That is extraordinary enough to excite my interest.'

'He didn't come in for a single word of criticism from her the entire time we were taking tea, which is more than can be said for the rest of us. Even you did not escape unscathed.'

'Yes, I am willing to admit I am intrigued by the unorthodox arrangement. I am also pleased to see Anne blossoming in his company.'

'Poor Mr Collins,' Lizzy said, smiling as they entered her chamber. 'He must be feeling severely neglected. His company will no longer be so desirable at Rosings now Lady Catherine has a more acceptable alternative. I owe Charlotte a letter. She has not told me much about Mr Asquith yet. I shall write to her in the morning and press her for more particulars.'

Will laughed, kissing the back of her hand as he headed for the adjoining door to his own room. 'Get some rest, my love. You will need it if you are to withstand my aunt's demanding company for a week or longer.'

'Longer?'

Lizzy sank onto a stool and surrendered herself to Jessie's capable hands, barely waiting for her maid to unfasten her hair and help her out of her gown before making her way to her bed and closing her eyes.

A week suddenly seemed like an eternity.

4

The following morning, Anne sat on a stool beside Georgiana and Miss Bennet on the edge of Pemberley woods. Biting her lip, she concentrated upon capturing the slant of sunlight filtering through the leaves. It was a difficult ambition to achieve using only charcoal, but Anne's companions did not seem deterred by Mr Asquith's suggestion and so she would attempt it too.

She was distracted by the lively discourse between Georgiana and Miss Bennet, to which Mr Asquith made frequent contributions. Laughing and dispensing advice as he walked behind them, he looked at their drawings and offered suggestions and encouragement. He had behaved in a similarly charming fashion at dinner the night before, not putting himself forward, but showing great sense and amiability that appeared to endear him to all members of the party. Anne was included in everything that was said, then and now, but struggled to respond spontaneously. Spontaneity had never had a place in her life, and she found it hard to adapt. Supposing she expressed an opinion and everyone else disagreed with it, or worse... laughed at her? No, it was much safer to remain quiet, concentrate on her drawing and say as little as possible.

'Your perspective is not quite right, Miss de Bourgh.' Mr Asquith peered over her shoulder and pointed to the area that was at fault. 'If you were to make those trees proportionately smaller, I think it would better serve.'

Anne tilted her head, but resisted the urge to glance at her companions' sketches. She was convinced theirs would be better than her effort, but preferred not to discourage herself by confirming the fact. Unlike her mother, she harboured no unrealistic ideas about her talent, such as it was, but she did enjoy sketching enormously and wondered why she had not been persuaded it try it before Mr Asquith had made the suggestion. She had so often been told she was not well enough to do anything that required the slightest effort for fear of making herself unwell that she had believed it was true. Now she knew better and regretted the lost time.

'Yes, you are right,' she said, sighing. 'I can quite see that now. Perhaps I should start again.'

'That would be a shame since you have captured the leafy canopy perfectly. Just a few minor adjustments here,' he said, pointing, 'would set the matter right.'

She was conscious of the size of Mr Asquith's body, of the robust strength and raw masculinity emanating from him as he stood directly behind her, and she breathed in the musky aroma she associated exclusively with him. She reacted to him in a manner she had never experienced before. A delicious sensation that made her blush ricocheted through her body. Perhaps it was desire. She had read a very great deal on the subject, but had never thought to experience it first-hand.

And neither would she, she reminded herself, briskly reapplying herself to her drawing. If her mama even suspected the nature of the thoughts occupying her brain, then Mr Asquith would be dismissed on the spot without a character, the blame for filling her head with inappropriate thoughts placed squarely at his door. That was a risk she could never take. Ensuring Mr Asquith retained the employment he clearly needed to survive was the one way in which she could repay him for all the positive changes that had occurred in her life since his arrival at Rosings.

Part of her was jealous because he treated Georgiana and Miss Bennet in exactly the same friendly, slightly deferential manner he showed towards her. She wanted to scream that he was *her* tutor, not theirs, but of course she would never reveal her possessive feelings. Besides, she wasn't surprised he admired them. Georgiana and Miss Bennet were both prettier than she was. They were also livelier and, unlike her, not afraid to express their opinions and laugh at themselves. How dull she must appear by comparison.

'Ladies, I think we should return to the house,' Mr Asquith said a short time later as he consulted his pocket watch. 'Mrs Darcy will be expecting us for luncheon.'

Anne felt ridiculously pleased when Mr Asquith insisted upon collecting up all her sketching materials and carrying them back to the house for her. Though he provided the same service for the other ladies, he took her things first and sent her one of his most devastating smiles as he did so.

'It looks like it might rain this afternoon,' Mama declared over luncheon. 'Oblige us by reading aloud this afternoon, Mr Asquith.'

'With the greatest of pleasure, Lady Catherine.'

Anne noticed a shadow flit across Mrs Darcy's features, presumably because Mama had taken it upon herself to decide how the ladies would pass the afternoon. It did not seem to occur to Mama that Mrs Darcy might have made alternative arrangements. Not that Anne was complaining about Mama's suggestion. Mr Asquith had a deep, velvety voice and managed to inject life and passion into even the dullest text, bringing it alive in ways the author probably never intended. Anne could have listened to him reading all day long. She loved the way his long, capable fingers curled around the side of the book, the way the colour of his eyes seemed to change in accordance with the words he read. She settled herself in the corner of a settee, with Kitty Bennet next to her, and availed herself of a legitimate excuse to feast her eyes upon the man with whom she had become obsessed.

Mr Darcy joined them when tea was served, and Mr Asquith finally got to rest his voice. Anne watched him, hoping he would come to sit with her. He did not. Instead, he stood up and joined Mr Darcy in front of the fireplace. They fell into easy conversation, but there was too much noise in the room for Anne to be able to hear what subject so enthralled them.

'Ah, here is Fitzwilliam,' Mr Darcy said, glancing out the window.

He and Mrs Darcy hastened to greet the new arrivals, while Anne quietly died a little inside. She had put all thoughts of Colonel Fitzwilliam's arrival out of her mind. If she considered it, she would also have to think about her mother's expectations. Not that Mama had actually said anything to her yet, but she was perfectly sure that happy state of affairs would not continue for very much longer. Her mother was nothing if not forthright in the expression of her views, and she expected to be obeyed absolutely, especially by Anne.

She glanced up and happened to catch Mr Asquith looking directly at her with a sympathetic expression. It was almost her undoing, and Anne looked away before it could affect her too much. A great many things had changed for the better in her life since Mr Asquith came into it, but she would never find the strength to disregard her mother's wishes, and that was an end to the matter.

Anne, along with all the other ladies with the notable exception of her mother, stood up when Colonel Fitzwilliam and his companions entered the drawing room.

Joshua dressed slowly for dinner, thinking about the scene that had greeted him in Pemberley's drawing room a little earlier. Word had reached him of Mrs Jenkinson's defection, as his aunt described it, but he had not realised her replacement was a man. Like Darcy, he was shocked and rather pleased. He had liked Asquith on sight. He was a man of great sense, considerable charm and apparently, no little mystery. In short, Darcy knew nothing about his history, and if Lady Catherine did, she was not saying. Joshua found it all rather extraordinary. Lady Catherine was nothing short of tyrannical when it came to protecting her daughter. He would have laughed in the face of any suggestion that implied she would risk exposing her to a man's continual company – and such an unusual man at that.

He noticed some differences in Anne, not least of all in her health, which appeared to have improved. But try as he might, he felt nothing for her other than cousinly affection. He sighed and made his way downstairs, responding to a request from his aunt for a private interview before the others came down. He did not need to ask what it was she wished to say to him, nor could he think of a reason to delay the inevitable.

'Might as well get it over with,' he said to his reflection, adjusting his neckcloth and then heading for the door.

'Ah, there you are at last, Fitzwilliam,' Lady Catherine said when Joshua opened the door to the small sitting room. She annoyed him by making it sound as though he had kept her waiting, which he had not.

'You wished to see me, Lady Catherine.'

'Indeed. Pray be seated.' Joshua swished the tails of his coat aside and took the chair beside his aunt. 'It's time to put Rosings' affairs in order,' she said without preamble. 'I am not getting any younger and I wish to oversee a smooth transition.'

'I do not have the pleasure of understanding you, ma'am,' Joshua replied, understanding her perfectly well. 'Do you require a new estate manager?'

'Don't be so obtuse, Fitzwilliam. It does not become you. It is time for Anne to marry so that her husband can get to grips with the management of the estate.'

'I see.'

'I had hopes of Darcy. To unite the great estates of Pemberley and Rosings had been his mother's greatest wish, as it was mine. However, we will not talk of his wilful disregard for his duty. Instead, we will discuss yours.'

'Mine, ma'am?' Joshua elevated a brow, his temper in danger of erupting. He knew his aunt thought nothing of organising everything and everyone who crossed her path, but the cavalier manner in which she appeared to think she could dictate the course of his entire life still rankled. 'Whatever can you mean?'

'Anne's health has precluded her from seeing much of the world and a secluded life has been forced upon her.'

'She appears a great deal better.'

'She is, thankfully. But if I were to launch her upon society now, she would be inundated with fortune hunters, and that I cannot allow.'

Joshua conceded the point with a nod. His aunt was certainly right in that respect. 'She does not know enough of the world to be able to make an informed choice.'

'Precisely. I engaged Asquith following Mrs Jenkinson's defection. His appearance in Kent was opportune, and he has done much to bring Anne out of herself.'

'What do you know of Asquith's background? He seems gentlemanly enough, and well educated to boot, but I have never heard of his family.'

'He is not a gentleman, although he received a gentleman's education. His father was Sir Marius Glover's plantation master in Jamaica. Asquith was born there, and Glover paid for him to be educated alongside his own son at Harrow and then supported him at university.'

'That was remarkably generous.'

'Sir Marius is philanthropic, and I trust his judgement.'

What an exceedingly enigmatic statement. 'And rightly so, it would appear,' Joshua replied, wondering what made his aunt speak so highly of Sir Marius. Joshua had never heard the name before.

'Asquith's father died when he was still a small boy and Sir Marius took him under his wing. I have advised him not to advertise his background and to allow his achievements to speak for him. It is nobody else's business but his and mine, as his employer. He would be looked down upon if the truth became public knowledge and I need him to help me bring out the best in Anne without distractions of that nature.'

'It must be difficult for Asquith to have enjoyed a gentleman's education but not be able to benefit from having a gentleman's background.'

'Enough of him.' Lady Catherine fixed Joshua with a gimlet gaze. 'I believe you know what I expect from you.'

'Indeed, ma'am, you are quite mistaken.' Joshua had no intention of making this easy for his aunt. 'I am unable to account for your wishing to speak privately with me.'

'Nonsense! I had hoped we could come to an agreement

quickly and sensibly. However, if you insist upon making me speak plain then I shall oblige you.' Lady Catherine squared her shoulders. 'You are the man I would see my daughter united with.'

'Me!'

'I am not taken in by your reticence. You must have been aware of what I had in mind when Darcy failed to oblige me.'

'Ah, so I am second best.'

'That is not what I meant and well you know it.' Lady Catherine made it sound as though she was discussing nothing more permanent than a trip to the theatre. 'Anne suffers from a nervous disposition and is not strong. She needs a husband with whom she feels comfortable and familiar. And I need her to be united with someone worthy of taking over the mantle of Rosings. Of course, you will need to resign your commission and dedicate your entire attention to the estate. There is much for you to learn and when you are married you can—'

'Wait if you please, Lady Catherine. You are being too hasty. I am very content with my military career and am not yet of a mind to marry.'

'Foolish boy! Think of Rosings and all the benefits you will enjoy from being master of that estate.' Lady Catherine tutted. 'Don't make this any more difficult than it needs to be.'

'Marriage is an emotional commitment between people who hold one another in affection.'

'Nonsense. Marriage is a business arrangement, as you are very well aware. I thought you had more sense than to be taken in by notions of true love.' Lady Catherine flapped a hand in dismissal of such a preposterous idea. 'Such felicity does not exist. Well, if it does, it never survives the first year. If you doubt my word, look no further than your brother and the way he was taken in by a pretty face that disguised a calculating brain and social ambition.' There was nothing Joshua could say to that and so he remained stubbornly silent. 'My suggestion would much better serve. Besides, you need to marry for money and we both know it.'

'Even if I were to agree, what does Anne have to say about this proposed contract?'

'She does not need to know about it until you and I have reached an understanding. I will tell her when the time is right and she will do as I ask. She is a dutiful child.'

'This has all come as a surprise, Lady Catherine. I am conscious of the honour but you must grant me time to think about it.'

'Don't take too long. Spend some time in Anne's company here at Pemberley, get to know one another better and think carefully about the advantages to yourself in such a union. The wealth and prosperity of the Rosings estate is quite on a par with Pemberley, you know.' Lady Catherine sounded a little desperate, presumably because she had expected to meet with immediate acquiescence rather than prevarication. 'Think of that.'

'I will readily give you my word to think about it, Lady Catherine.' Joshua stood up and offered his aunt his arm. 'But now I think we should join the others. They will wonder what has become of us.'

Joshua brooded on his conversation with his aunt throughout the evening, glad at least to see his friends Halstead and Turner enjoying themselves in the company of Georgiana and Kitty Bennet. Turner's unfortunate stammer didn't seem so much in evidence on this visit to Pemberley, perhaps because he felt more at his ease, having visited once before. For his own part, Joshua was restless and angry about the clinical nature of his aunt's suggestion. He was equally conscious of the great honour she had offered to bestow upon him, and was aware that most men would jump at the opportunity.

He glanced across the table at his cousin, caught her eye and smiled at her. She returned the gesture and quickly dropped her eyes to the plate in front of her. It wouldn't be so very bad, he supposed. Anne was biddable and would not give him any trouble, which was a great deal more than could be said for her mother.

Joshua knew he had little choice but to do as Lady Catherine suggested, and he ought to count himself fortunate. Even so, every bone in his body protested at the prospect of becoming leg-shackled to a lady he did not love.

5

'You handled Lady Catherine well.' Will touched Lizzy's cheek as he removed himself from her bed the following morning. 'She was unpardonably rude when she expressed her dissatisfaction with the dinner you served, for which I apologise. It can't have been easy for you to withstand her spite.'

'Her remarks did not come as a great surprise and I was prepared for them.' Lizzy smiled. 'She was testing me, hoping for a wild reaction so she could tell herself, and you no doubt, that she had been right about me all along. However, she did not get her way and I believe we understand one another much better now.'

Will laughed. 'If she ever doubted her inability to bully you, she can no longer harbour any unrealistic expectations in that respect.'

'Never mind Lady Catherine. Colonel Fitzwilliam seemed a little distracted and lacking in his customary poise. I assume Lady Catherine has already told him he is expected to marry Anne.'

'Yes, so I understand.' Will tightened the belt on his robe and nodded. 'Most men in his position would jump at such an opportunity but I can understand why he hesitates. He is more accustomed to issuing orders than he is to obeying them.'

'The colonel does not strike me as the type to satisfy himself with a marriage of convenience, however dire his circumstances.'

'Possibly, but he does not have the luxury of pleasing himself in that respect.'

'How very dispassionate of you.'

'Facts must be faced, my love.'

'Yes, I suppose they must.' Lizzy smiled because she knew Will spoke the truth. 'Still, the improvements in Anne are so very remarkable that perhaps it will not be so bad. She is more intelligent than I realised. I actually heard her contribute to a conversation without being asked *and* she expressed her opinion very sensibly.'

'She certainly talks more than she once did.'

Lizzy marvelled at her husband's lack of perspicacity. She wasn't such an old married lady that she had forgotten how it had made her feel and look when she had supposed herself to be enamoured with a gentleman. She shuddered when she recalled the object of her affections had been Mr Wickham, but that was beside the point. Lizzy had observed how Anne... well, observed Mr Asquith with ill-disguised adoration.

The man was an enigma, and Lizzy would like to know a great deal more about him. Jane and Mr Bingley were due to arrive in the afternoon and planned to stay for two nights. Lizzy would value Jane's opinion about Mr Asquith's character. It would be quite like old times when they had sequestered themselves in one of their bedchambers at Longbourn for hours at a time, discussing various gentlemen – specifically Jane's prospects of securing Mr Bingley, and Mr Wickham's unfortunate situation. The only difference this time would be that they were contemplating the suitability of gentlemen for women other than themselves. God forbid that they were turning into their mother.

'Mr Asquith is responsible for the changes.' Lizzy canted her head. 'It seems odd Lady Catherine would employ a man about whom she knows so little, and one who could so easily turn her daughter's head in directions Lady Catherine almost certainly would not wish it to take.'

'I believe Lady Catherine knows a fair amount about him. She told Fitzwilliam he is the son of Sir Marius Glover's plantation manager in Jamaica. That gentleman valued Asquith so highly that he paid for his son to be educated in England alongside his own boy.'

'Really?' Lizzy arched a brow. 'Well then, Mr Asquith will have much to talk to Mrs Sheffield about when she comes to dinner tonight with the Briars. I understand her late husband made his fortune in Jamaica.'

'Perhaps Mrs Sheffield is known to him. That ought to make for interesting discourse.'

'Ah, so you think there is something about Mr Asquith's background he doesn't wish to have commonly known?'

Will leaned over Lizzy and kissed her brow. 'I did not say that.'

'You didn't have to.' She reached up and stroked his jaw. 'My letter to Charlotte Collins, asking her what was known about him in Kent, has already been sent. Hopefully, Charlotte will satisfy my curiosity and reply by return.'

Will sent her a teasing smile. 'Which will do nothing to stop you from asking your own questions.'

Lizzy had no reply to make. She was too taken up with her husband's lovely smile to find the breath for words. Whenever he looked at her in that particular way, her insides melted, desire blossomed, and she fell in love with him all over again.

'I know what you are thinking.' He wagged a finger at her. 'And the answer is no. You have a houseful of guests, and you are in a delicate condition. I will not place added demands upon you.'

'I thought I was the one doing the demanding. Besides, it will do the baby no harm.'

'I have business to attend to and must leave you for the morning.' Damnation, Lizzy thought. He really did mean to reject her. So much for her feminine wiles. They appeared to be losing their appeal already. 'Promise me you will not over-exert yourself.'

'Your aunt will ring a peal over me if I attempt to do so. The thought of a tedious lecture about the responsibility I bear for the Pemberley heir will be enough to keep me in line.'

'Then for once I have reason to be obliged to my aunt, provided you do not treat her lecture as a challenge and disregard it.' Will's expression darkened. 'I beg you not to make me worry about you, my love.'

Lizzy reached up and kissed his lips. 'You have just said the only thing that will make me obey you. You start to understand my character and know precisely how to treat me.'

'Thank you. Now I must go. I will see you at luncheon.'

Lizzy watched her husband leave, then laid back and closed her eyes for a moment, breathing in the masculine aroma that lingered on his pillow and which was so uniquely him. It was ridiculous really. They had been married long enough that she ought to be over her initial infatuation with him. Goodness only knew being mistress of Pemberley ensured that she had plenty with which to occupy her time. Lizzy hugged Will's pillow to her breast, making a mental note to ask Jane if she still felt obsessed with her Mr Bingley and missed him the moment he left the room.

Laughing at her foolishness, Lizzy rang the bell. Jessie brought up her breakfast tray and then helped her to wash and dress. Lizzy went down but none of her guests were anywhere to be seen. She glanced out of her sitting room window and noticed Anne de

Bourgh sitting alone in the herb garden, a sketch pad on her lap. Anxious to speak with her alone and equally anxious to avoid Lady Catherine, Lizzy slipped out a side door and joined her.

'I hope I am not disturbing you.'

'Not in the least, Mrs Darcy.'

'Oh, please call me Lizzy. We are related now, after all. And I hope I may address you as Anne.'

'I would like that. So few people do. They are too afraid of what my mother will say if they presume to be familiar. Besides, I have never had any close friends.'

'Well, I am not afraid of your mother and so Anne it is. And you now have a friend in me if you will allow it.'

'With the greatest of pleasure.'

'That's settled then.' Lizzy smiled. 'What are you drawing?'

'I was trying to capture a likeness of those herbs growing against that fountain, but I think I am being too ambitious.'

'Let me see.'

Lizzy examined Anne's sketch. It was rudimentary, but still better than anything Lizzy could have achieved.

'What do you think? There is no necessity to be kind. I know I have a long way to go before I will not be ashamed of my efforts,' Anne said. 'If that ever happens.'

'I am no expert, but there is a certain rustic charm in your image. I am sure Mr Asquith will be able to tell you what to do to improve it, but you wouldn't thank me for offering you advice. I cannot draw to save my life.'

Anne appeared surprised by the admission. 'I thought there was nothing you could not do.'

'Did you really?' Lizzy blinked. 'What a very strange image you have of me, but it is hardly deserved. I am not nearly as accomplished as you appear to think. I am very outspoken, I suppose, which people often mistake for confidence. It is just that I never have been able to hold my tongue, especially if I think someone else has spoken out of turn or has been unjust. That trait has landed me in all manner of trouble.' Lizzy emitted an embarrassed little laugh. 'But it is hardly my fault if I always have firm opinions upon every conceivable subject.'

'Whereas I never have anything to say that people wish to hear.'

'That once might have been true, about you're not speaking, I mean. But since your health has improved, I can see a vast difference in you.' Lizzy smiled. 'I believe Mr Asquith must take some credit for that.'

Anne blushed. 'Yes. I was terrified of him when Mama first engaged him as my tutor. I never would have expected her to do such an unorthodox thing.'

'I must say it surprised us too.'

'He was very kind right from the start and very patient. Most surprisingly of all, he did not treat me like an invalid.' Anne paused, lost in reflection, her sketch abandoned. 'People had been treating me as though I was a weakling for so long that I had started to believe it must be true. But Mr Asquith made no allowances for my supposed infirmities and I gradually started to feel... well, normal.'

'Then he is to be congratulated, because I see a completely different side to you now, and like what I see.'

'Thank you, but I am still very dull and uninteresting.'

'No you are not.' Lizzy patted her hand. 'Never think that way.'

'Mr Asquith has taught me to aspire to things I had always supposed were beyond me, but now I... well, perhaps that wasn't such a good thing. If one does not have expectations then one cannot be disappointed when they are not realised.'

'Because you cannot have your heart's desire?'

Anne's head shot up. 'Whatever do you mean?'

Lizzy smiled. 'Mr Asquith is very elegant, very charming. Were you to have formed an attachment towards him, I could quite understand how it would have happened.'

'Is it that obvious?' Anne shot Lizzy a startled look. 'Mama would dismiss him on the spot if she had the slightest notion. I am here because... well, I am not supposed to know, but I'm not quite the numbskull Mama supposes me to be.'

Lizzy's heart went out to the poor girl. 'I am sure your mother only has your best interests at heart.'

'Yes, I dare say.'

'You must not feel pressured to do things you would prefer not to do.'

'I am not you, Lizzy. Besides, I have always known what is expected of me.'

Lizzy didn't quite know how to respond, but seeing Mr Asquith approaching, their intimate conversation had to end anyway, which was probably just as well.

'We are friends now, Anne,' Lizzy said, standing. 'Please feel free to talk to me about anything at any time.'

'Thank you. That means a great deal to me.' Anne paused. 'As I said before, I have never had a friend to confide in and I am only now beginning to realise what I have missed.'

Lizzy returned to the house thinking that was one of the saddest, most poignant statements she had ever heard. Having grown up surrounded by four sisters, not having a confidant would have been unthinkable. Poor Anne. Born into all that money and privilege and yet she was lonely and completely lacking in self-confidence.

* * *

Jane and Mr Bingley arrived in the middle of the afternoon. Lizzy and Will greeted them with informality and great affection. Jane looked tired and drawn.

'I should not have asked you to come,' Lizzy said, feeling guilty as the sisters embraced. 'The journey was too much for you.'

'You are as bad as Charles. It is only ten miles. Besides, I am curious to meet Lady Catherine.'

'She terrifies me,' Kitty said, taking her turn to hug Jane. 'I don't know how Lizzy finds the courage to stand up to her.'

'It is that or allow her to dictate, which is unthinkable.'

'Who is that gentleman?' Jane asked, glancing through the drawing room window and seeing Mr Asquith assisting Lady Catherine and Anne from the carriage that had taken them into the village.

'A very good question,' Lizzy replied. 'And one I would like to know the answer to myself.'

* * *

Joshua spent the day with Darcy, which gave him a legitimate excuse to avoid squiring his cousin Anne. Seeing Darcy at his most efficient, handling the management of his estate with skill and intelligence, reminded Joshua that a similar future was his for the taking. All that was required of him was to marry his cousin. Common sense told him to grasp the opportunity with both hands and thank Lady Catherine for her benevolence.

So why did he hesitate?

Darcy made no mention of the possible union, but it was as though he was trying to show Joshua what he could expect if he decided to go ahead. He would be a fool not to, he thought, sitting astride his horse and surveying Darcy's land which stretched as far as the eye could see. So too did the land attaching to Rosings.

Joshua could see changes for the better in his cousin. She was no longer a timid church mouse, and occasionally offered up an opinion of her own when there was the least likelihood of its being heard. She made no effort to single Joshua out and her response when he had addressed a remark to her the previous evening had been stilted, almost indifferent. It was evident the prospect of their union held no more joy for Anne than it did for Joshua. It had not previously occurred to him that she might be as averse to the idea as he was, having assumed she would do as she was told by her mother simply because she always had in the past.

Joshua slid his arms into the coat his man held out for him and stood still as Cox brushed imaginary specks from the shoulders. His next move ought to be to speak privately and candidly with Anne, discover precisely how she felt about her mother's proposal and then decide how best to proceed. Anne looked a great deal better than she usually did and no longer hid beneath several layers of shawls for fear of catching a chill. She had altered in subtle ways and as Joshua tripped lightly down the stairs, he was determined to discover who or what had wrought such remarkable changes in her. He was equally determined that Anne would speak honestly about her feelings. He understood Lady Catherine's determination to see the Rosings estate pass into capable hands, but those hands would not be Joshua's if they came at the expense of her daughter's happiness. He did not love Anne de Bourgh but he did feel a duty of care towards her and would not force her into a loveless marriage against her will.

Darcy, Bingley, and Asquith were already in the drawing room. Joshua was received warmly by his host and accepted a glass of whisky from him with a nod of thanks. Turner and Halstead followed on his heels and were provided with refreshment also.

'Our neighbours are joining us for dinner this evening,' Darcy told them. 'Lord and Lady Briar and Lady Briar's sister, Mrs

Sheffield. Did you happen to know Mrs Sheffield's late husband, Asquith? I believe he made his fortune in Jamaica.'

'The name is not familiar,' Asquith replied, shaking his head. 'But then a lot of Englishmen have interests in Jamaica. I am acquainted with only a few of them.'

'Yes, of course, but sometimes these coincidences happen.'

Joshua's instincts told him Asquith had not answered Darcy's question honestly, but what possible reason would he have to lie about it? Not that it mattered to Joshua. He had problems of his own to wrestle with, and he dismissed the matter from his mind.

'How are you enjoying your new estate, Bingley?' Joshua asked instead.

'Very much indeed,' Bingley replied with great enthusiasm. 'It is exactly right for us in all respects. I shall enjoy sharing it with my family, although my sisters seem quite determined to remain in London for the present time, which I admit surprises me.'

'They probably want to give you time to adjust to married life,' Darcy said hastily. 'After all, they were always with you in Hertfordshire, as was Mrs Bennet.'

Bingley pulled a wry face. 'That is certainly true.'

Joshua said nothing, but he knew the real reason why Bingley was denied his sisters' company. Miss Bingley had recruited Wickham to help her undermine Eliza's position during a house party at Pemberley a few weeks previously. Supposing Darcy to have made a mistake in marrying Eliza, which she believed he himself had come to regret, she had also convinced herself that she was the true object of Darcy's affections. It was Darcy's contention that she was quite mad, an opinion which was supported by the best medical brains in the business.

Darcy's price for not informing Bingley of his sister's treachery was that she underwent treatment for her condition. Mrs Hurst had taken it upon herself to ensure that happened. Miss Bingley would never be invited to Pemberley again of course, so how that could be avoided if she returned to the north and resided with her brother was a problem Joshua didn't envy Darcy having to wrestle with. There could be no doubt that Bingley, if he discovered the truth, would be devastated. Joshua knew Eliza was especially keen for it not to come to light, at least until after her sister's confinement.

The ladies joined them, and the conversation became more general. Even before their neighbours arrived, they were a lively party. Lady Catherine attempted to dominate proceedings but was generally ignored as proper deference was shown to Mrs Darcy. Joshua considered joining his cousin but she was engaged in animated conversation with Asquith, causing Joshua to wonder if that gentleman could be the cause of the changes in Anne's demeanour. Indeed, looking up at him as she was at that moment, eyes sparkling, cheeks slightly flushed, she appeared almost pretty.

Joshua noticed Lady Catherine watching them, a slight frown marring her brow. He moved to join Anne and her tutor and engaged the pair in polite conversation. If that was the way the wind blew then Joshua would not stand in his cousin's way, provided of course Asquith wasn't just a fortune hunter. He would make it his business to find out a great deal more about his circumstances and satisfy himself on that score.

Still unsure why he felt so relieved to have possibly talked himself out of a comfortable future, the answer became obvious when the door opened and Simpson announced Lord and Lady Briar and Mrs Sheffield. His eyes were drawn to Mrs Sheffield as a moth to a flame, and the breath left his body in an audible whoosh. It felt as if his entire life had been leading up to this moment, and his disinclination to marry his cousin now made perfect sense.

The lady who captured his complete attention was extremely

beautiful, with a profusion of dark blonde curls, and an adorable air of vulnerability that made Joshua yearn to protect her, even though he was unsure if there was anything she needed to be protected from. Her face was dominated by large, exceedingly blue eyes that showed intelligence and strength of character. Although no longer in mourning, she was modestly gowned in grey silk which clung to her svelte form and sent Joshua's mind spiralling in all sorts of inappropriate directions.

Joshua Fitzwilliam waited patiently for the introductions to be performed.

6

As a general rule, Anne found crowded drawing rooms rather daunting. Either she was dismissed as an irrelevance or people insisted upon talking at her incessantly, ingratiating themselves for reasons of personal advancement. No one seemed interested in her for her own sake and she could think of nothing amusing or interesting to say when people insisted upon singling her out. How very dull they must think her.

This evening, she felt very differently. Everyone appeared relaxed and comfortable with one another, not a sycophantic social climber in sight. One of the advantages of being invisible in a crowd, she soon discovered, was that she could look at Mr Asquith for as long as she wished, admiring his elegant person and pleasing manners without anyone noticing her growing obsession with that gentleman.

'Are you enjoying the change of scenery, Miss de Bourgh?' As though sensing her watching him, Mr Asquith approached her and instigated a conversation. Mesmerised, she watched his long fingers curling around the stem of his glass, much as she enjoyed watching them curl around the sides of a book when he read aloud to them, wishing they could be embracing her hand instead. Ye gods, what was happening to her? 'Your relatives appear relaxed this evening.'

'Oh... er, yes. I was just now thinking the same thing.' She summoned up a smile, conscious of her mother observing them closely from across the room. She was simultaneously quizzing Georgiana about something, but that did not prevent her from also glaring at Anne. She must take better care not to allow her true feelings to show. Lizzy had already noticed, but if Mama had done so surely she would have said something? Still, it would be better not to give her any reason to suspect. Her days with Mr Asquith were numbered, she knew that very well, and she was determined to make the most of every last one of them before they were separated for good. 'It is a long time since I was last at Pemberley. I had forgotten how much I like it here. Mr Darcy seems so much less severe since his marriage.'

'From what little I know of Mrs Darcy, it is my opinion he could not have chosen a more suitable wife.' Mr Asquith fixed her with a probing glance. 'I am so very glad he found her.'

What could he mean by that statement, Anne wondered. Was he aware that her mother had hoped to see her married to Mr Darcy? Could it really be? Her heart swelled with hope, even though such hope was... well, hopeless. 'Yes, as am I.'

'The countryside is very different from Kent.'

'Yes, indeed. The peaks are rugged yet quite starkly beautiful.'

Anne's heart lurched when she noticed Colonel Fitzwilliam approaching them even though it was unreasonable to suppose that she could keep Mr Asquith to herself for long. She assumed Mama had already spoken with him and he was here to press his suit. Why would he not be? Rosings was a rich prize, well worth a little effort on his part. Anne was surprised and a little ashamed at the uncharitable turn her thoughts had taken. Were it not for Mr

Asquith, she supposed she would not have minded marriage to her cousin too much. He would most likely treat her with kindness. He did not possess Mr Darcy's taciturn disposition and had on one or two occasions during his annual visits to Rosings actually made Anne laugh.

Even so, the thought of committing herself to such a man – to any man other than Mr Asquith – appalled her. She had fallen deeply and passionately in love with a person whom her mother would never permit her to marry.

'Rain is expected tomorrow,' Colonel Fitzwilliam said, 'and Mrs Darcy is proposing amateur dramatics to keep us all entertained.'

'A play?' Anne frowned. 'If you are suggesting I should take part, Colonel, I am not sure I could—'

'I have been asked to organise something, but it looks as though we will not have enough willing players. Can I persuade you to take pity on me, Miss de Bourgh, and help to make up the numbers?' Mr Asquith flashed a charming smile that caused Anne to go weak at the knees and sent colour rushing to her cheeks. When he looked at her in that particular manner, making it seem as if only she could save the day, it was impossible to deny him anything. 'It would be a sorry way for me to repay Mrs Darcy's hospitality if I cannot even interest sufficient players, and so I must throw myself upon your mercy.'

'I have never tried anything like it.' Anne shook her head, horrified at the thought of putting herself forward. 'I don't think I have any natural talent for acting.'

Colonel Fitzwilliam laughed. 'That doesn't stop half of those treading the boards in Drury Lane.'

'It's the greatest fun imaginable,' Mr Asquith assured her. 'You get the opportunity to pretend to be someone else, which can be quite liberating.'

He spoke as though he appreciated the daily torment she felt at being herself, which should not have surprised Anne. Mr Asquith understood her in a way no one else ever had, or so she chose to think.

'Well, perhaps a minor role, if it would help you.'

'Mr Asquith!' Mama's voice cut through the hum of conversation and several heads turned in her direction. 'A word, if you please.'

'Excuse me please. Lady Catherine has need of me.'

Mr Asquith bowed and strolled across the room. If he felt annoyed to have their discourse interrupted by Mama's autocratic command, he gave no indication of it. Anne watched his retreating back, only tearing her gaze away when she realised Colonel Fitzwilliam had addressed a remark to her and she had not responded.

'I beg your pardon,' she said, aware that she was blushing again. 'I did not hear what you said.'

'I merely remarked that Mr Asquith appears to be a first-class chap. How long has he been with you?'

'A little more than three months.' Anne's smile was probably less guarded than it ought to have been, but whenever the conversation turned towards Mr Asquith, she was unable to control her reactions. 'And I agree with you. He is very interesting and informative.'

'Then I am glad, for your sake.'

A commotion at the door caused all heads to turn in that direction. Lord and Lady Briars and Mrs Sheffield were being announced and Anne could sense she had lost Colonel Fitzwilliam's attention. She noticed Mr Asquith glancing at the new arrivals, and as quickly look away again. How strange. It was almost as if he didn't wish to be seen by them. She noticed her mother dismiss him with a negligent wave of her hand because Mr

Bingley had joined her. Mr Asquith pleased Anne by returning to her side.

'I understand Mrs Sheffield's late husband made his fortune in Jamaica,' she said. 'Did you know him, Mr Asquith?'

'I do not recall the name.'

'I am sure you would not have forgotten Mrs Sheffield had you met before. She is very beautiful.'

Asquith inclined his head. 'I must take your word for that. I had not noticed.'

'Your gallantry does you credit, Mr Asquith, but it is hard for me to believe any gentleman would be blind to such beauty. Indeed, why should he be? Beauty in all its forms ought to be admired.'

'Then if you insist, I shall admire Mrs Sheffield, but only after we have been introduced.'

* * *

Lizzy and Will greeted the new arrivals with the greatest of pleasure. Introductions were made, with sufficient deference shown to Lady Catherine to satisfy even her exacting standards. Lizzy stifled a smile, imagining how vexing it must be for Lady Catherine not to be able to find anything obvious to criticise about her conduct. She was not foolish enough to imagine she would escape unscathed, but if Lady Catherine wished to find fault with the manner in which she discharged her social duties, then Lizzy would not make it easy for her.

With their relaxed manners and natural charm, Lord and Lady Briars were soon engaged in polite conversation. Lizzy, whose back was aching, felt she could safely leave them and joined Jane, seated on a chaise beside the fire. The sisters had not yet had an opportunity for private discourse. This was hardly the time or the place, but Lizzy was well aware that would not deter them. Whenever they found themselves in one another's company they picked up where they had left off, almost as though they had never been separated.

'You look hot, my dear. Are you quite comfortable?'

Jane winced. 'Not entirely, as you will discover for yourself in another month or so.'

'I should not have asked you to come.'

'I would not have missed it for the world. I so enjoy seeing the improvements in Kitty. She really does seem quite taken with Captain Turner, and he with her.'

'Yes, but we ought not to get our hopes up. The chances of the captain's father permitting such a match are slim.'

'Why? Because we are not good enough?' Jane smiled. 'That might once have been a valid argument, but my marriage, and especially yours, have raised our status as a family.'

'True enough I suppose, but it might all come to naught.' Lizzy smiled at her sister. 'Let us leave Kitty and her captain to enjoy one another's company without interference from their old married sisters and talk of other matters. What do you make of Lady Catherine?'

'You would do better to ask me what I make of Mr Asquith. Now there is an interesting gentleman if ever I saw one.'

'Yes, Anne de Bourgh is very taken with him and doesn't quite know how to disguise her feelings. He is by far the best thing that could have happened to her. He has brought her out of herself no end. However, I believe Lady Catherine might have cause to regret her decision.' They watched as Lady Catherine called Mr Asquith to her side for the second time in five minutes so he could perform a menial task that ought to have been executed by a footman. Presumably she was making a point. 'I sense trouble brewing.'

'Especially if Lady Catherine has settled upon Colonel

Fitzwilliam for her daughter.' Jane hid a smile behind her hand. 'Have you observed that he hasn't been able to remove his gaze from Mrs Sheffield since she entered the room?'

'Yes, I did notice that.' Lizzy grinned. 'Oh dear. Lady Catherine failed to bend Will to her demands and now it looks as though she might fail for a second time.'

'Only if Mrs Sheffield is attracted to the colonel and has funds of her own. Is not the colonel required to marry for money?'

'I got the impression that Mr Sheffield left his widow well provided for, but of course I know nothing of the particulars.' Lizzy patted her sister's hand. 'Now, tell me about Campden Park. What did you decide about the small sitting room? Shall you change the décor?'

Jane spoke enthusiastically about her new home. Lizzy had viewed the property shortly after Mr Bingley decided to purchase it and liked what she saw. It was a fraction of the size of Pemberley, but still a substantial estate, albeit a trifle neglected. Jane was enjoying herself, bringing it up to date.

'I shall take pleasure in showing it to Louisa and Caroline when they next join us.' Jane frowned. 'In fact, I cannot think what could have detained them in London for so long.'

'Perhaps they are being thoughtful and leaving you and your Charles to enjoy one another's company. Besides, I recall Mrs Hurst telling me she and her sister planned a visit to Brighton.' Lizzy felt wretched lying to Jane, but it was necessary. 'And bear in mind, your purchase of Campden Park and removal north all happened very quickly.'

'That is how Charles does things. Once he makes up his mind about something, he cannot wait to act upon his decision.' Jane grinned. 'Do you recall when he took Netherfield? One moment we heard rumours a gentleman was considering it, the next he was installed. He also quit it equally quickly when he thought I did not enjoy his society.'

Lizzy winced. 'That is certainly true. No one can accuse your husband of not being a man of action.'

'I would not say this to anyone except you, Lizzy, but much as I enjoy Louisa's and Caroline's society, I have also enjoyed making up my own mind about things at Campden Park. I know their opinions would most likely not have coincided with mine but I would have felt duty bound to take them into account. This way I cannot be accused of ignoring them since they have been invited but have not chosen to come.'

'Well, there you are then.'

'But it is so strange, don't you think? Caroline was so insistent that Charles purchase an estate in this part of the country. She would keep reminding him to do so. But now that he has, she seems to have lost all interest. You are right to say we have only been here for a few weeks but I didn't think that would deter her. Charles has not said anything to me but I know he finds it curious too.'

'Did I mention I received a letter from our Aunt Gardiner?' Lizzy asked in a hasty change of subject.

'No. Do tell.' Jane sat forward. 'How are Lydia and Mr Wickham managing in town? I dare say my uncle already regrets his generosity. You and I both know how difficult Mr Wickham can be and what high expectations he has.'

Mr and Mrs Gardiner had come to the rescue following Wickham's infamous attempt to manipulate Lizzy a few weeks previously. Having quit the army altogether, Wickham found himself without occupation, unable to support his wife. They had offered Wickham a position as manager of one of Mr Gardiner's warehouses, which had a small apartment attached to it. Wickham had been scathing of the offer, but Lydia had surprised Lizzy by showing great maturity and insisting upon her husband grasping the opportunity. Neither Lydia nor Jane knew the full particulars of Wickham's spectacular fall from grace and Lizzy had no intention of enlightening either of them. Even so, Lizzy had an uncomfortable feeling they had not heard the last of Wickham, and she believed he would somehow find a way to interfere in her life again.

'Wickham is as idle as always, but Lydia has apparently taken to the life with great enthusiasm.'

'Ah, but will it last?' Jane shook her head, looking concerned. 'You know Lydia. She has fads.'

'Surprisingly, I think she understands this is their last chance and will ensure Wickham does as he is told. It will be harder for him to stray now that he is constantly in her company. Besides, Lydia enjoys all the fabrics that pass through the warehouse and is already becoming quite an expert upon the best establishments to sell them on to.'

'Well, I suppose fashion is the one subject guaranteed to hold our sister's interest.'

'It also helps that they are in London,' Lizzy added, smiling.

'Yes, I dare say.'

Will and Mr Bingley approached them.

'Are you here to scold me for gossiping with my sister and neglecting our guests?' Lizzy asked Will with a smile.

'Actually, my suspicions were aroused by your both sitting down, as you ought to be.'

'And why should that make you suspicious?'

'Since when did you ever do anything that was expected of you?'

'That is grossly unfair!' Lizzy cried in mock anger.

'Be that as it may, dinner is about to be served. I must attend to Lady Briars, and Bingley has kindly offered to take Lady Catherine in. We shall seek them out now so that Lady Catherine has no time to organise people the way she wishes to.'

'And you accuse me of meddling,' Lizzy said, smiling.

Will sent her an enticingly intimate smile. 'Indeed, my love,' he said softly. 'I would not dare.'

Lizzy was still laughing when she entered the dining room on Lord Briar's arm.

7

'I recall you being rather partial to roast pigeon, Anne. Allow me to serve you a small portion.'

'Thank you, Colonel.'

Joshua did so and then passed the platter further down the table. He could not recall the last time he had enjoyed a dinner more, or one at which time had passed so quickly. The food was excellent, the wine a perfect vintage, but he would expect nothing less at Pemberley, and those considerations had little to do with his animation. Indeed, he scarcely noticed what he ate or drank, or what the general subjects of lively conversation happened to centre upon.

He had dutifully escorted his cousin Anne to the table, ensured her needs were met and kept her entertained with polite discourse. His efforts were occasionally rewarded with a smile but it was obvious her attention was all for Mr Asquith, seated on her opposite side. She was hopeless at dissimulating, but Joshua could hardly object because his own attention was all for Mrs Sheffield, seated directly across from him between Halstead and Turner. It was a pleasure to feast his eyes on her lovely features each time he glanced across the table, which was frequently, but he remained frustrated since he was unable to speak with her. Conversing across the table would be the height of bad manners and Joshua wouldn't dream of being so crass.

Perhaps it wasn't such a bad thing they were unable to speak, he decided as the meal progressed and the glances they shared became more probing and prolonged. Mrs Sheffield had more than a passing interest in Joshua, it seemed. Was she attracted to him, or did she have ulterior motives? Joshua gave himself a mental shake. What ulterior motives could she possibly have?

Being unable to converse with her now gave him a legitimate excuse to seek her out in the drawing room after dinner. He knew something of Jamaica himself, having spent a few months there at his late father's behest before returning to England and purchasing a commission in the army. It gave them an interest in common that would be both natural and polite to discuss, given they had barely exchanged more than a handshake and a few words thus far. He listened to her lilting voice as she responded to questions put to her, keen to hear what subjects engaged her attention so that he would know what else to talk to her about when their time came.

Anne's company was relatively undemanding, leaving Joshua free to watch his fellow diners. The mood was elegantly relaxed, for which Joshua gave Eliza credit. She had a natural way about her – far less stiff and formal than Darcy's. It was playful almost, and put people at their ease. There was a marked difference in Darcy too since Joshua's last visit just a few short weeks ago, and he appeared less reticent than usual. He gave Eliza the credit for that change too.

His fellow officers were taken up with Georgiana and Eliza's sister, but did not neglect Mrs Sheffield. As their commanding officer, Joshua would have seen them cashiered had they forgotten their manners to such an extent. The only person who appeared less than delighted with the evening's progress was his aunt, presumably because Joshua had not yet given her an answer. It would be unreasonable for her to expect one so soon after she had made her proposition, but then his aunt was not known for being reasonable when it came to getting her own way.

The other possibility was that she disliked her daughter's growing interest in Asquith. Well, what the devil had she expected when she brought a male tutor – and such a charming and worldly one at that – into her sheltered daughter's life? Lady Catherine seldom did anything without a reason, but Joshua suspected on this occasion matters had not gone the way she had hoped. She sat sour-faced on Darcy's left, not dominating the conversation because Darcy would not allow her to. He cut her off politely but firmly whenever she got into her stride and gave her opinion a little too forcibly. That would not sit well with Lady Catherine, who expected to be at the heart of any gathering.

Each time Joshua glanced up, he caught Mrs Sheffield studying him. He was encouraged by her interest in him until it occurred to him that the lady was not fascinated by him. Instead she appeared to be avoiding looking in Asquith's direction. Now, that was interesting. When Mrs Sheffield first entered the room, Asquith had stiffened and muttered something unintelligible beneath his breath. He had denied knowing her but Joshua would bet what blunt he possessed the man had not told the truth. Mrs Sheffield and Asquith were not strangers, but neither of them wanted the company to know that they were acquainted. A hot shaft of jealousy pierced Joshua when the possibility of their being secret lovers occurred to him. He as quickly dismissed the idea. If they were, Asquith would have had no reason to seek employment with Lady Catherine, keeping him separated from the object of his affections. He had no way of knowing he would come to Pemberley at the same time as Mrs

Sheffield was in the district. Satisfied on that score, Joshua pondered upon what other reasons there might be for the pair to deny their acquaintance.

When the meal came to an end, he had reached no definitive conclusions.

'Have you decided what performance you and your players will entertain us with, Mr Asquith?' Mrs Darcy asked.

'I have settled upon a light comedy, ma'am, but must beg you not to ask me for more particulars, mainly because I have not yet decided upon them.'

'A comedy, Asquith,' Joshua said. 'That ought to be just the thing.'

'I hope you are not thinking of anything too modern,' Lady Catherine said, frowning. 'I do not hold with all these new-fangled ideas people find so amusing. I find them vulgar in the extreme.'

'Indeed not, Lady Catherine. I have a particular piece in mind but unfortunately I am one lady short.'

'You are planning theatricals?' Lady Briars asked.

'Yes, ma'am. The weather is supposed to deteriorate and we thought it an amusing way to fill the time.'

'Could not one lady play more than one part?' Mrs Darcy asked.

'Unfortunately that would not work since the players are required to appear together at all times.'

'Perhaps my sister would oblige,' Lady Briars said. 'Did you not do that sort of thing in Jamaica, Celia?'

'No,' Mrs Sheffield replied.

'I could not ask Mrs Sheffield to inconvenience herself,' Asquith replied at the same time.

'Nonsense.' Lady Briars appeared determined. 'It is just what you need to bolster your spirits, my dear. I absolutely insist.'

Mrs Sheffield's smile was brittle and did not trouble her lovely eyes. 'And I am equally determined not to spoil the production by having anything to do with it.'

An awkward silence ensued, broken by Mrs Darcy when she glanced down the table to ensure everyone had finished, placed her napkin aside, and pushed back her chair. 'Come, ladies, let us leave the gentlemen to their port.'

Every male in the room was instantly on his feet helping the ladies with their chairs. Joshua flattened himself against the wall as the ladies filed past his position. He hoped for a look, a sign of interest of some sort from Mrs Sheffield. When she did not glance his way, he felt severely disappointed. It was as though she was punishing him for not defending her when she seemed so desperate to be excluded from the play. His first instinct had been to do so but he held back for fear that it would arouse too much interest in... well, in his interest in her, and create unnecessary difficulties for him. He sent her an apologetic look but she was on the other side of the table and didn't see it. His only reward was a waft of her light floral perfume as she left the room.

The gentlemen did not linger over their port. When they returned to the drawing room and Joshua looked for Mrs Sheffield, she was nowhere to be seen. Nor was Asquith. He had preceded Joshua from the dining room, Joshua himself having been detained by a question from Darcy. Where the devil were they both? It was beyond his imagination, given the tension he had sensed between them, that they should be the only people missing and not be together. Presumably, they were clearing the air. Joshua slipped back out of the drawing room before his aunt could demand his company for her daughter and sauntered over to the door of the small adjoining sitting room. It was the most obvious place for Asquith and Mrs Sheffield to have taken refuge. He was rewarded by the sound of voices – a man's and a woman's – coming from within, and he didn't scruple to eavesdrop.

'It is most unfortunate we should meet in this way,' Mrs Sheffield said. 'I had no idea you would be here, or I would have—'

'Indeed.' Asquith said the one word with a marked lack of the charm Joshua was accustomed to hearing in his voice.

'What do you intend to do?'

'I have not yet decided.'

A long pause, and then Mrs Sheffield spoke again. 'Thank you at least for not making your suspicions public so far. I have told you many times they are unfounded, but if you do not choose to believe me, there is nothing I can do about it. However, such a slur, even if it is not supported by evidence, which it cannot be because there is none, would show me in a bad light.'

'We made a mistake in pretending we do not know one another. People are already suspicious.'

'I did not know what to do and followed your lead. I had no idea you were here, whereas you must have realised who I was when Mrs Darcy mentioned my name.'

'Yes.'

'Please do me one kindness, even though I have no right to ask it of you. If you do decide to voice your suspicions, at least warn me in advance and give me an opportunity to tell my sister myself. She suffers from a nervous disposition and such a slanderous allegation would make her condition worse. I would leave here and return to my husband's estate, but I am not free to do so. My husband's brother seeks to—'

'Yes, I heard something about that.' Perdition, why the devil did Asquith have to interrupt? Joshua wanted to know a great deal more about the slanderous allegations Asquith was considering levelling against Mrs Sheffield. Damn his impertinence! 'Come, we ought to return to the drawing room before we are missed.'

Joshua was shocked by Asquith's abrupt tone and complete lack of sympathy when it was obvious Mrs Sheffield was in some sort of trouble. Trouble that was visited upon her in Jamaica. He concealed himself when the two of them left the room and delayed his return to the drawing room, slipping in virtually unseen.

His tardiness meant any opportunity to converse with Mrs Sheffield was again denied to him. Music had been suggested, and it appeared Mrs Sheffield played, as did Georgiana and Eliza. The three ladies conferred and Mrs Sheffield was persuaded to perform first. Joshua enjoyed music and it soon became evident that Mrs Sheffield was a proficient pianist. It was equally obvious, but unsurprising given the conversation he had just overheard, that she was preoccupied and gave her performance less attention than it deserved. Even so, he joined in the warm applause at the end of her piece, when she gave way at the instrument to Georgiana.

Mrs Sheffield found a seat at the side of the room and Joshua strolled across to join her. People had got up and moved around when Mrs Sheffield quit the instrument, so Joshua's movements went unnoticed by the rest of the gathering since their attention was now focused on Georgiana.

'May I?' He indicated the vacant seat beside Mrs Sheffield.

'Please do, Colonel.'

Joshua swished the tails of his coat aside and seated himself. It was impossible for him to establish from her demeanour whether Mrs Sheffield welcomed his company or if she had hoped for solitude.

'You play very well.'

'You are mistaken, sir. My performance was unremarkable. These surroundings are rather daunting.'

'I cannot believe you are a stranger to elegant salons.'

'The salons in Jamaica are not on this scale, and since returning to England I have been in mourning. I am still reacquainting myself with society's mores.'

'Your absence has been society's loss.'

'It is very gallant of you to say so, sir, but quite unnecessary.' She lifted her gaze to his face and smiled at him. The effect that simple gesture had on him took Joshua completely unawares. Desire spiralled through him in a unique and disquieting manner. It had been a very long time since he had felt such a fierce attraction and such torrents of protectiveness towards any female. 'I am fully aware of my limitations as a musician.'

'You do yourself an injustice.' Joshua paused, wondering what more he could say to her. The subject of music had already been exhausted between them, and he could sense he was losing her attention. Now, he decided, was not the time to mention Jamaica. She was skittish, afraid of something, and he had no wish to scare her off. 'How do you find Derbyshire?'

'Cold,' she said with another smile.

'Quite, but rather beautiful also.'

'Yes, what I have seen of it so far. I enjoy riding very much. It is something I missed during my years in Jamaica. It was too hot and not safe enough. But now I am back, I am intent upon exploring the countryside here.'

'Then allow me to offer my services as a guide.'

'Oh, thank you, but I did not mention my plans in order to beg for a companion.'

'I am sure you did not, but it would be my pleasure. I spent a lot of time here as a boy and know the area like the back of my hand. Really, I would enjoy the excuse to show off my local knowledge.'

'Well, if you are sure—'

'Absolutely sure. Would tomorrow morning be too soon?'

She raised a brow, and Joshua cursed his impatience. As a good military tactician, he knew rushing an unplanned strategy through was a recipe for disaster, but the blame rested entirely with Mrs Sheffield. There was something about her that caused him to act impulsively. 'Do you not have responsibilities to detain you at Pemberley?'

God's beard, did everyone know what his aunt expected of him? 'Not that I am aware of,' he replied casually.

'Even so, I—'

'You need not concern yourself with the proprieties if that is what makes you hesitate. This is the country, not the *ton*, and if it would make you feel better we could take a groom with us.'

'That particular difficulty had not occurred to me, but now that you mention it—'

'You are in need of a friend hereabouts, are you not, Mrs Sheffield?'

She gasped. 'Whatever do you mean by that?'

Joshua glanced at Asquith, standing beside the piano and singing, accompanied by Mrs Darcy. In view of the conversation he had just overheard, Joshua reviewed his opinion of Asquith and was annoyed that he appeared to do absolutely everything he attempted with consummate skill. Did the blaggard have no faults? 'I sense antagonism between you,' he said softly, 'and would like nothing more than to be your friend. Do not suspect me of ulterior motives, madam, because I have none. I merely wish to be of service to you.'

She closed her eyes and then nodded. 'You are very perceptive.'

Or a damned good eavesdropper. 'I live to serve.'

'Really, it is nothing. I have no wish to visit my trifling problems upon you.'

'Not so very trifling, I think,' he replied softly, holding her captive with his eyes.

Mrs Sheffield turned away from him, as though she was worried about what he might read from her expression. 'Very well, Colonel. Thank you. I shall be pleased to ride out with you in the morning, but have we not been warned to expect bad weather?'

Perdition; so they had. 'Weather permitting. Let us hope the rain obliges us by holding off until later in the day.'

Her spontaneous laughter enchanted Joshua and drew curious glances from several others in the room. 'I ought to remind you, Colonel, that the elements do not answer to anyone, not even colonels, and will do whatever they like.'

Joshua responded with a wicked smile of his own. 'They would not dare to disappoint me,' he said, rising to his feet and reluctantly excusing himself.

8

'Leave us.'

The sound of Mama's voice at its most autocratic caused Anne's heart to sink. Her maid bobbed a hasty curtsey and vacated the room, but escape for Anne would not be so easily achieved. Anne had hoped that by rising early she would be able to avoid seeing her mother and facing the questions she sensed her formulating. She pushed her breakfast tray aside and summoned up a smile.

'Mama, I did not expect to see you about so early.'

'The same could be said of you. I thought you would still be sleeping.'

And yet you came to disturb me? 'I agreed to join the other ladies this morning. We are to start work on the play.'

'I did not give you leave to participate. It is not the sort of thing you ought to be doing.'

'My role will be a minor one, and I would hate to disappoint everyone.'

Mama fixed Anne with a penetrating glare. 'Everyone or someone in particular?'

Anne swallowed, unsure what she had done to give herself

away and occasion her mother's suspicions. She was not in the habit of disobeying her formidable parent, but for once she wanted something badly enough to stand up for herself. She had probably not chosen a good moment to act rebelliously, but there was no help for that. Mama had broken her self-imposed exile from Pemberley grudgingly, and now that she was here, she did not like seeing Mrs Darcy as its mistress. She had been bad tempered and highly critical of that lady's conduct since her arrival, but refrained from expressing her displeasure in public for fear, presumably, of causing further tension between herself and Mr Darcy. In spite of all that, Anne's strong desire not to be excluded from Mr Asquith's planned entertainment gave her courage.

'I feel so much stronger nowadays and look it too,' Anne said, avoiding a reply to her mother's question, mainly because there was nothing she could possibly say short of an outright untruth that would not condemn her. 'Everyone says as much.'

Mama narrowed her eyes. 'I miscalculated when I permitted Mr Asquith into your life. He has turned your head and made you forget your duty. I can quite see that now.'

'Does that mean you plan to dismiss him?' Anne could hear the despair in her own voice.

'That rather depends upon you.'

'Me?' Anne opened her eyes very wide. 'I have a say?'

'You are old enough now to understand what is expected of you.'

'I have always known that, Mama,' Anne replied quietly.

'You have been protected and cossetted all your life, which is partly my fault, and partly a consequence of your fragile health.' Mama paced around the chamber, looking uncharacteristically flustered. 'You have never seen anything of the real world, nor do you understand its ways. I was hoping Mr Asquith would give you some insights, make you understand just how privileged you are, and prepare you for the next stage of your life.'

'He has taught me a great deal.'

'More than I anticipated, clearly.'

Anne had no idea how to respond. 'I do know how fortunate I am,' she said instead. 'How could I not?' *Especially when I have you to constantly remind me.*

Mama turned and fixed Anne with the full force of her determination. 'With privilege comes responsibility, Anne. Never lose sight of the fact that many people rely upon Rosings for their livelihoods. Since your papa died I have done my level best to maintain the estate and keep it profitable, but it is no easy task and it has sapped my strength.'

Anne sat a little straighter. Her mother had always appeared indefatigable and certainly was not in the habit of admitting to her weaknesses, supposing she had any. 'Are you feeling unwell, Mama? You did not say anything. Have you seen a doctor?'

'I am merely tired, nothing more. It is time to start ceding my responsibilities to you, or rather to your husband. Which means I must choose the right man to keep the Rosings estate running smoothly. Many men would aspire to own it, but most would fritter its wealth away because they are too idle to keep proper control. I cannot allow that to happen.'

'No, of course not.'

Anne did understand that perfectly well. What was less clear was why she could not be allowed to make her own choice, or at least have a say in the matter. She did not bother to pose a question that would only lead to a serious disagreement between mother and daughter, but she still wanted to scream that it was unfair. She did not care about wealth, privilege, or even Rosings. She would settle for a very great deal less if only she could choose her own husband. But then again, if she did not have wealth and privilege, what man would be interested in her?

'May I ask why you chose to replace Mrs Jenkinson with Mr Asquith, Mama? It was an unusual arrangement that raised more than one set of eyebrows. I overheard Mr Collins advising you quite forcibly not to take the chance.'

'Mr Collins sometimes assumes too much. Besides, he does not know Mr Asquith's history.'

'Whatever do you mean?'

Mama's expression became distant. She was quiet for so long, Anne thought she wouldn't answer her question. When she did speak again, her tone was remote, her expression even more so.

'Mr Asquith's mentor in Jamaica, Sir Marius Glover, was a very close friend of your papa's.'

'Oh, I did not realise.'

'No one does. It is not something I choose to talk about. Sir Marius and your father, Sir Lewis, were inseparable as young men. I knew them both very well.'

Anne had never heard her mother sound so wistful before, or seen her look so pensive. She understood then that she probably had loved both men. How extraordinary. Mama clearly had hidden depths, deeply buried secrets that accounted for her inexplicable decision to employ Mr Asquith. Anne sat forward expectantly, hoping her mother would say something more to throw light on the matter. Perhaps Sir Marius had been her first choice but he had not felt the same way about Mama, or Mama had found herself in a similar position to Anne and had not been permitted to make her own choice. It took a great deal of imagination to think of Mama as young and in love – not with one gentleman, but with two.

'When Mr Asquith returned to England looking for a position as a teacher, Sir Marius suggested he tried Hunsford and sent a letter of recommendation, which Mr Collins received. At the same time, Sir Marius wrote to me urging me to give the young man an opportunity.' Mama stared through the window, her back turned to Anne, still lost in the past. 'Mrs Jenkinson had just left us. I interviewed Mr Asquith, liked what I saw of his manners and intellect, and thought he might be just the person to imbue you with a little self-confidence.' Mama paused, screwing her features into a more recognisable expression of distaste. 'He seems to have managed the task a little better than I anticipated.'

'Mama, I do not mean to—'

'You will marry Colonel Fitzwilliam, Anne.' Mama whirled around, her earlier pathos replaced with a look of stark determination. 'Mr Asquith is charming and I can quite see why you are so taken with him, but he is not well born. Rosings cannot be entrusted to his care and neither can you.' Mama's voice softened. 'Do not imagine me to be quite so heartless that I care nothing for your happiness, since nothing could be further from the truth. Even so, we must all make sacrifices in this life.' She paused. 'Even you.'

'I do not believe Colonel Fitzwilliam wishes to marry me, Mama. He has not shown the slightest partiality towards me.'

'But he will, once he has had the opportunity to consider the advantages of the match. He will ensure that Rosings prospers. I can trust him absolutely in that respect.'

Anne said nothing, quelling a rare burst of temper she knew better than to reveal. She wondered if her mother could even begin to imagine how worthless it made her feel to have it confirmed that gentlemen had to be tempted by the prize of Rosings into matrimony with her. Even then, it appeared Colonel Fitzwilliam was still hesitating.

'Mr Asquith may remain with us,' Mama continued, presumably mistaking Anne's silence for acquiescence, 'provided you promise me you will remember your duty and do as I ask.'

'Colonel Fitzwilliam does not love me, nor I him.'

Mama flapped a hand. 'Love has nothing to do with the matter.'

'Did you not love Papa?' Anne canted her head as she dared to ask the question. 'You always speak of him with great affection.'

'I married him because my father said he was the right man for me, much as I am telling you Fitzwilliam is right for you. My father knew best, and so do I.'

Which does not answer my question. 'I had always hoped to fall in love with the man I marry.'

'Don't be such a fool! That only happens in penny novels.'

'Mr Darcy married for love.'

'Darcy is a great disappoint to me.' Mama pursed her lips. 'I thought he had more sense than to be swayed by a fine pair of eyes. I am happy my sister is not alive to see who has become mistress of Pemberley in her place.'

'I like Mrs Darcy,' Anne said, surprising herself by showing great daring she was unaware she possessed. In danger of incurring her mother's ire, she persevered, mainly because Mama had never spoken to her so frankly before and Anne thought it important to show that she did have a mind of her own. 'And I believe she makes Mr Darcy happy.'

Mama snorted. 'For now, perhaps, but it will not last, and he will then be at leisure to regret his foolishness. But enough of the Darcys. I never thought I would have occasion to remind you of your duty but it seems I was wrong about that. And now I need you to assure me that you will accept Fitzwilliam when he offers for you. Only if I have your word will I permit Mr Asquith to remain for a moment longer.'

Anne paused, sorrow and resignation twisting her insides into a vicious knot of disappointment because she knew she had no real choice in the matter. 'Yes, Mama,' she replied, suppressing a sigh which nevertheless managed to slip past her guard. 'Of course I will behave as you expect me to.'

Joshua awoke to a sky heavy with dark clouds that threatened rain. However, it was not raining for now, which was all that mattered to him. He broke his fast early and was out on horseback long before the hour when he had agreed to meet Mrs Sheffield. She had insisted Joshua not call for her at Briar Hall and excite the interest of her sister. Joshua had willingly agreed and now walked his horse around the spinney that separated the two estates, anxious with anticipation. He felt like a callow youth about to confront an attractive lady for the first time rather than the seasoned campaigner that he actually was.

Ye gods, Celia Sheffield had a lot to answer for.

He heard her approaching before he actually saw her, which gave him a moment to quell his ridiculous nerves. He raised a hand in greeting when a pretty bay mare appeared on the path ahead of him, with Mrs Sheffield perched elegantly on a side saddle. She wore a form-fitting pale blue velvet habit with matching hat that sported a whimsical plume. Significantly, she was alone, no groom in sight. Joshua took that to be an encouraging sign.

'Good morning, Mrs Sheffield.' Joshua raised his hat.

'Good morning, Colonel. I trust you have not been waiting for long.'

'I only just this moment arrived myself.' He turned his horse in the opposite direction. 'If we go this way, we will reach the folly on the top of the hill. It is quite a climb, but the view makes the effort worthwhile.'

'It is not us who will be making the effort,' she replied, patting her mare's neck. 'But I have often wished to see that folly, and Molly is keen to stretch her legs.'

'Well then, we are agreed.'

They rode side by side in silence as the horses commenced the upward incline. Joshua cast sideways glances at his fair companion, feeling ridiculously privileged to have her to himself. She looked fresh this morning, but there was evidence of strain around her eyes, as though she had not slept well.

'Darcy and I spent hours playing in these woods as boys,' he said. 'We set up camps, enlisted boys from the farms to our respective sides, and plotted to breach one another's headquarters.'

Mrs Sheffield's smile lit up her eyes, banishing the sadness that had resided there. 'So you were a soldier in the making even then.'

'Perhaps I was. The alternatives were the church or the law. Neither appealed. Besides, wearing a red coat held a certain appeal to a young man who did not understand the brutal realities of soldiering.'

'And yet you rose to the rank of colonel.'

'Indeed.'

'Seldom have I met a gentleman better suited to soldiering than you are.'

'How can you tell? You barely know me.'

'Oh, I can tell. I have led a very active life and had a lot of contact with military men over the years.'

Joshua laughed. 'You make yourself sound as old as the hills.'

She wrinkled her nose. 'I feel that way sometimes.'

'A positive old crone,' Joshua said, laughing at her.

'Thank you, but I was not fishing for a compliment when I made that remark.'

'Certainly, I am aware of that, but nonetheless the situation calls for plain speaking. I am sure you don't need me to tell you that your presence here is like a breath of fresh air.'

Mrs Sheffield shot him a sideways look. 'With such charming manners, I find it hard to believe you are still unmarried. I feel persuaded more than one young lady must have set her cap at you before now.'

'Since we appear to be speaking frankly, you might as well know I am a younger son.'

'Yes, I thought that must be the case. You are obliged to make your own way and marry for money.'

'If I marry at all.'

'You definitely should,' she replied, sending him a shrewd glance. 'You would do a disservice to my sex by remaining single.'

'Now it is my turn to assure *you* I was not looking for compliments.'

'And mine to confess I already knew your circumstances. My sister, you understand. You are Lord Braithwaite's younger son, are you not?'

'Yes. But my father died some years ago. My brother now holds that title.'

She offered him a wry smile. 'You do not think highly of your brother?'

'Good heavens, your sister is well informed.'

Mrs Sheffield's laughter filled the air. 'No, not my sister this time. You just gave yourself away. You glanced to the left when you mentioned your brother and a look of extreme distaste crossed your face.'

'Ah well, there you have me. I can see I shall have to guard my expressions more closely while in your company.'

'For my part, I hope you do not.'

Their conversation came to a halt when the path narrowed and they were obliged to ride in single file, with Joshua leading the way. He glanced back to ensure Mrs Sheffield was keeping up with him, impressed with the easy way in which she handled her mare. It was clear she was no stranger to the saddle. Her balance was precise, her seat elegant, her hands light on the reins.

'I can see that you really do enjoy being on horseback,' he said when they were able to ride side by side again. He watched her as she steered her mare around a rut in the path, still wondering what to make of her previous comment and how to respond to it. 'You certainly ride well.'

'Thank you. I enjoy being outdoors. While I have been here it has been frustrating not to be able to ride without a groom. We are in the country, so it ought not to matter, but frustratingly I don't know the lie of the land and it would be so easy to get lost. My sister does not ride and Lord Briar doesn't have the time to oblige me.'

'Ah, I see.' Joshua sent her a smile of mock reproach. 'Now I understand why you accepted my offer. And there was I thinking that my sparkling wit and engaging personality were the attraction.'

She hooted with laughter and Joshua found her uninhibited personality refreshing. 'Colonel Fitzwilliam, I hope you do not expect me to respond to such an infamous remark.'

Joshua laughed as well. 'Forgive me, Mrs Sheffield. I cannot imagine what came over me. However, I blame you.'

'Me?'

'Indeed you. Your outspokenness appears to have rubbed off on me.'

'Oh no, you must do better than that if you wish to impress me.'

'I certainly wish to do that, and so I shall reapply myself.'

They reached the top of the hill. Mrs Sheffield looked around and gasped. 'This is wonderful! Thank you so much for bringing me here. One can see for miles.'

'It's the wrong weather for it. As you can see, the dark clouds are rolling in and we shall have the promised rain. On a clear day, it is so much more worth the effort of coming up here.' He threw his leg over the pommel of his saddle and jumped athletically to the ground. He secured his horse's reins to prevent them being trodden on and turned him loose to crop at the thin grass. 'Shall we walk?'

Joshua reached up his hands, placed them on Mrs Sheffield's waist, and lifted her down. He paused when her face was on a level with his. Drinking in the sight of her lovely features, her skin slightly flushed from the exertion of the ride, he was slow to place her on her feet. Their gazes locked and a strange feeling gripped Joshua – a premonition, a sun responding to a gravitational pull; something. She felt it, too. He could tell as much by the way her sculpted lips formed a perfect 'O', and he suspected that the deeper colour now invading her cheeks had nothing to do with their recent exercise.

'There we are.'

His voice sounded thick and raw as he turned his attention to her mare. Satisfied that the horses could not stray far, he offered Mrs Sheffield his arm, and they slowly strolled along the crest of the hill. She continued to admire the view, exclaiming every so often as Joshua pointed out landmarks. He preferred to admire his companion rather than the vista opening up beneath them, willing the rain to hold off and time to stand still.

'You can see the entire layout of the Pemberley house,' Joshua said, pointing in the appropriate direction.

'My goodness, it is extensive.'

'It certainly is.'

'I hear Lady Catherine was set upon combining Pemberley and her own estate in Kent.'

'Yes, but as soon as Darcy met his wife, there was not the slightest possibility of that ever happening.'

'Oh dear, that cannot have pleased Lady Catherine. She seems like a lady who is accustomed to having her own way.'

'That is certainly true, and she has sufficient wealth and consequence to ensure most people do as she wishes.'

'But not her nephew, it seems.'

'My aunt failed to take into account that Darcy inherited the same stubborn streak as Lady Catherine's from his mother, Lady Catherine's sister.'

'I was not referring specifically to Mr Darcy.'

'Ah, I see.'

But Joshua did not see – not precisely. Who had Lady Catherine told about her expectation of Joshua wedding Anne? It seemed unlikely she would speak about it, especially to strangers, until terms had been agreed. There again, perhaps she sensed Joshua's reluctance and was trying to make it happen by openly implying it was all but settled. Either way, it was clear Mrs Sheffield knew, or suspected. So why was she here with him now?

'And what of your own plans, Mrs Sheffield? How long do you intend to remain in Derbyshire?'

She sent him a teasing smile. 'Are you tired of my society already, Colonel?'

'Quite the contrary, I do assure you, but I understood you inherited an estate from your husband.'

'Yes, in Buckinghamshire.' Her laughter abruptly faded. 'But I have no immediate plans to return there.'

'Your husband made his fortune in Jamaica, I collect.'

'Yes.'

'Did you enjoy living there?'

Mrs Sheffield absently plucked a leaf from a bush as she considered the question. 'At first, but I soon became homesick.'

'I understand. I have spent some time on the island myself and confess I found it rather limiting after a while. If you enjoy riding, and you clearly do, I can understand why living in Jamaica would have been frustrating. As you said last evening, you cannot ride out alone and it's usually too hot to ride at all.'

'Precisely.'

They had reached the end of the path and paused to admire a different prospect. 'You and Mr Asquith met one another in Jamaica, I imagine,' Joshua suggested as they turned to retrace their steps.

Her entire body tensed. 'Why ever would you think that?'

'Tell me to mind my own business if you like, but if we are to be friends I would prefer it if you did not prevaricate. I am a colonel, Mrs Sheffield, a leader of men. It is my job to recognise, or at least suspect, when things are not all they seem to be.'

'You take a very great interest in my affairs, Colonel.'

He covered the hand that rested on his sleeve with one of his own hands and was slow to remove it again. 'Yes,' he said. 'I do. You must forgive me but I cannot seem to help myself. I know you are in trouble, have anxieties that keep you from your own property, and if I can be of service in any way you have but to say the word.'

She swallowed several times, and Joshua thought her eyes appeared moist. 'Thank you,' she said softly. 'I was not aware I was in such very great need of a confidante, until now.'

'You are assured of one if you will honour me with your trust.'

They walked in contemplative silence for several minutes. Joshua was unsure whether he had overstepped the mark. No, that was not precisely true. He *knew* that he had. In fact, the tenor of their entire conversation had not exactly been correct. It had however felt exactly right. What was less sure was whether Mrs

Sheffield would turn away from him or look to him for the help she clearly needed. There was nothing more he could say or do to persuade her and so he remained silent. It was now up to her.

'Mr Asquith and I are acquainted,' she said eventually, 'but we do not choose to advertise the fact. There was nothing improper about our relationship in Jamaica, but for reasons I cannot share with you, we prefer others not to know it.'

'In which case, you can rely upon my discretion.'

'Again, I am indebted to you.' She stepped around a rut in the path. 'That is why I was so keen not to take part in the play Mr Asquith is producing and why he did not wish me to be a part of it. I understand he has made alternative arrangements to fill the vacant role.'

'You dislike one another so much that you cannot bear to be in the same room?' Joshua flexed a brow. 'Now I am really intrigued.'

'You read too much into that particular situation.'

'What business was your husband in? What took him to Jamaica is what I am asking, I suppose?'

'Oh, the usual. He and his younger brother were involved in the exportation of sugar.'

'He had his own plantation?'

'Yes. He was known to Sir Marius Glover, Mr Asquith's mentor, which is how I came to know Mr Asquith.'

'But there is a very great deal more to your acquaintanceship than that, I think. Your husband died in Jamaica.'

'Yes, a fever went round and he unfortunately caught it.'

Again, Joshua was convinced she was holding something back. She certainly didn't appear to mourn her husband genuinely. 'I am very sorry,' he said.

'And the correct response would be for me to say I am too, but it would be untrue.' She flashed a brittle smile. 'My husband was a bully and a tyrant and I would be a hypocrite if I pretended to be sorry he was dead. If we are to be friends, Colonel Fitzwilliam, I ought to be able to trust you with that secret at least.'

'It is refreshing to hear you admit it, Mrs Sheffield, and you can certainly trust me with as many of your secrets as you are willing to share.'

'You make me sound as though I am leading a double life.'

'I assume your family persuaded you to marry him since it is clear that you did not do so voluntarily.'

'Yes, he was a charming gentleman from a good, if impoverished, family, and my father thought well of him. I had neither the will nor inclination to go against my father's wishes and so we were married. With the benefit of my dowry, Albert and his brother became involved in Jamaica.'

'His brother is still alive?'

'Unfortunately, yes.'

'And living on your estate in Buckinghamshire?'

'Precisely.'

'I see.'

And this time he did, to a degree. The brother was at least as loathsome as the dead husband, and probably had designs upon Mrs Sheffield. However, she was no longer the subject of parental dictate and wished to have nothing to do with him. Be that as it may, the property obviously belonged to her and she ought not to be afraid to occupy it. Joshua was filled with a violent need to be of service to Mrs Sheffield, and wondered how to make the suggestion. Before he could think of a way, a fat raindrop bounced off the brim of his hat. He glanced up and noticed a black cloud directly overhead. He had been so entranced by Mrs Sheffield's engaging company that he had not noticed the weather closing in. He stripped off his coat, held it over her head, and together they rushed for the shelter of the folly.

By the time they reached it, Joshua, now in waistcoat and shirtsleeves, was soaking wet. Mrs Sheffield, with the protection of his coat, had fared a little better. Even so, the plume on her hat wilted across her face, bedraggled and probably ruined. She blew it out of her eyes, and then laughed.

'Thank you,' she said, moving from beneath the protection of his coat. 'That was kind of you, and now you are soaked through.'

'Better I should be, than you.'

'How very gallant.' She crossed her arms over her torso and hugged herself, laughing as she watched the rain pounding onto the hard earth. 'I love rain. We had a lot of it in Jamaica, but that was tropical rain, of course. Not the same thing at all.'

Joshua stood directly behind her, somehow managing not to touch her. God's teeth, but it was a hard temptation to resist! Never had he felt a greater urge to embrace a woman. Never had circumstances conspired to make it so easy and yet impossible. He wanted her to trust him, not fear his intentions. He wanted that trust very badly indeed.

'Then I am glad to have been able to summon up a rainstorm for your enjoyment,' he said. 'Unfortunately, it is unlikely to last for long. I can see clear skies directly behind the raincloud.'

'Perhaps that is just as well. My sister will wonder what has become of me and worry. Besides, my solicitor is due from London today. He has matters to discuss with me regarding Albert's estate.'

'Mrs Sheffield.' Joshua removed his hat and ran a hand through his damp hair, unsure how to phrase what was on his mind, aware he ought not to but unable to help himself. 'I know you have difficulties. I know they somehow have to do with Asquith and your brother-in-law. We are virtual strangers but I feel as though I have known you for a long time.'

'Yes,' she said softly. 'I can understand that because I feel it too.'

'Then will you not let me be of service to you? Whatever troubles you, you have clearly not confided in your sister or her husband. Please treat me as your confidante. You ought not to feel so alone.'

'Thank you, Colonel Fitzwilliam, but I could not burden you. You have enough problems of your own to be going on with.'

'If you refer to my aunt then let me put your mind at rest. I might not have Darcy's resources but I share his stubbornness. No one will make me do that which I do not wish to do, regardless of the monetary rewards.'

'Fine words, sir, and finer principles are at play here, but even younger sons must have something to live on.'

Strange, Joshua thought, but he recalled saying more or less the same words to Eliza Bennet as she still was when they'd first met at Rosings more than a year previously. Mrs Sheffield obviously saw more than he realised and understood what was only just becoming apparent to him. He would probably have married his cousin and made the best of it even though his heart wasn't in it. Since meeting Mrs Sheffield, every bone in his body rebelled at the thought. He had no reason to suppose that lady would entertain an offer from him, especially so soon after being widowed, but making her acquaintance had reminded him that money was not the path to happiness.

He placed a hand on the small of her back, sensing her body heat searing through his glove, and turned her towards the door.

'Come,' he said. 'The rain has eased. I will escort you home.'

The horses had had the good sense to seek cover when the rain came and their saddles were only a little damp. He easily lifted Mrs Sheffield into hers and helped her to find her stirrup. Satisfied that she was comfortable, he swung himself onto the back of his own horse.

'I must see you again,' he said as they descended the hill and turned in the direction of Briar Hall.

'I would like that, Colonel.'

When they reached her destination, he kissed the back of her hand as he bade her *adieu.*

'May I call on you tomorrow?' he asked.

'Certainly you may, although what my sister will make of my entertaining gentleman callers, I can't begin to imagine.'

'Would your sister have you live a life of seclusion? You are, after all, out of mourning for a man you did not love. Presumably your sister knows there was little affection in your marriage and will rejoice in seeing you making new acquaintances?'

Her teasing smile illuminated her eyes, banishing their haunted expression. Joshua's reaction to it was profound, and he shifted his position in his saddle, anxious to conceal its physical manifestation.

'I believe you are right about that, Colonel, just as you appear to be right about so many things. You see a great deal. I shall have to remain alert when in your company if I wish to retain even a degree of mystique.'

Her gaze clashed with his and Joshua was conscious of the deep longing that whipped through his bloodstream. He had supposed himself to be infatuated by a lady on several previous occasions but the feelings he had entertained then were nothing to the way he felt for this feisty, mysterious, and slightly vulnerable widow.

'For you, Mrs Sheffield, I shall ensure my insight is selective.'

She laughed, waving over her shoulder as she rode through the gates to Briar Hall. 'Where would be the fun in that?' she asked.

Joshua bit back the flirtatious response that sprang to his lips, waited until she had disappeared from view, and then turned in the direction of Pemberley, wondering what the devil he was supposed to do about his situation now.

9

'You are sisters. Dolores, Dorothea and Daphne Downton all have their individual interests set upon the same man,' Mr Asquith explained. 'Originally there were four of you, but I was unable to persuade Mrs Sheffield to become Doris. No matter, three will work just as well, if not better.'

'Don't t-tell me,' Captain Turner said, laughing. 'The object of their affections is Mr David Doolittle.'

Georgiana and Kitty linked arms and smiled at Anne. 'I feel sorry for the poor gentleman, being bombarded with our attentions,' Georgiana said.

'But at least he only has to endure three of us now, instead of four,' Kitty pointed out.

'I shall gladly play the part of that gentleman,' Major Halstead said. 'I think I can tolerate the attention.'

Everyone laughed.

'At first, there is lively competition between you,' Mr Asquith continued. 'But each of you secretly believes she will triumph. When none of you makes progress, you become less civilised and start sabotaging one another's campaigns.'

'Goodness,' Anne said. 'It all sounds rather brutal.'

'That is the beauty of comedy, Miss de Bourgh. One takes an ordinary situation and makes it farcical. I mean, how far would you go, what stratagems would you employ, to secure the affections of a man you supposed yourself to be in love with?'

Anne's cheeks warmed. She wished Mr Asquith's question could be personal rather than hypothetical. He was so handsome, so elegantly relaxed amongst Anne's relations and Mr Darcy's distinguished guests, almost as though he had been born to a position of consequence himself. He assumed the role of gentleman as though he actually *was* one, making it necessary for Anne to remind herself that appearances could be deceiving. He was so intelligent, Anne would never tire of listening to his voice as he effortlessly instructed the players in their individual roles. She watched his fingers curling around the edges of the book, as she so often had before, while he read out parts of the play. The thought of those same long fingers stroking her skin had kept her awake on countless occasions as deep feelings of intense longing gripped her body, sending tremors down the length of it, awakening a part of her she had previously been unaware existed.

He looked at her so intently as he waited for her answer, she wondered if his question was personal and if he had guessed her shameful secret. Oh dear, this was all so confusing. She had so little experience with the male gender that she had no way of knowing, and no one whom she could go to for advice. Unless, perhaps... Lizzy Darcy had been so kind to her, so patient and understanding. Could she dare to ask her? Anne's blush deepened at the very idea of exposing herself to ridicule. If Mr Asquith had found her out, then this ought to be a tragedy, not a comedy, since Anne had much to fear from any future that did not measure up to her mother's rigid standards, and little to laugh at.

'Would you really put itching powder in your sister's clothing,

Miss de Bourgh?' Kitty asked, giggling as she skimmed through her lines.

'Or ruin the trim on her best ball gown when there was no time left to repair it?' Georgiana added. 'Oh dear. I am afraid we are not very nice sisters at all, Mr Asquith.'

'Which of the sisters finally triumphs?' Jane Bingley asked from her chair in the corner of the room, from which she acted the part of chaperone.

'None of them,' Mr Asquith replied, smiling. 'Major Halstead's character is already secretly married to a woman his father does not approve of. He has to pretend to court the Downton sisters, just to put his father off the scent, you see.'

'I s-say, what a bounder,' Captain Turner said, grinning.

'Shall we run through the parts?' Mr Asquith stood up and indicated the dais at one end of Pemberley's ballroom. 'The opening scene sees the three sisters sitting together when their brother, played by Captain Turner, brings his friend Major Halstead to the house for the first time. Are we all ready?'

They read for half an hour, with much laughter and many errors being made. At first, Anne was nervous, and her voice could barely be heard. When it occurred to her no one was laughing at her efforts or deferring to her in the manner she was accustomed to, and which so irked her, she gradually relaxed and actually enjoyed herself.

'Well done, all of you,' Mr Asquith said when a maid came in with refreshments. 'I think I can safely say there is only room for improvement.'

Everyone laughed.

'I thought we made a passable first attempt,' Major Halstead said. 'Although I will be the first to admit we are a long way from making a living through treading the boards.'

'Just as w-well we d-don't need to,' Captain Turner added.

Georgiana settled herself behind the teapot and poured for everyone.

'We need to think about costumes and scenery,' Mr Asquith said as he sat down and elegantly crossed his long legs at the ankle. 'Mrs Darcy has kindly said it will be all right to stage our performance in the music room, although it is better if we rehearse in here where we won't be in anyone's way.'

'Since we shall have such a small audience,' Kitty said, 'the music room is a good idea.'

'Quite.' Mr Asquith shared a smile between them all, but Anne chose to believe it lingered upon her for longer than anyone else. 'Your own clothing will be perfectly all right, ladies, but we do need to think about painting some scenery. A lot of the action takes place in the garden, you will recall.'

'We could hang up old sheets and paint garden scenes on them,' Kitty said.

'Absolutely,' Georgiana agreed. 'I shall speak with Mrs Reynolds and see if she can supply us with sheeting.'

The conversation was lively with suggestions, many of them fatuous, some actually helpful. Only Anne remained silent, mainly because she was unable to think of anything sensible or amusing to contribute.

Everyone drifted away once tea was finished and Anne found herself alone with Mr Asquith. That was not unusual. It had happened on many occasions since his appointment as her tutor, even though she was supposed to be chaperoned at all times. She had never felt nervous before but today things were different. Something had changed between them. The atmosphere was charged with a feeling Anne was unable to identify – the one that normally only crept up on her when she was alone in her bed at night and her thoughts dwelt upon the man who had captivated her.

'Are you glad I persuaded you to take part, Miss de Bourgh?'

'I beg your pardon.' Anne snapped out of her reverie and gave her full attention to Mr Asquith, although she was unable to meet his gaze for fear of what he might read in her expression. Instead she looked at her hands clasped together in her lap.

'I merely thanked you for agreeing to participate. The play would not work nearly so well with only two sisters instead of the original four.'

'I enjoyed this morning. I did not think I would, and so that surprised me. Unfortunately I was not very good.'

'Nonsense. You were every bit as good as the others.'

'You deceived me, Mr Asquith. You promised I would only have a small part to play, but that doesn't seem to be the case.'

The corners of his lips lifted. 'Would you have agreed to do it if you had known?'

'Probably not.'

'Then you must forgive me for the small deception. I am employed in part to help you overcome your shyness. What better way?'

She shook a finger at him, astonished by her brazenness. To her precise knowledge, she had never in her entire life shaken a finger at anyone before now. 'You are very devious, Mr Asquith.'

He chuckled. 'I live to serve, Miss de Bourgh.'

A heavy silence ensued. In her desire to break it and prolong her moment alone with Mr Asquith, Anne asked the first question that popped into her head. 'What shall you do when your position at Rosings comes to an end?' *Whatever possessed me to bring that subject up?*

'Find another one, I suppose,' he said with a shrug of his impossibly broad shoulders, seeming disconcertingly unconcerned about leaving Rosings, and her, at some future date.

The thought of another young lady being the recipient of his wisdom and charm filled Anne with a virulent jealousy. 'In a school perhaps?'

'Wherever there is a place for my talents, such as they are.' He cocked his head to one side and sent her a lopsided smile. 'Are you in such a very great hurry to get rid of me?'

'Oh no!' How could he possibly think that? 'I was just curious. You are so very good with people, I cannot imagine you having any difficulty when the time comes, that is all, and I wondered where your preference lay. Mama would, I am sure, give you a glowing character.'

'You are to marry Colonel Fitzwilliam, which is the reason for your question.'

His was not a question, Anne realised, but more a statement of fact. It annoyed her that everyone seemed to think the matter was settled, when the colonel had not said a word to her and she had not actually agreed to anything.

'Why does everyone seem to think that?' she asked crossly.

'Excuse me if I speak out of turn. Before we left Kent, Lady Catherine told me that was the purpose of this visit, and, well, I just assumed—'

'The colonel has not spoken to me, and even if he does, I...'

Anne became too choked with emotion to continue speaking. To her great mortification, she felt tears trickling down her face. Mr Asquith knelt beside her and took one of her hands in his. He had never touched her so intimately before, and the gesture took her completely by surprise. It occurred to her now that he had always gone out of his way *not* to touch her. He drew patterns on her palm with his thumb, while passing her his handkerchief with his other hand.

'There, now I have overset you. Accept my apology, if you can. I assumed too much.'

'You thought, like everyone else including Mama, that I have no mind of my own.' Anne blew her nose, very conscious of the fact Mr Asquith still held her hand and that his handsome face was creased with seemingly genuine concern. She ought to have enjoyed the moment, because it would soon be consigned to history, but she was too upset and too confused by the strength of her feelings for this enigmatic man to live for the moment. 'You just assume I will do as my mother tells me to.'

'On the contrary, I know you have a very fine mind, are a deep thinker and have more strength of character than most people give you credit for.'

'Thank you, at least for that.' She dried her eyes and squared her shoulders. Somehow, she also found the strength to withdraw her hand from his. 'There, I am better now, and we shall not refer to the matter again.'

'May I ask you a personal question?'

She looked at him askance. No one had ever asked her permission to question her before. 'You may certainly ask,' she replied cautiously, wondering what he could possibly wish to know.

'How do you feel about Colonel Fitzwilliam? Do you wish for his addresses?'

'No,' Anne replied without hesitation. 'But he needs a rich wife, and I have a duty to marry someone who will take good care of Rosings.' She rolled her eyes, something else she was not in the habit of doing, but which she now discovered to be a very expressive way to show her feelings. 'My mother never tires of reminding me of that fact. She did intend Mr Darcy for me.' Mr Asquith shook his head, looking appalled. 'I agree with you. He frightens me and we never would have suited. The colonel does not frighten me quite so much, but... Oh, never mind.'

'Please, Miss de Bourgh, say what is on your mind. I fancy you don't often get the opportunity.'

She offered him a wry smile. 'That is certainly true.' She

straightened her spine and found the courage to meet his gaze. 'I see a very different side to Mr Darcy since he made such a happy marriage. He was always so severe before, you see, but he clearly feels deeply for his wife. His entire demeanour has changed as a consequence. Mr and Mrs Bingley are a less extreme example. I never knew Mrs Bingley before her marriage, and Mr Bingley has always been agreeable. Even so, it is obvious to anyone with eyes in their head that they are completely happy with one another.' She fixed Mr Asquith with a candid gaze. 'Is it such a very bad thing to want that sort of felicity for oneself?'

'To marry for love?' Anne nodded. 'Not in the least.'

'Not that I ever shall, of course.' She spread her hands. 'Even if I was free to receive addresses from admirers, I would never know if they liked me for myself or merely hankered after the rich prize that is Rosings. Or rather, I would know.' She averted her gaze. 'Who would look at me for any other reason? I am dull, unworldly, not especially handsome and my health is frail. In other words, I have absolutely nothing to recommend me.'

'Oh my dear girl!' he cried passionately. 'I feel so very sorry for you.'

Anne elevated her chin. 'I do not require your pity.'

'I was not pitying you. I was merely expressing my despair at your self-image.'

'Why?' His statement surprised her. 'You have known me long enough to appreciate it is true.'

'I disagree.' He sat beside her, and she felt the full weight of his dark gaze resting on her profile. 'You are intelligent, thoughtful, exceedingly well read and show promise as an artist.' His expression lightened. 'You also have the makings of a fine actress.'

Anne laughed. 'I would hardly go that far, but thank you for trying to make me feel better about myself.'

'Has it occurred to you that you are actually free to make up your own mind about your future, or at least have a say in it?'

'If I did, I would not only upset my mother but also risk being disinherited.'

He stood up and paced the width of the room, standing at its opposite side with his back turned towards her so that she was unable to read his expression. 'You have no money of your own on which to live?'

'Well, yes, my father left me provided for, but my mother has control of those funds. I am not sure how much is involved, but I think there is enough to live modestly.' She lifted her shoulders. 'I had not considered that before.'

'Then my advice, if you will accept it, is to think about yourself for a change. Think about your own hopes and aspirations, and don't rush into anything you find distasteful.'

'That is easy for you to say, Mr Asquith, but what can I hope to achieve without Rosings? I become invisible. Even more invisible than I already am, and anyone I find interesting would no longer be interested in me.'

'I find you interesting.'

His back was still turned towards her, and he spoke so quietly Anne could not be sure she had heard him correctly. Her heart soared but she told herself not to be foolish. She was upset and he was trying to make her feel better. She had probably read more into his words than he had intended by them, perhaps because they were what she so desperately wanted to hear. The thought of disobeying her mother terrified her, and she simply could not contemplate such a daring action – unless her future was with Mr Asquith. That would put a very different light on matters. She loved him with a deep passion that overrode all other considerations.

But it was impossible to believe he could love her in return.

He was a fortune hunter, albeit a charming and agreeable one. Unless he could convince her that his feelings mirrored her own, she would never take the extreme measure of defying her mama. Ergo, she would most likely accept Colonel Fitzwilliam and make the best of it.

'You are compassionate, thoughtful and kind,' he said softly, turning to face her again. 'Do not let others dictate the way you live your life, Anne.'

She gasped when he used her name. Never had it sounded sweeter as it slipped past his dear lips. She wanted him to say it again, to take her hand again and reiterate his advice. When he failed to speak, she felt compelled to fill the silence.

'Thank you,' she stuttered inadequately. Lord, she was handling this all wrong! She must appear immature and maladroit to a man of his sophistication.

'Your mother would dismiss me on the spot if she heard what I just said to you.'

'She will never hear it from me, but in return you must answer a question.'

'Gladly.'

'How well do you know Mrs Sheffield?'

'What makes you think I know her at all?'

'You disappoint me, Mr Asquith.' Anne shook her head. 'I opened my heart to you, but you are unwilling to return the favour. I thought we were speaking as equals, not as tutor and pupil.'

'I knew Mrs Sheffield slightly when I was in Jamaica, but I knew her husband rather better.'

'Thank you.' She dredged up a smile, amazed at her own brazenness in forcing this conversation. 'There, that was not so very difficult, was it? And yet last night you treated one another as strangers. Why would you do that?'

'I will tell you about it one day, I promise you. But in the meantime I must ask you to keep what I have told you to yourself.'

'You have not told me anything.'

'I want to be your friend, Anne,' he said, his eyes burning with sincerity. 'Not because of what you are, but because of who you are. There is a huge difference. Always remember, my dear, in this world there is one man who does appreciate you for yourself, even if he is not in a position to do anything about it.'

'Mr Asquith.' Anne clapped a hand over her mouth, totally surprised. 'Whatever can you mean by—'

The door opened, Georgiana burst through it with a question for Mr Asquith, and the opportunity to pose her question was lost. In retrospect, she decided, that was probably just as well.

With the actors occupied in the ballroom, and the rest of their guests otherwise engaged, Will and Lizzy enjoyed a moment's respite in front of the fire in the small sitting room. His arm circled her shoulders as he held her close and rested his chin on the top of her head.

'You look tired,' he said sympathetically.

'Not tired precisely, but your aunt makes me anxious. All the time I sense her watching me and mentally criticising everything I do. Naturally, I don't achieve anything as well as your mama did, and she congratulates herself on always having known I would pollute Pemberley by becoming its mistress.'

'If she thinks that way, which I doubt, she knows better than to say so to me. Besides, she must sense she is very much in the minority. Everyone else here loves you.' Will removed his chin from the top of her head and fixed her with an intense gaze. 'Especially me.'

'You always know exactly the right thing to say.' Lizzy lifted one hand and ran a finger down the cleft in his chin. 'Even so, I shall be glad when she is gone.'

'Which won't be until she gets her way and matters are settled between Fitzwilliam and her daughter.'

'Then she will be with us for a long time.'

Will placed a protective hand over the slight swell in Lizzy's belly. 'Whatever do you mean?'

Lizzy laughed. 'Honestly, you men are supposed to be the superior sex but you seldom see what is beneath your noses.'

Will rested his forehead against hers, his eyes heavy-lidded and seductive. 'What is it that you think you saw?'

'I don't think. I am perfectly sure. Your cousin is enamoured of Mrs Sheffield.'

Will appeared taken aback. 'Good God, is he really?'

'Few men would not be. She is very beautiful, and if even half of what I hear is true, also of independent means. He will not be the first man to have set his cap at her since the death her of husband, of that I am perfectly sure.'

'Even so, that doesn't mean Fitzwilliam would—'

'And he spent half the evening watching her across the dining table, then spent a long time in private conversation with her while we had music.'

'Oh lord, you don't think he plans to defy Lady Catherine's wishes too?'

'I think he might have been persuaded to go along with her wishes, although as I told you before, he was less than enthusiastic at the prospect. That is a great pity for Anne. I feel very sorry for her. It must be hard to be in her position, never knowing if she is admired for herself.'

'Georgiana will be able to sympathise.'

'Georgiana is an heiress, but not Pemberley's heir.'

Again, Will's hand touched her belly. 'Certainly she is not.'

'I think Mr Asquith has done his job a little too well, and your timid cousin is developing a mind of her own.'

'I am very glad to hear it. Even so, I wish she would do it somewhere else.'

Lizzy poked her husband in the ribs. 'Don't try to pretend you are not enjoying the drama almost as much as I am.'

'I shall be sorry to see Lady Catherine discomposed again. When she is roused to anger, it is not a spectacle for the faint-hearted, and I don't want you exposed to it. Not in your delicate condition. However, I also think Fitzwilliam ought to do what is right for him, and Anne too for that matter, regardless of the repercussions.' Will's lips twisted into the parody of a smile. 'It's just I would prefer if they did it elsewhere and left us in peace to anticipate the arrival of our first child.'

Lizzy flexed her brows. 'Would that life was that simple.'

'Where is Fitzwilliam now? Don't tell me he has been dragged into Asquith's play too.'

'I happened to see him go out on horseback quite early this morning.' Lizzy sent her husband an impish smile. 'I am willing to wager he left early to avoid Lady Catherine, and that he is escorting a certain female neighbour over the estate even as we speak. I happen to know Mrs Sheffield is fond of riding.'

'You like Mrs Sheffield, do you not?'

'Very much,' Lizzy replied without hesitation. 'If she and your cousin were to... But what am I doing? It is absolutely none of my business.'

'Romantic speculation is every lady's business,' Will replied, running his forefinger gently down the curve of her face.

'Only because we are not permitted to do anything important and have no better way to occupy our time.'

'Running this house does not occupy you?'

'Mrs Reynolds pretends to need me, but she is only being kind. She and Simpson have the place running like clockwork. I hesitate to interfere.'

'Are you suggesting you would take no interest in our friends' romantic intentions if I asked for your help in running the estate?'

Lizzy waved a hand in vague agreement. 'I would not give such matters another thought.'

Will's deep, throaty chuckle echoed through the room. 'Then let me seize the moment while your mind is still veering in that direction and ask you about Turner. The last time he was here, Kitty was depressed because he had been summoned by his father, who intended to marry him off to some suitable woman. What happened?'

'I have absolutely no idea.'

'Lizzy!'

She treated him to an innocent look. 'But you have no interest in rumour and speculation.'

'On the contrary, I thrive on the latest *on dits*. Besides, I bear some responsibility for your sister's welfare while she is under this roof, and I would not see her anticipation unnecessarily excited if nothing is to come of it.'

'My father was fond of telling us that next to being married, all young ladies enjoy being disappointed in love.'

'Your father spoke in jest.'

'Very possibly.'

'So will you enlighten me or leave me to guess?'

Lizzy laughed. 'In other words, you are as curious as I am but can't bring yourself to admit it.' She lifted her head from its comfortable resting place on Will's shoulder and placed a delicate kiss on his lips. 'Very well, I will tell you what I know, which is precious little. I have not spoken to Captain Turner on the subject. It is really for him to discuss it with me if he feels the need.

However, Kitty tells me he will not be marrying the lady his father chose for him. Whether he balked at the idea or the lady decided against the match, I cannot tell you since that is all Kitty knows herself.'

'Well, that is encouraging, I suppose. It is evident he enjoys Kitty's society, and she his. Let us hope for a happy outcome.'

'Yes, by all means let's hope for that. I want everyone to be as happy as we are.'

'I hesitate to spoil any pleasure of yours but I fear that would be impossible. No man could be as fortunate in his choice of a wife or as content in his marriage as I am, Lizzy.' His fingers played with the escaped curls at her nape. 'I am sorry if that makes me sound selfish, but there's no help for that.'

'Then I am selfish too. I feel exactly the same way and pity the rest of my sex since none of them are destined to be as happy as I am.'

Booted footsteps rang out on the tiled floor of the vestibule. Lizzy glanced over her shoulder, through the open doorway, and saw a dishevelled Colonel Fitzwilliam there, watching them embrace with a pensive expression on his face.

'You look as though you were caught in the rain, Colonel,' she said, removing herself from Will's arms. 'Pray come and warm yourself in front of the fire and tell us about your morning.'

'Idle curiosity?' Will whispered, raising an ironic brow at her.

'I showed Mrs Sheffield the folly,' he said, striding into the room and holding his hands out to the flames.

Lizzy shot her husband a triumphant smile. 'It is not the best day to appreciate the view.'

'That is what I told Mrs Sheffield.'

'But the weather did not detract from your enjoyment?' Lizzy asked, smiling.

'The weather did not,' the colonel replied, seating himself

opposite Lizzy and Will, 'but I am concerned about Mrs Sheffield's welfare.'

'Why?' Will asked.

Succinctly, the colonel outlined what he had learned of Mrs Sheffield's unhappy marriage and her disinclination to return to her own estate because her husband's brother was in occupation of it.

'Something unpleasant happened in Jamaica,' the colonel said in summary, 'but Mrs Sheffield either does not know the full particulars or is unwilling to share them with a comparative stranger. Either way, I am willing to wager her husband did not die of a fever.'

'I got the impression she and Mr Asquith are acquainted, even though they pretended otherwise,' Lizzy remarked.

'They do know one another, but that is all I could persuade Mrs Sheffield to say.' The colonel frowned. 'The lady is out of her depth, in danger of being cheated, and I'm damned if I will stand back and allow that to happen. Oh, I beg your pardon. Please excuse my language, Mrs Darcy.'

'That's perfectly all right, Colonel. I can see you are upset by the prospect, as I am. But what shall you do about it?'

Colonel Fitzwilliam ground his jaw. 'I have not yet decided. Mrs Sheffield's solicitor calls to see her this afternoon. I myself am engaged to call upon her again tomorrow, when I shall endeavour to gain her confidence.'

'What of Lady Catherine, Fitzwilliam?' Will asked. 'If you have definitely decided against Anne then you ought to tell her so and get the business out of the way.'

'I shall not marry Anne, regardless of how things develop between Mrs Sheffield and myself. I had my doubts before, for her sake as much as my own, but now I am perfectly sure. But you are right, I ought to tell our aunt of my decision sooner rather than later.'

'Please let me know when you intend to do so, Colonel, and I shall make sure I am elsewhere,' Lizzy said, making them laugh and lightening the sombre mood.

'Are you absolutely sure, Fitzwilliam?' Will asked. 'Think of the benefits.'

'Do you imagine I have not already done so? Lady Catherine has been dropping endless hints about her wishes ever since you and Mrs Darcy married. I have had ample opportunity to reflect.' He paused to rub his chin in thoughtful contemplation. 'If Anne was still the same frail, docile creature we are accustomed to seeing, with barely a word to say for herself, then I might well have gone ahead. But Asquith has had a very beneficial effect upon her and her personality has blossomed as a consequence. That changes everything.'

'That is certainly true,' Lizzy said. 'I do not know her nearly as well as you and Will do but I can see remarkable changes in her too.'

'Quite so. I don't believe marriage to me would please her very much but she would go through with it for her mother's sake if I was willing. I refuse to put her in that position.'

'But Lady Catherine will choose her husband however noble your intentions, Fitzwilliam. She could finish up with someone far less sympathetic to her feelings than you are.'

'Oh, I wouldn't be so sure about that,' Lizzy said. 'I have a feeling Anne de Bourgh is only just starting to realise she has a mind and will of her own.'

'God help us if Anne defies her mother too,' Will said, rolling his eyes.

'I don't relish the idea of your aunt not having her way, but at the same time I do feel very strongly that Anne is entitled to have some say in her future.'

Will laughed. 'Not all young ladies are as strong-minded as you are.'

'Then I feel very sorry for them.'

Their private conversation came to an end when Kitty and Georgiana joined them, laughing, faces flushed with excitement.

'How go the rehearsals?' Lizzy asked.

'I am Miss Dolores Downton,' Georgiana said with an exaggerated curtsey.

'And I am Miss Dorothea,' Kitty added, curtseying also.

'Anne is Daphne, and all three of us are enamoured of the same gentleman.'

'Then the poor gentleman has my sympathy,' Lizzy replied, laughing.

'Save your sympathy, Lizzy, he is—'

'No, Kitty, you must not tell. It is to be a surprise.'

Lizzy shared a glance with Will. Neither of them had ever seen Georgiana quite so animated, or so quick to put herself forward before. It was clear Mr Asquith's theatrical production had the same effect upon her as his tutoring did upon Anne, causing both young ladies to feel less inhibited. Perhaps Lady Catherine knew what she was about, after all. Then again, she might have grossly underestimated her daughter's reaction to the glamorous young man, thereby creating more difficulties than his presence solved.

'Ah, that it is,' Kitty agreed. 'Do not ask me a single thing more about it, Lizzy, in case I forget myself and reveal all.'

Lizzy laughed. 'Now I am really intrigued.'

'Mr Asquith has us painting scenery,' Georgiana explained. 'And we also have to remember our lines.'

'It's exhausting,' Kitty added, throwing herself into the nearest chair.

'Then have the servants do it for you,' Will suggested.

'Oh no.' Georgiana shook her head. 'Where would be the sense of achievement in that?'

'Well, it is almost time for luncheon,' Lizzy said, glancing at the clock and standing up. 'I dare say a good meal will restore your energy.'

10

Torrential rain fell for the entire afternoon but failed to dampen the spirits of Pemberley's residents. The actors threw themselves wholeheartedly into the play and barely noticed the weather. Joshua passed the closed door to the ballroom and heard raucous laughter coming from within. To his considerable satisfaction, Lady Catherine had taken over chaperone duties from Mrs Bingley.

'I insist upon knowing how the play ends,' he heard his aunt say. 'How can I be sure it is suitable for Anne to be involved with if I do not know the particulars?'

Joshua heard Asquith reply in a low voice but could not make out what he said.

'That is all very well, Mr Asquith, but I do not see why Mrs Bingley should know it all, yet I cannot be trusted with that information.' She paused briefly, permitting Asquith to speak. 'Yes, yes, I understand she has been sworn to secrecy but I am well able to keep a secret myself.'

Having satisfied himself that Lady Catherine had no intention of leaving the ballroom, Joshua did not linger to hear how the matter was resolved. His aunt being otherwise engaged gave him a legitimate reason to delay telling her of his decision not to marry Anne. He strode away from the ballroom, thinking about Rosings. If he were to become master of such a rich estate, his future would be secure. He would also be in a position to help his ungrateful brother restore the Braithwaite estate to its former glory. Why the devil was he even hesitating?

A small part of his brain wondered if he had taken leave of his senses. He then thought of Darcy and the beneficial effect a happy marriage had had upon his character and temperament. The changes in his previously taciturn cousin's demeanour were nothing short of remarkable. He thought also of Mrs Sheffield and the instant attraction he had felt towards her the first moment he saw her. He had never known anything like it before. If Darcy's wife stirred his passions as violently as Mrs Sheffield affected Joshua's, then he could understand why he had been prepared to shock society and disappoint his relations by marrying a lady some considered beneath him.

Not that Joshua was considering offering for Mrs Sheffield, nor was she likely to accept him if he did, but the feelings she had engendered in him made it impossible to put financial expediency ahead of desire. He could survive on his army pay if need be. Money was not everything. He had nothing against Anne de Bourgh, but she was not in love with him and she deserved to find happiness every bit as much as Joshua himself did.

With his conscience salved, Joshua whiled away the afternoon with Darcy and Bingley in the billiards room, losing a modest sum to those gentlemen because he was unable to concentrate on the game. His thoughts were at Briar Hall instead. He wondered if Mrs Sheffield's solicitor had arrived and what possible business could have brought him all the way from London. It had to be more than a routine affair or he would have consigned it to writing. He knew

Mrs Sheffield was concerned about the impending visit, much as she tried to pretend otherwise. Joshua ground his jaw. When he saw her on the morrow, he would be at his most convincing and would somehow persuade her to place her trust in him. Unless Joshua's judgement had become severely impaired, she had never had greater need of a confidante or a reliable friend. For reasons of her own, he suspected she had not revealed the true nature of her difficulties to her sister and Lord Briar, affording Joshua the privilege of standing protector in their stead.

Dinner that evening was a cheerful affair with the players full of laughter at their afternoon's efforts. Even Lady Catherine seemed to have picked up on their flamboyance and only made the occasional complaint about the folly of the production, wondering aloud why young people nowadays could not find a more seemly way to occupy their time.

'Anne is proving to have remarkable talent for acting,' she informed the rest of the diners. 'You ought to have seen her, Fitzwilliam.'

'I would have been glad to watch, Lady Catherine,' Joshua replied, 'but the door to the rehearsal room is barred to those of us not participating.'

'Acting is hardly a ladylike quality I would wish to encourage,' Lady Catherine continued. 'But since she is determined to try it, and my daughter and niece are performing here at Pemberley for an audience of family and close friends only, I can see no harm in it.'

'No harm whatsoever,' Mr Asquith agreed.

'Are you enjoying yourself, Anne?' Joshua asked.

'Actually I am, but Mama has greatly exaggerated my talents.'

'I am not given to exaggeration, child. I merely speak as I find.'

'Yes, Mama, but you are biased. I am not nearly so good as Georgiana and Kitty.'

Good heavens, Joshua thought. It was the first time he had ever heard Anne contradict her mother. Asquith was to be congratulated. Presumably it was he who had persuaded her to form opinions of her own, and he who had given her the courage to voice them.

'At least you remember your lines.' Kitty wrinkled her nose. 'I have to be prompted all the time.'

'I would exchange a good memory for a louder voice,' Anne replied with feeling.

'Really, it does not in the least matter if your voices are too low or if any of you forget your lines,' Mrs Darcy said, smiling at all the players. 'It is only us who will be there to admire your performance and I am perfectly sure we shall find none of you wanting.'

Kitty laughed. 'I shall remind you that you said that when I dry up.'

'Y-you will n-not forget your lines, M-Miss Bennet,' Captain Turner assured her. 'I s-shall be glad to help you remember them and make sure y-you are w-word perfect.'

'For my part,' Joshua said, 'I intend to persuade Mrs Bingley to confide in me. I have a great desire to know how the play ends and to discover which lady gets her heart's desire.'

'Oh no, I could not possibly tell.' Mrs Bingley smiled an apology. 'I would never be forgiven if I gave the ending away.'

'Who wrote the play, Asquith?' Joshua asked. 'Perhaps there's a copy in Darcy's library and I can look it up.'

'Don't spoil the surprise, Colonel,' Mrs Darcy said, smiling. 'Just like the rest of us, you must contain your curiosity until the players are ready to perform.'

'You ask a lot.'

After dinner, the card tables were placed. Joshua found himself partnering Anne, thanks no doubt to Lady Catherine's influence. He anticipated a dreary time with Anne barely saying a word, but actually he rather enjoyed the game. Anne's new sense of self-worth manifested itself and she proved to be engaging company. Joshua forgave her for constantly stealing glances at Mr Asquith who was seated at one of the other tables, partnering Georgiana.

'Well done,' Joshua said when the game came to an end and he and Anne triumphed.

'We were lucky,' Anne replied.

'My advice, for what it's worth,' he said, helping her with her chair and speaking softly so only she could hear him, 'is that one ought to make one's own luck.'

Anne looked at him with confusion. 'Whatever do you mean?'

Joshua glanced at Asquith. 'I think you know.'

'Oh.' Colour invaded Anne's cheeks. 'Colonel, I do assure you… Besides, Mama would never permit—'

'What are you speaking to Anne about?' Lady Catherine demanded loudly from an adjoining table where the game was still in progress. 'I must know why you feel the need to whisper, Fitzwilliam.'

Lady Catherine appeared to have overlooked the fact that young people who were attracted to one another tended to do a great deal of whispering. By drawing attention to it, Lady Catherine could have been accused of hampering Joshua's campaign, had he decided to launch one.

'We were discussing our strategy at whist, ma'am.'

Joshua inclined his head to Anne, offered her the ghost of a wink, and strolled away to join Darcy in front of the fire. By reminding him of her autocratic, interfering manner, Lady Catherine had just eradicated any lingering doubts Joshua might otherwise have entertained regarding his decision not to become the master of Rosings.

* * *

The following morning was blighted by heavy clouds and overcast skies. There was no rain, but it wouldn't hold off for long and the already sodden ground would become more like a bog. Joshua didn't care. He would ride to Briar Hall even if his horse sank hock-deep in mud and he became soaked to the skin in the process. The players were again hard at work in the ballroom, fully engrossed in their activities, and Lady Catherine had not yet shown herself. Joshua made his escape while he could.

Mrs Sheffield and Lady Briar received him with great civility. Lady Sheffield's countenance showed signs of strain and there were dark circles around her eyes. She clearly had not slept well for the second night in succession. Seeing her so discomposed renewed Joshua's determination to win her trust.

'Celia told me you planned to call this morning, Colonel, but I did not expect you to keep the engagement in such appalling weather.'

Wild horses could not have kept me away. 'I am a soldier, Lady Briar,' he replied, sending Mrs Sheffield a brief, reassuring smile. 'Weather conditions seldom deter me when I make up my mind on a course of action.'

'How is everyone at Pemberley, Colonel?' Mrs Sheffield asked.

'They are all in the best of health, I thank you. Speaking of which, I come with an invitation for you all to dine in six nights' time. As you are aware, the young people are combatting the inclement weather by putting on a play.' Joshua smiled. 'We are to be the audience, if you can bear it.'

'It would be our pleasure.' Lady Briar clapped her hands. 'I once enjoyed play-acting myself when I was younger and possessed some aptitude as an actress, though I do say so myself.'

'Are you not taking part, Colonel?' Mrs Sheffield asked. 'I can just see you as a dashing hero, riding to the rescue of the hapless heroine.'

'I hesitate to disappoint you, ma'am, but my services have not been offered, nor are they required. They can manage very well without me. I gather there are three heroines and I lack the courage to take all three of them on at once.' Joshua shuddered, making the ladies laugh. 'Give me an enemy regiment to face on the battlefield instead. That is a situation over which I might be able to exert some control.'

'Really, Colonel, do you expect us to believe that?' Lady Briar asked, smiling.

'You ought to, ma'am. The players are rehearsing in strict seclusion in the Pemberley ballroom. Even so, they have managed to turn the place on its head. No one except Mrs Bingley, who has bravely offered her services as chaperone, knows how the play ends, and she refuses to give a single hint.'

'I should think so.' Mrs Sheffield laughed, and some of the wariness left her eyes.

'Then you will come?'

'Certainly we shall. Please thank Mrs Darcy for including us and assure her we would not miss it.'

The conversation turned more general as tea was served. When Lady Briar finished hers, she excused herself on some pretext and at last Joshua found himself alone with Mrs Sheffield. As soon as their gazes clashed, an air of expectancy sprang up between them and she abandoned all pretence of normality. She looked so crestfallen that Joshua impulsively reached for her hand.

'I cannot bear to see you looking so unhappy,' he said passionately. 'Will you not tell me what has overset you so? You can be assured of my secrecy.'

'What is the point?' She flapped her other hand. 'There is nothing you can do.'

'I may not be able to act, Mrs Sheffield, but I am very resourceful in all other respects. I have yet to encounter a situation that cannot be resolved with a little guile or, if necessary, brute force.'

She managed a wan smile. 'Always the soldier.'

'No, not in this situation.' His fingers closed more firmly around her palm, and she made no attempt to pull her hand free. 'I am simply a man who wishes to be of service to a lady who has attracted his interest.'

'You would do better to go back to Pemberley and pay court to your cousin. I am an entirely lost cause.'

'Hang my cousin!' Joshua fixed her with an intense, probing look. 'It is you whom I wish to serve, and unless I mistake the matter, you have seldom had greater need of a confidante and friend. Whatever troubles you, you have not told your sister or Lord Briar about it, have you?'

'No.' She shook her head. 'They cannot help me and I would not worsen my sister's nervous disposition by visiting my problems upon her.'

'Always putting others ahead of yourself.' Joshua drilled her with a look. 'Do you not trust me? Perhaps I am being presumptuous but I thought there was something between us and that you feel the connection every bit as much as I do.'

Mrs Sheffield moistened her lips with the tip of her tongue, clearly trying to come to a decision. Joshua said nothing more. He had all but declared his feelings for her, and she had not laughed in his face. Encouraged, he waited her out in silence.

'My husband's brother is claiming that my estate in Buckinghamshire is rightfully his,' she said with a heavy sigh. 'And as things stand, I am unsure how to refute that claim.'

Joshua wasn't entirely surprised. Her unwillingness to return to Buckinghamshire because her brother-in-law was in residence there and her obvious dislike and mistrust for the man had set him wondering.

'What does your solicitor suggest?'

Mrs Sheffield's despairing look gave way to one of anger. 'That I should leave the negotiations to him, because as a feeble woman I cannot be expected to understand these things, or words to that effect.'

'There is absolutely nothing feeble about you.'

She offered him a humourless smile. 'I believe Mr Higgins is now aware of that fact.'

'The man sounds incompetent. What made you choose him?'

'I did not. He was engaged by my husband when he purchased the estate and took care of Albert's interests in this country while we were in Jamaica.'

'That was to be my next question. If the estate was not previously in your husband's family and was only purchased after your marriage, then presumably your dowry paid for it.'

'Well, no.' She looked away from him and spoke evasively. 'We only acquired the house after we had been married for several years. His work in Jamaica was sufficiently profitable to make the purchase possible.'

'And I imagine his brother was a-party to that work, which makes him think he now owns the estate?'

'Yes, that is precisely what he thinks.'

Joshua sighed. This was clearly not as straightforward as he had at first imagined and his suspicions were on high alert. 'Did your husband leave a will?'

'Yes, I am his sole beneficiary. His brother is not mentioned.'

'Then he has no claim.'

'That is what I tried to tell Mr Higgins, but of course he disagrees.'

'Then you had better tell me everything from the beginning.'

Mrs Sheffield glanced out of the window. The intermittent rain had been blown away by a strong wind that caused tree branches to bend against it and sent a scattering of leaves bowling across the recently cut lawns. 'Can we walk outside and talk about this? I feel trapped in here, restless and... oh, I don't know. I think better outdoors.'

'I understand completely. Go and fetch a warm cloak. I shall wait for you in the vestibule.'

Five minutes later, they strolled along the gravel walkway that surrounded Briar Hall and headed for the reflecting pools. Even though it was such an overcast day, their images were still cast back at them in the water's surface, as was the edifice of the house itself. The Pemberley estate had similar pools, but on a grander scale, and they had always fascinated Joshua as a boy.

Mrs Sheffield placed her gloved hand on Joshua's proffered arm and they proceeded walking at an easy pace. He said nothing, sensing the fresh air would galvanise his fair companion, and she would speak when she had taken a moment to gather her thoughts.

'Albert and his brother had a signed partnership agreement regarding their work in Jamaica that I knew nothing about until yesterday afternoon,' Mrs Sheffield said after a prolonged pause.

'That seems rather strange, if you don't mind my saying so. Surely your husband would have mentioned the arrangement to you, even just in passing?'

'He didn't ordinarily tell me anything about his work, but I agree with you. He should have told me at least that much.'

'You think the agreement is bogus?'

She lifted her shoulders. 'I don't know what to think. Albert's signature looks genuine but I am no expert on such matters.'

'Let us leave aside the validity of the agreement for now and consider your brother-in-law's claim. I imagine he says he was not paid monies owed to him and so plans to take the estate instead.'

'Something like that.' She screwed up her features into an

expression of disdain. 'Out of Christian charity he claims I can still live there if I so wish.'

'How very obliging of him.' Joshua was consumed by a murderous rage, well able to imagine what this vile-sounding individual had in mind once he had Mrs Sheffield beneath the same roof as him. Outwardly, he remained perfectly calm. 'We will not allow that to happen. You will live there again, of course, but your husband's brother will have to find alternative accommodation.'

She gasped. 'You make it sound straightforward but how can you be so sure?'

'Let us start at the beginning. Excuse me for asking such personal questions, but I was under the impression that your dowry was quite adequate enough to enable the purchase of an estate.'

'And so it should have been.' They turned at the end of the walk and took a different direction, further away from the house. 'What my father did not know until we were married and it was too late to do anything about it was that Albert had very large debts to discharge. Not of his own making. Albert was many things, most of them disagreeable, but one thing he was not was careless with money. Quite the opposite, in fact. Unlike his father, he never went near a gaming table, nor did he squander money unnecessarily. When his father passed away, Albert inherited his debts, which he felt honour bound to settle.'

Joshua grunted. 'I want very badly to dislike your late husband, Mrs Sheffield, and you are making it difficult for me.'

'Oh, don't worry, he was not a kind person and I can tell you plenty of things about him that would validate your dislike. However, I was attempting to be fair. He ought to have explained those debts to my father before Papa gave Albert permission to address me. That was remiss of him and I dare say Papa would not have entertained his suit if he had known about them.'

'Which is precisely why he didn't tell him.' Joshua found a bench beneath an ancient oak that was in the lee of the wind and steered Mrs Sheffield towards it. 'Your husband's father did not own an estate of his own.'

'He did at one time, but—'

'Let me guess. He gambled it away.'

'Precisely.'

'And so after Sheffield discharged his father's debts, there was not much of your dowry left and you were obliged to rent lodgings.'

'Yes. We were in London but didn't show ourselves much in society. There was no money to spare for that. Besides, Albert would have considered it money wasted. He was not afraid of hard work and established himself as a commodities broker. He opened an office close to the docks and found markets for products that were brought in speculatively by independent vessels. You can have no idea how many such ships there are, and he did reasonably well at it, although his gains were nothing exceptional.'

'I suppose that is where he got the idea for going to Jamaica?'

'Yes. His brother Percival worked with him when the fancy took him, but he is cut from the same cloth as their father. Albert wasn't one to tolerate shirkers but he had a blind spot when it came to Percival, I know not why, and the same rules didn't seem to apply to him. Basically, he did as little as possible and claimed a great deal of the profits. Albert once referred to an event in their childhood; I don't know what happened, but I think Percival somehow saved Albert from a life-threatening situation. Albert felt obligated to Percival because of it and allowed him to do more or less as he pleased.'

Joshua disciplined himself to pay close attention to Mrs Sheffield's account. That was no easy resolve since he was totally transfixed by the delicacy of her profile and greatly moved by the desolation in her luminous eyes. Brother Percival was trying to swindle her. He knew it as surely as he sat beside this lovely, vulnerable lady, doing his level best not to pull her into his arms and comfort her in the manner that sprang spontaneously to mind.

'It was Percival who first heard about the opportunity in Jamaica. He used to go to the dockside taverns, drink with the sailors and heaven knows what else. Percival is a viper but blessed with the appearance of an angel. He is universally popular with the ladies and manages to remain on good terms with most men he meets as well. One of his sea-faring acquaintances told him about a plantation in Jamaica that was in decline because the owner had died unexpectedly. His heirs had no interest in going to the island and required someone to purchase the plantation at a bargain price because they needed the money quickly. Albert wasn't prepared to take the risk but Percival kept on and on at him. He said the market for sugar was thriving and only a simpleton could fail to make a success of it. Percival had no money of his own. He frittered away whatever he earned with Albert and eventually Albert gave in and agreed.'

'Without knowing anything about managing a plantation?' Joshua flexed a brow. 'Was that not rather risky?'

'I thought so, and I tried to persuade him not to do it, but he would never listen to anything I said. I hated the idea of going to the Indies and asked him to leave me behind, but of course that was out of the question. I was his property, you see, a bit like one of the commodities he traded so profitably, and he would never have left me to my own devices.'

'But your husband made the plantation profitable?'

'He must have done so because a year after he acquired it we returned to England and he purchased Everton Park outright. I have not spent more than two months beneath the roof of the house we now own because we returned to Jamaica again almost immediately.'

'How large is your estate?'

'Nothing compared to Pemberley, or even to Briar Hall. It is a large manor house with about fifty acres.'

Joshua could imagine the place. A modest establishment, but also very desirable, and fairly easily managed. The sort of establishment any man would be proud to call home. Joshua reined in his imagination, scowling when he thought of the scoundrel, Percival Sheffield. Sheffield was relying upon Celia's lack of knowledge of her late husband's affairs in order to pull off this deception, but he had not counted upon Joshua's involvement. He hardened his jaw, silently vowing it would never happen while he had breath in his body to prevent it.

'You doubted your husband's ability to turn the plantation around, and yet he purchased an estate from the proceeds after little more than a year?'

'Yes, and paid for it with his life.'

'What were the conditions like on the plantation?'

'Deplorable. Our slaves were a wretched band of creatures who had been so badly treated and were so under-nourished that they could barely work.' She shuddered. 'It was awful. I felt so very sorry for them and tried to persuade Albert to treat them better, give them more food so they would be more productive. He would not listen to me, of course. His way of getting more out of them was to have the overseer whip them into submission.'

'If Sheffield made money with such a poor workforce, only imagine how much more profitable a well-run plantation with well-treated workers would be.'

'Quite so. Sir Marius Glover, Mr Asquith's mentor, is a case in point. He called to see us soon after we arrived and was closeted with Albert and Percival for a long time, offering them the benefit of his advice, which included better food and housing for the slaves. Unfortunately, the Sheffield men thought they knew better.'

There were a dozen more questions Joshua wished to ask, but he suspected she would not know the answers to them. Asquith, on the other hand, almost certainly would and Joshua planned to have a frank conversation with that gentleman upon his return to Pemberley. Of immediate concern was the agreement between the brothers. Mrs Sheffield's solicitor seemed to think it was genuine, and had travelled all this way to talk to her about it.

'You say your husband's signature appeared genuine on this supposed partnership document between the brothers, so I presume you saw the whole thing?'

'Yes. It was witnessed by a solicitor in Kingston, Jamaica whom I had never heard of. Nor did I ever hear Albert mention his name. There was a will also drawn up by that gentleman, dated after the one in England naming me as Albert's sole heir.' She wrinkled her brow. 'It is very peculiar.'

'What were the precise provisions of the agreement?'

'Albert was the senior partner and Percival worked for an agreed percentage. That was all straightforward enough and hardly needed to be stated in writing. They had always worked that way. The agreement also said that in the event of the demise of one brother, ownership of the plantation would revert to the other.'

Joshua sat a little straighter. 'I see. But in that case, why cannot Percival simply take control of the plantation?'

'Because the slaves revolted, for which I don't in the least blame them. Their conditions were nothing short of a disgrace, and when people run out of hope and have nothing to lose... well, I tried to warn Albert that feelings were running high, given all the talk about abolition. Word had reached us of slaves on other plantations taking matters into their own hands, but it was all rumour and speculation which Albert chose to dismiss without trying to get to the truth. Anyway, the plantation was razed to the ground; all the buildings and the crop. Albert died trying to save his property.'

'Ah, I thought there was no fever.'

'It is an explanation that satisfies most people and saves all the inevitable questions.'

Joshua lost the battle to remain passive and raised a hand to gently stroke her face. 'I, my dear, am not most people.'

'No,' she replied after a long pause. 'You are not, but I must know, why are you so anxious to help me?'

'Mrs Sheffield... Celia.' Joshua paused, too acutely aware of her close proximity, of the intoxicating aroma of her floral perfume, of an overwhelming torrent of protective feelings, to act with discretion. 'I will resolve this problem for you one way or another, on that you have my solemn word, and you owe me absolutely nothing.'

'That does not answer my question.'

'Is it so unnatural for a man of integrity to wish to offer his services to a lady in distress?'

She offered him the ghost of a smile. 'You are attracted to me, Colonel Fitzwilliam?'

He chuckled. 'Am I so very transparent?'

'You make me feel safe. Safer than I have for a very long time. I am not sure if that is such a good thing.'

'You have nothing to fear from me,' he replied, gently stroking her cheek with a gloved finger. 'Just so long as you refrain from looking at me in the way you are at this precise moment. There is only so much temptation a man can be expected to withstand.'

'I cannot help the way I look.'

'And I cannot help the way I respond to that look.'

Her eyes burned with unfathomable emotion, robbing Joshua

of what little common sense he had managed to retain. With a smothered oath, he pulled her into his arms and covered her lips with his own, kissing her with determination and brutal passion. She responded with a sweet urgency that drugged his mind. Joshua deepened the kiss, disciplining himself to accept that this would be the first and only time he allowed his feelings to get the better of him. Her arms had worked their way around his neck, and her upper body was pressed against his. He could feel the softness of her breasts, even through the thick layers of their clothing. Ye gods, he should not have done this!

Joshua broke the kiss and released her, breathing heavily. Her eyes were now muddy with passion and she looked at him with a combination of surprise and total confidence in his abilities.

'I did warn you,' he said softly, taking her hand and pulling her to her feet. 'Come, I will take you back to the house. Have the goodness to give me the name of your solicitor, his direction and written authority to act on your behalf.'

'What do you intend to do?' she asked in a husky voice.

'I shall speak with Asquith first. See what light he can shed on matters.'

'He did not like my husband or brother-in-law.' They walked slowly towards the house. 'He disapproves of me, too.'

'Be that as it may.'

A short time later, Joshua was in possession of the information he had requested and had no further reason to delay his departure. Anyway, Lady Briar had rejoined them and so the intimacy of the moment was lost.

'I shall call again tomorrow,' Joshua said, kissing the back of Celia's hand before taking formal leave of Lady Briar.

'I look forward to it,' Celia replied.

As Joshua rode away, mulling over all he had just learned, he doubted whether her anticipation could be greater than his own.

11

'A word if you please, Asquith.'

Joshua caught Anne's tutor just as luncheon came to an end and the ladies had already vacated the dining room. The young man turned to face him with an affable smile.

'How can I be of service to you, Colonel?'

'Let's talk in here.'

Joshua led the way into the library and closed the door after them. He took a chair on one side of the fire and gestured Asquith towards its twin.

'I won't keep you long. I dare say you have rehearsals to keep you occupied and enthusiastic players to keep amused.'

Asquith chuckled. 'They are certainly enthusiastic. So much so that the ladies are painting scenery this afternoon and so I am entirely at your disposal.'

Joshua admired the elegant manner in which Asquith draped himself in his chair. He seemed perfectly at his ease in august surroundings that would have intimidated most men, and he mingled with people of quality as though he had been doing so his entire life. It occurred to Joshua he was a gentleman by instinct as well as education and could well understand why such a sheltered girl as Anne would be so taken with him.

'What can you tell me about Sheffield?' Joshua asked without preamble.

If the question took Asquith by surprise, he gave no sign of it. 'What do you wish to know about him?'

'Anything you can tell me about the plantation he purchased, and about the manner of his death.' When Asquith merely raised a brow, Joshua felt the need to explain himself. 'Sheffield's brother is attempting to swindle Mrs Sheffield out of her property.'

'Hmm, is that so?'

'You don't appear surprised.'

Asquith twisted his lips into an expression of distaste. 'Nothing that blaggard does would surprise me.'

'Ah, so you dislike him. I am pleased to hear you say so. I don't know him myself, of course, and I only have Mrs Sheffield's word that he does not hold a legitimate claim to her property. All I do know is he has a cowardly way of staking that claim, hiding behind solicitors instead of coming straight out and discussing the matter with Mrs Sheffield.'

Joshua's outburst elicited more than an elegant shrug from Asquith, who looked genuinely startled. 'He has not communicated with Mrs Sheffield himself?'

'Not in connection with his claim to the property. That came as a complete shock to her. He told her when they arrived back from Jamaica that he would need to live there until her husband's affairs were put in order. She imagined he would receive something from his estate and anyway, he had nowhere to live until he was in funds again. Anyway, Mrs Sheffield had no wish to live in the same house as him and chose to come here to her sister. Perhaps she ought not to have done, since it gave the impression she was happy for Sheffield to take her property. However, I suppose that is better than the alternative.' Joshua stood up and braced both arms against the mantelpiece. 'Tell me more about this Percival Sheffield.'

'Presumably you have Mrs Sheffield's permission to ask such questions?'

Joshua shot Asquith a castigating glance, taking exception to the fact that he would assume otherwise. Gentlemen did not question gentlemen's motives in such a manner. But there again, in spite of appearances to the contrary, Joshua reminded himself Asquith was not a gentleman. 'In writing,' he said curtly. 'I will show you if you doubt my word.'

Asquith waved the suggestion aside. 'That won't be necessary. Forgive me if I caused offence, but you have put me in an awkward situation. One cannot be too careful.'

'Is that why you pretended not to know Mrs Sheffield when she dined here the other evening?'

'Ah, yes, that was deuced awkward. I wasn't sure how to play it, but to understand why, perhaps I had better start at the beginning.'

Joshua resumed his chair and fixed Asquith with a steady gaze. 'That would be best.'

'Then I shall start by telling you a little more about my background. My father worked as Sir Marius Glover's plantation manager, but died when I was very young. I don't remember much about him. My mother died when I was ten.' Asquith crossed one booted foot over his opposite knee and settled himself more comfortably in his chair. 'I assumed I would be sent back to England after her death. I still had relatives here who might have taken me in, but Sir Marius wouldn't hear of it. His eldest son and I were of a similar age and played together. Sir Marius kindly paid for me to be schooled in England alongside his own son, and then supported me at university.'

Rather as old Mr Darcy supported Wickham, Joshua thought. 'He clearly thought highly of you,' he remarked aloud.

'And I hope I have gone a small way to repaying his trust in me by serving him well.' Asquith paused. 'At one stage, Sir Marius spoke of me following in my father's footsteps and eventually managing his plantation, but by the time I finished university, talk of abolition was gaining momentum and everything in Jamaica had become unsettled.' He waved an elegant hand. 'Don't get me wrong, I shall be as happy as the next man to see an end to slavery, but at the current time the entire Indies are a maelstrom of uncertainty and unrest. It no longer feels safe and no one knows quite what the future will hold. All I can say for certain is that things will never be quite the same again, and I am not so sure I wish to be a part of that particular revolution.'

Joshua inclined his head, thinking Asquith was exceedingly astute. 'I'm with you there.'

'Sir Marius and I discussed the situation, and he understood my feelings because they closely mirrored his own. He understood I needed gainful employment and so had me school his younger children and then escort his youngest son to England when it came time for him to complete his education here.'

'And you stayed on.'

'Yes, instead of relying on Sir Marius's charity, it was time to support myself.'

Joshua nodded his approval. 'Very commendable. Most men in your position would have taken advantage of Sir Marius's affection for you.'

Asquith waved the suggestion aside with a casual flip of his wrist. 'Sir Marius has a large family, eight children all alive and well. He does not need me adding to his burden.'

'You were still in Jamaica when Sheffield arrived?'

'Yes.' Asquith leaned an elbow on the arm of his chair and

rubbed his chin in his cupped hand. 'Badly run plantations such as the one Sheffield purchased against Sir Marius's advice were worked by half-starved slaves incapable of doing a full day's work through no fault of their own. That didn't prevent their previous master from trying to beat them into working harder, which of course only made them weaker. Several died from untreated wounds that turned septic.'

Joshua nodded. 'I have heard many such barbaric tales.'

'When the owner of the plantation died, his sons couldn't wait to sell and leave the chaos that Jamaica had become. They were unable to believe their good fortune when Sheffield made them an offer for the place greatly in excess of its value.'

'But in spite of what you say, it must have been profitable because Sheffield made enough money from it to purchase the estate back here in England that his brother is now trying to lay claim to.'

'Because he didn't play fair.' Asquith flashed a humourless smile. 'What do you know of the Jamaican Maroons?'

'Not a great deal.' Joshua stretched his legs out in front of him, taking a moment to recall his history. 'Going back a hundred years, the Spanish colonists fled Jamaica and left a large number of African slaves behind. Rather than be re-enslaved by the British, they escaped into the mountainous regions of the island, joined forces with... er—'

'Very good, Colonel. They joined forces with the Tainos, intermarried with Amerindian natives and established independence in the back country, surviving by subsistence farming and by raiding plantations. Inevitably there were wars because the Maroons were ruthless and becoming increasingly powerful as a consequence – a threat to authority, in other words – and had to be stopped. Eventually, the British governor signed a treaty with the Maroons promising them two thousand five hundred acres of land in two locations in exchange basically for living beneath their own chief and a British superintendent.'

Joshua nodded. 'I recall something about that.'

'In return, the Maroons agreed not to harbour runaway slaves but to help catch them. They were actually paid a bounty of two dollars for each returned slave, which was the start of a lot of tension between rival black communities.' Asquith ran a hand across the back of his neck. 'To summarise, another war recently ensued. Some Maroons remained neutral and were left alone; others were viciously hunted down and deported. Tensions were running high, and still are, hence the reason for a lot of British settlers selling up and leaving.'

'Yes, I can see the attraction of the place would be on the wane. A lot of people in this country have been made anxious by talk of abolition.'

'Mainly because they don't want to pay the slaves,' Asquith said with a cynical snort. 'Now that the place is in chaos, they are claiming they were in the right of it. Anyway, where was I?'

'Deportations.'

'Right, well, of those left behind, a large enclave of rogue Maroons occupied the hills close to Sheffield's plantation. They could see he had a decent crop but no manpower to harvest it. They struck a deal with the Sheffields, or to be more precise, with Percival. They would pick the crop and make sure it got refined and exported without the necessity to pay the usual taxes. In return, they wanted half the profits.'

'That was highly illegal, I take it?'

Asquith shrugged. 'And also highly profitable. It is not an uncommon practice, especially in these anarchic times when slaves are starting to organise themselves and make demands.'

'How do you know it was Percival's idea?'

'I overheard him on one occasion, talking to the Maroons and assuring them he would talk his brother round.'

'Ah, I see.' Joshua would give a great deal to know what hold Percival had over his older sibling. It must have been something vital to persuade Albert, who had been described to Joshua as a methodical and cautious man, to go along with such a risky scheme. 'What happened to the slaves who lived on the plantation?'

Asquith shot Joshua a look. 'What do you think?'

'Percival left them to fend for themselves?'

'Exactly, but in so doing, he miscalculated badly. To this day I don't know how they managed it, but they went off somewhere in the hills, were taken in, and recovered their strength. Then they were on the lookout for revenge, against the Maroons, but more especially against Sheffield, whom they blamed for making them homeless.'

'It was they who destroyed the plantation?'

'Yes, but here's a question for you, Colonel. Was Mrs Sheffield's husband killed trying to save his property? Did his former slaves finish him off, or—?'

'Or did Percival see an opportunity to take everything for himself?'

The two men locked gazes and neither spoke for several moments as the full implication of Asquith's suggestion struck Joshua.

'Quite so,' Asquith said, breaking the brittle silence.

'You really think Percival Sheffield is capable of fratricide?'

'I assume you haven't met him?'

'No, I have not had that pleasure.'

'If you had, you wouldn't have asked the question. He is perfectly charming, a great favourite with the ladies, but cunning as a fox, totally ruthless, and doesn't possess a single moral in his entire body. Both brothers were that way, but Percival had an added something about him that made him especially dangerous. If you pressed me to say what it was, I would have to guess that he enjoys cruelty.'

Joshua's blood ran cold at the thought of this man having anything to do with Celia Sheffield. 'As I already told you, he is trying to claim Mrs Sheffield's property here in England as his own, saying he had a written agreement with his brother to that effect.'

Asquith shook his head. 'I wouldn't believe a word of it if I were you.'

'I can assure you that I do not.'

'There is nothing he would like more than to have Mrs Sheffield beholden to him.' Joshua scowled at having his suspicions confirmed. 'I saw the way he used to look at her with such hunger in his eyes, but she never wanted anything to do with him and it infuriated the man. He wasn't used to failing with the fairer sex, you see.'

'I am certainly beginning to form a very disagreeable picture of the cove.'

'So what will you do about him?'

'What can I do?' Joshua lifted his shoulders, feeling better informed but just as helpless as he had been at Briar Hall. 'I don't suppose you have any way of confirming what you have just told me?'

'Unfortunately not. It is all speculation and conjecture. As you can imagine, it was pretty confusing at the time. Sir Marius's plantation was some distance away from Sheffield's. By the time news of the fire reached us and we dashed over to see if we could help, the damage had already been done. Even so, we thought it rather odd that while both brothers supposedly fought to save their home, Albert perished in the attempt, but when we got there Percival barely had a singed whisker.'

'Hmm, that does seem rather odd. Perhaps Mrs Sheffield knows more. Presumably she was there.'

'No, she was visiting ladies on an adjoining plantation that afternoon. I have always wondered if Percival had some say in the timing of the attack and ensured it occurred when Mrs Sheffield was not at home.'

'Or she might have been hurt too?'

'Exactly, and if my suspicions about Percival wanting her for himself are true, then he would not have taken that risk.'

Joshua fell to thoughtful contemplation. Asquith left him to ruminate for several minutes before speaking again.

'Sir Marius would probably agree to give a sworn statement regarding events but that would take a long time to reach us here in England. Besides, he can only relate the facts, much as I have just done. He cannot swear under oath that Percival murdered his brother because of course none of us have anything other than our instincts to persuade us that he did.'

Joshua stood up and paced the length of the room, mulling this latest intelligence over. 'Why did you pretend not to know Mrs Sheffield when she dined here the other night, and then treat her almost with disrespect, Asquith?'

'I behaved very badly, and I regret it.' Joshua watched Asquith closely as he answered and had the satisfaction of seeing him look abashed. 'I shall apologise when next we meet. It was just that seeing her here brought all those awful memories back. It was not a happy time, and many other people besides Sheffield died in that fire, a lot of them slaves who found themselves trapped when the blaze spread far more quickly than they had anticipated. I know the slaves were the ones who started it, but they had good reason to feel aggrieved, and—'

'Excuse me, but I overheard the two of you speaking privately in this very room. She thanked you for not giving her away. What did she mean by that?'

Asquith now looked ashamed and shifted awkwardly in his seat, failing to meet Joshua's gaze. 'I knew she did not much like her husband, and I couldn't blame her for that. But he *was* her husband, and she showed little remorse at his demise.'

Joshua scowled. 'She didn't pretend a grief she did not feel, and you blame her for that?'

'Well, yes. Several people were shocked by her attitude.' Joshua snorted. He had never been one to conform and he applauded Mrs Sheffield's refreshing honesty. 'She also made little secret of the fact she hated Jamaica and couldn't wait to return to England.'

'But you just mentioned a lot of other people felt the same way.'

'True.' Asquith inclined his head. 'To her credit, she also had endless battles with her husband and his brother about the appalling manner in which they treated their slaves. She didn't try to hide her disgust from the rest of us, but it did her no good because the Sheffield brothers adamantly refused to do the right thing by them. So all Mrs Sheffield could do was spend time with the women and children, doing what she could for their illnesses and sneaking food to them when she was able.'

'And you hold that against her?' Joshua asked, feeling his temper rising.

'No, I applauded her efforts, but... excuse me, I did wonder if she encouraged her slaves to rise up against her husband and the Maroons who moved in. They would do absolutely anything she asked of them, you see.'

'Careful!'

'I was wrong, I know that now, but you must see how it looked. She got what she wanted, which was release from an unhappy marriage, return to England, and financial independence. She wasn't to know that Percival would try to claim her property.'

'I am very glad you did not spread false rumours about Mrs Sheffield's character,' Joshua said, narrowing his eyes at his cousin's tutor.

'I would never do that.'

No, Joshua thought, perhaps not. But he would not have imagined the young man he thought so well of being capable of jumping to such erroneous conclusions either. Joshua might be in love with Mrs Sheffield, and therefore justifiably considered biased, but it must be obvious even to the slowest-witted she was incapable of such duplicitous behaviour.

'I assume Mrs Sheffield is aware of what you thought about her.'

'Things were said in the heat of the moment that I now regret,' Asquith replied evasively.

'Apologise when you next see the lady, throw your support behind me in my efforts to restore her property to her, and we will say no more about the matter.'

'Thank you, Colonel. That is very generous of you.' Asquith paused. 'Now we have cleared that matter up, will you permit me to ask you a personal question, sir?'

Joshua sighed, suspecting he knew what was coming. 'Ask away.'

'Miss de Bourgh. Er, Lady Catherine told me why she wished to come to Pemberley, and why you are here also.' He cleared his throat. 'Excuse me, but you obviously have a personal interest in Mrs Sheffield. Where does that leave Miss de Bourgh?'

Damn the man's impertinence! 'Anne and I would not suit,' he replied shortly.

Asquith elevated both brows. 'You would pass up the opportunity to be master of Rosings?'

'Apparently so.'

'Have you told Lady Catherine of your decision?'

'Not yet, and nor shall I for a few days more.' Joshua slapped the younger man on the shoulders. 'That ought to give you time.'

'Me?' Asquith laughed. 'If Lady Catherine even suspected—'

'I have watched you and Anne together. She is clearly besotted with you and deserves to be happy. You have done a great deal to bring her out of herself. I hardly recognise her any more.'

'It is what I am paid to do.'

'Anne is no longer quite so afraid of Lady Catherine, thanks in part I think to your opening her eyes. If there is something she wants enough, my impression is she might even defy her mother in order to get it.'

Asquith shook his head. 'Lady Catherine would disinherit her.'

'I doubt that very much. Lady Catherine likes you. She has softened greatly since I saw her last.' Joshua paused. 'There is something in her attitude when she looks at you, especially when you mention Sir Marius.'

'They knew one another when they were younger.'

'I suspect my aunt liked him, which accounts for her taking you on as Anne's tutor. The question is, do you return Anne's feelings?' Joshua waved a hand. 'I don't expect you to answer that. It's none of my damned business. All I would ask is that you do not excite her expectations if that is not the case.'

'I am very fond of her, but she will never believe I have anything other than the acquisition of Rosings in mind if I tell her so.' Asquith expelled a long breath. 'She told me once she will never know if anyone really likes her for who she is, simply because of the material benefits that she holds within her gift. She looked so sad when she said it, I felt very sorry for her.'

'Be that as it may, she knows she must marry soon to someone of her mother's choosing.' Joshua grinned. 'Someone like me. You have to be a better alternative. You make her happy, that much is very obvious.'

'Only if she can be made to believe I like her for herself, and how the devil am I supposed to convince her of that?'

'Well then, you have some work ahead of you.'

The two men shook hands at the door to the room and went their separate ways. Joshua was unsure what he had just set in motion, and where the repercussions might lead. All he knew was that everyone, no matter what their circumstances, deserved a chance of happiness. If he could achieve that for his cousin by encouraging Asquith to think the unthinkable then so be it, and the devil take the consequences.

12

Painting huge areas of sheeting to resemble a garden was exhausting yet exhilarating work. Within half an hour, Anne had almost as much paint on her as she had managed to apply to the sheet, but she was enjoying herself too much to mind. She couldn't remember the last time she had actually got dirty, or if she ever had. Games in the garden that normal children enjoyed had been denied to her because she was too frail, and chances could not be taken with her health. It never once occurred to her to question her mother when she insisted Anne had a sickly disposition. Mama always knew best.

When Sir Lewis had died and Mama showed no inclination to remarry, she made it clear Anne would be her heir because the de Bourghs did not discriminate against female succession. What she failed to mention was that Anne's life would never be her own from that point onwards. The slightest sniffle might develop into influenza, and so Anne was required to take to her bed for a fortnight, just as a precaution. If she coughed the doctor was immediately summoned. If she cut herself it put the entire household into an uproar. Anne had become so accustomed to the fuss made of her that it became ordinary, and she began to assume all young ladies of consequence were similarly cossetted.

Being here at Pemberley with Georgiana and Kitty, Anne started to realise what she had missed all these years.

'You have paint on the end of your nose, Anne,' Georgiana said, laughing.

'We all have paint on our exposed parts,' Kitty pointed out. 'It is fortunate these pinafores cover our gowns or they would be ruined.'

Georgiana stood back to examine the rose garden she had just painted. 'It looks more like a rambling jungle,' she said, screwing up her nose in disgust.

'Oh no, Georgie, it looks fine.' Kitty examined Georgiana's efforts with a critical eye. 'Don't forget, Mr Asquith explained that when the sheets are lining the walls, they will look very different. Something about perspective, I think he said.'

'Dim lighting would better serve,' Georgiana replied, grimacing.

'Or else we will put on such a dazzling display of acting no one will notice the scenery,' Kitty suggested hopefully.

'Unfortunately, there is more chance of our scenery appearing realistic than of that happening.'

'When we put the scenery up in the music room, I think Mr Asquith said something about having potted palms put in front of it,' Kitty remarked.

'Ah, so he anticipated our miserable efforts.' Georgiana flashed a rueful smile. 'How very wise of him. How are your trees coming along, Anne?'

'About as well as your roses.' Anne stood up and stretched. 'Where is Mr Asquith, by the way? I thought he would be here to advise us.'

Anne noticed Georgiana and Kitty share an amused glance. 'I

think he was detained by Colonel Fitzwilliam,' Kitty said. 'Don't worry, Anne. He is devoted to you and I am sure he will not neglect you for long.'

Anne felt heat invade her face. 'You misunderstand me. I simply wanted to ask him something about the trees.'

'Of course you did.'

'It's all right,' Georgiana said. 'We are only teasing you, even if we can't help wondering what the two of you find to talk about when you are closeted together for so many hours at a time.'

'Literature,' Anne replied, causing both girls to burst out laughing. 'It's true,' Anne protested. 'We both share a love of the written word, but I have had no one with whom to discuss what I read before now. If Mama knew how much time I secretly spend with my nose in a book, she would scold me for straining my eyes, but really, I cannot think of a better way to pass the long hours in each day. Escaping into a literary world is... well, my guilty secret.'

'That is so sad,' Georgiana said. 'I am very glad you now have someone to share your... er, passion with, and we promise not to tease you about it any more.'

'Thank you.' Anne actually giggled, something else which she couldn't recall ever having done before. Mama did not approve of young ladies who giggled. Come to that, there were a lot of things Mama did not approve of.

'You are entirely welcome.' Georgiana smiled before turning her attention to Kitty. 'Talking of passions, has Captain Turner said anything more about his duty visit to his father?'

'No, surprisingly little.' Kitty pouted. 'All he said was that the meeting with his father had not gone well, and that he would not be marrying the lady his father wishes him to.'

'That is a good thing, surely?' Anne couldn't understand why Kitty seemed so glum. 'It is obviously you he wants for his wife.'

'I wish I shared your optimism. He has not said a word, or done anything to suggest a preference.'

This time it was Georgiana and Anne who shared a laugh at Kitty's expense.

'You goose,' Georgiana said affectionately. 'The captain adores you. Whenever you are in the same room together, his gaze seldom leaves you.'

'You exaggerate.'

'Indeed, she does not,' Anne said. 'Even I have noticed.'

'I think he does like me,' Kitty agreed modestly. 'But he has never said a word about his feelings or tried to... well, anything.'

'I should hope not.' But Georgiana laughed as she said it. 'My brother would skin him alive if he behaved inappropriately.'

'Besides,' Anne added, 'you have not known one another for very long. This is only your second meeting, I understand.'

'Yes, but even so. If he was as sure of his feelings for me as I am of mine for him, there would be no occasion for delay,' Kitty replied glumly. 'I think there is something, some difficulty, he has not shared with me that is preventing him from declaring himself.'

'Give him time,' Georgiana said. 'He has clearly had a falling out with his father. Even if he has independent means, I am sure he would wish to be on good terms with his family before admitting to his feelings.'

'Yes, I suppose you are right about that, Georgie. However, you must not think I don't know your game.' Kitty shook a paint-stained finger beneath Georgiana's nose. 'You are deliberately turning the conversation towards mine and Anne's aspirations in the hope we will not cross-question you about yours.'

'Is that what she is doing?' Anne asked, raising a brow in speculation.

'Undoubtedly.' Kitty grinned at Anne. 'As though we didn't both know she is madly in love with Major Halstead.'

'Then you are both wrong.' Georgiana sighed. 'I like him very much and enjoy his society, but love... well, it is a very serious commitment. Besides, I don't think my brother would allow me to become betrothed quite yet, even if the major declared himself.'

'What do you want, if not Major Halstead?' Anne asked.

'I want what my brother and Lizzy have,' she replied without hesitation. 'Seldom have I seen more complete and absolute love. I envy them so much. You know, sometimes I can be in the same room as them but they are so completely involved with one another they don't seem to realise I am there. Nothing persuades me I could feel that way about the major.'

'Yes,' Anne said. 'I have noticed that about them. Even with a houseful of guests, they still seem to be totally absorbed with each another.'

'Lizzy didn't feel that way at first,' Kitty said. 'So perhaps your feelings for the major will change.'

'Oh, it is entirely possible. I am not saying he isn't the man for me. I am just not as sure of my feelings as you two appear to be.'

The door opened to admit Mr Asquith, bringing their intimate conversation to a close. Anne was pleased to have been included in it and to offer her advice, such as it was. She had never had the pleasure of another female to swap confidences with before. It had been illuminating, even if she had little by way of personal experience to bring to the discussion.

'How are you progressing, ladies?' Mr Asquith asked.

It was Georgiana who answered him. 'Not terribly well, Mr Asquith, as you can see. Sketching is one thing but painting on this scale is entirely another. I had not realised it would be quite so challenging.'

'Could we not just close the drapes in the music room and make do with them as a backdrop?' Kitty asked.

Mr Asquith took a close look at their handiwork and nodded

his approval, but Anne sensed he was distracted about something. She knew him well enough to be sure he was not giving the matter in hand his complete attention. Whatever could he and the colonel have been discussing?

'You underestimate your abilities,' he replied. 'From a distance, this will look very well indeed. Who is responsible for painting the sun dial?'

'That was me,' Anne admitted reluctantly. 'I know it is too large. I got a little carried away. Unlike with sketching, it is impossible to start afresh if things go awry.'

Mr Asquith turned towards her and offered her the benefit of a dazzling smile that pointedly excluded Georgiana and Kitty. 'I beg to differ, Miss de Bourgh. I think it a very realistic touch, skilfully executed and not at all out of proportion.'

Anne blossomed beneath such lavish praise. She seemed unable to snatch her gaze away from Mr Asquith's even though there was no occasion to continue looking at him. 'I am not sure about that. Besides, it was Kitty's idea.'

'Well, I have had quite enough for one afternoon,' Georgiana said, putting aside her brush and unfastening her pinafore. 'I had no idea painting scenery could be quite so exhausting.'

'No, nor I,' Kitty agreed, also abandoning her painting equipment. 'Please excuse us, Mr Asquith. I for one intend to idle the rest of the afternoon away. Oh, and study my lines, of course,' she added, giggling.

'As do I,' Georgiana said.

Mr Asquith opened the door for the girls. Anne blushed when Kitty looked back over her shoulder and winked at her. It was clear they were not really tired. Anne had wondered about that. She was supposedly the weakest of the three and yet she felt full of energy and vigour. This was their clumsy attempt to leave Anne alone with Mr Asquith. The silence hung heavily between them once the girls' chattering voices had faded.

'Are you tired as well, Miss de Bourgh?' Mr Asquith asked. 'I have been working you all very hard.'

'Not in the least. Although I dare say Mama will come looking for me sooner or later and insist I rest before dinner.'

'What is it?' he asked softly, moving to stand closer to her. 'You look very pensive.'

'Oh, take no notice of me. I was just thinking how much I have enjoyed my time here with Georgiana and Kitty. I have never had friends my own age before, you see. But I also can't shake the feeling we are all marking time, waiting for something significant to happen.'

'You refer to Colonel Fitzwilliam, perhaps.'

'Yes.' Anne twisted her hands together, wondering what could have possessed her to instigate this line of conversation. She had become accustomed over the years to keeping her thoughts and opinions to herself for fear of earning her mother's disapproval. With Mr Asquith she seemed to say whatever came into her head despite the fact he probably thought her immature and undeserving of her privileged position. 'Mama warned me to expect an offer of marriage from the colonel while we were here and yet he has made no effort to single me out or speak to me alone.' She wrinkled her brow. 'I don't know what to make of that. Does he find me so unattractive that he simply cannot make himself do it even though he would have Rosings to make up for his disappointment?'

Mr Asquith looked very agitated, as though there was something he particularly wished to say to her. Or maybe he was simply embarrassed by her candour but couldn't actually say so. After all, he was her mother's employee.

'Take no notice of me,' she said, turning away from him. 'I am not feeling myself today.'

'You are anxious to receive the colonel's addresses after all?'

'You know I am not, but I *am* most anxious not to have an argument with Mama if he fails to ask me. She would probably say the fault is mine for not encouraging him.'

'The blame is definitely not yours.'

Anne shuddered. 'Mama will not see things that way. I feel so much stronger nowadays but the prospect of arguing with her is enough to sap my energy and resolve.' She managed a droll smile. 'I have always found it easier to do whatever Mama asks of me. Rosings is a much pleasanter place when Mama is in good humour.'

Mr Asquith glanced out of the window. Anne followed the direction of his gaze and saw the earlier rain had given way to patchy blue skies.

'We have been cooped up in here for two whole days,' he said. 'Shall we take a walk together in the grounds?'

The suggestion was as surprising as it was welcome. 'By all means. Give me a moment to fetch my bonnet and pelisse. Providing I can avoid Mama and her intrusive questions, I shall meet you in the vestibule in ten minutes.'

'Lady Catherine is in the conservatory writing a letter. You ought to be able to slip past her if you are quick.'

Mr Asquith was right about that. Anne managed to reach her chamber, don her outdoor clothing, and run back down again without encountering her mother or her maid. She wondered why she felt the need for secrecy. There was nothing out of the ordinary about her walking with Mr Asquith. They did it all the time at Rosings, even if they did take a servant with them. There was really no necessity for that, but Mama would insist, or worse, inflict her company upon them and then dominate the conversation.

'You were very quick,' Mr Asquith said when she returned to the hall and found him awaiting her.

'Mama has eyes and ears everywhere,' she said in a conspiratorial whisper that made her handsome tutor smile.

He led her to a side door, presumably so they wouldn't be seen leaving together. The wind was brisk and yet invigorating. The air smelled fresh and clean. Damp leaves, whipped up by the wind, whirled around their feet and clung like natural decoration to the hem of Anne's gown.

'I love this time of year in England,' he said. 'It was one of the things I missed most while in Jamaica.'

'And yet you were born in Jamaica. I should have thought you would have found our autumn and winter far too cold for your taste.'

'I did when I first came over here to school. I actually thought I might freeze to death but I soon learned to prefer it to the heat and humidity of the tropics.'

'I have never set foot outside of England so I am not qualified to give an opinion. However, I am sure I would not enjoy being too hot all the time.'

They turned a corner that brought them close to the famous Pemberley maze.

'Have you ever tried this?' he asked.

'Goodness no. I would get lost for a month.'

'Nonsense.' He offered his arm, and she placed her hand on it. 'Come along, Miss de Bourgh. Let us be brave. We shall either triumph or be lost together for all time.'

Anne would greatly have preferred the latter alternative; then her other problems would just have to take care of themselves. 'Very well, Mr Asquith, I shall place my trust in you,' she said. 'Lead on.'

Smiling, she set off beside Mr Asquith as he plunged into the confusing construction of beech hedges.

'The trick is always to turn in the same direction and never deviate. What shall it be, Miss de Bourgh, left or right?'

'Oh, right, by all means.'

He briefly covered the fingers that rested on his arm with his opposite hand. 'I shall never knowingly do wrong by you,' he said with a gaze of dark intensity.

Anne turned away, unsure what to make of that statement. Probably nothing. She was determined not to spoil this rare time alone with Mr Asquith by reading more into this conversation than was there, or to think about what her mother would have to say if she knew about it. She would consider it a highly inappropriate situation and Anne would receive a scolding. She simply didn't care. She felt light of heart, free almost. Being defiant definitely had its advantages.

'Are you sure about this, Mr Asquith?' she asked when they had taken several turns that took them deeper into the maze with no clear end in sight. The hedges were far too tall even for Mr Asquith to see over them. 'I am sure we just passed down this walkway in the opposite direction.'

'Have faith.' He dropped his voice to a soft purr he had never used with her before. 'Have I ever guided you wrong?'

'Well, no, but perhaps not all mazes are designed the same way.'

'Don't tell me you are nervous.'

'Not nervous precisely, but it is a little daunting.'

'We could leave markers as we go to ensure we find our way out. A ribbon from your hair, my handkerchief, things like that, but it would be cheating, do you not think?'

'Yes, I suppose it would be.' It would also make Anne feel a lot safer but she had been consumed by a capricious mood and had no desire to be safe.

'If all else fails, we will simply wait to be found.'

'But no one knows where we are so how would they know where to look?'

'Ah, so they do not.' He sent her a charming smile, the one that always seemed to melt her insides and send agreeable sensations rioting through her body. 'In which case, we must hope I know what I am doing. Now which way, I wonder.'

They had reached a crossroads. The path they were on continued straight ahead, but there were also turnings to the left and right.

'Right,' Anne replied, without hesitation. 'This junction is supposed to confuse us I think, and trick us into not turning.'

'Exactly so.'

The right hand turning took them to a large clearing in the centre of the maze. It boasted a magnificent statue of a winged horse with a bench beneath it.

'Oh, it is beautiful!' Anne stared at the statue, awestruck. 'I should love to draw it.'

'Do you not recognise it?'

'Should I?' Anne tilted her head, examining the statue from all angles. 'Pegaz?'

'Yes, from the ancient Persian legend we read together.'

'Did you know it was here, Mr Asquith?'

'No, but it occurred to me that Mr Darcy would put something special in the centre of his maze to reward those brave enough to make their way through all the wrong turns.'

A bit like her life, Anne thought, briefly closing her eyes and pretending she was here with Mr Asquith because he intended to go down on bended knee and request her hand in marriage. That would make the agonies of her lonely childhood and the confusion of impending adulthood more than worthwhile. She shook her head to dislodge the thought, telling herself not to be so foolish. Even if he did pretend affection for her, that is all it would be. Pretence. It wasn't her he wanted, but Rosings. That was all everyone saw when they looked at her. She shivered at the thought and her pleasure in the moment was spoiled.

'Are you cold?' he asked.

'Not really.'

'Then what is it?'

He took her hand in his, and she felt compelled to meet his gaze. What she saw there unbalanced her. There was sympathy and understanding in his eyes, and compassion too. It was as though he grasped the reasons for her turmoil and cared, really cared, about her as a person. Of course that was not possible, but it did no harm to pretend. She didn't want to tell him the truth and admit to her pathetic weaknesses, but the manner in which he was regarding her with an expression of such deep intensity made it impossible to keep her uncertainties to herself.

'I am afraid,' she said simply. 'Afraid of what will happen if Colonel Fitzwilliam addresses me, but even more afraid of what will happen if he does not.' She swallowed, wondering whether she ought to go on. One look at his resourceful features and she threw caution to the wind. Let him laugh at her if he wanted to, she no longer cared. 'But whatever happens, I will have to part with you,' she said, turning her head away. 'Mama never intended for you to remain with me for long, we have both always known that, but the truth of the matter is that you have taught me far more than she could have bargained for. You have opened my eyes to the world beyond Rosings, given me the courage to think and to hold opinions of my own I am no longer afraid to express and... well, I have said too much.'

'My dear girl!' he cried passionately. 'You need never concern yourself about my leaving you.'

She blinked, unsure she had heard him right. 'You have to earn a living, Mr Asquith. We both know that.'

'Miss de Bourgh... Anne.' He reached out an arm and pulled her against him. Anne was breathless with delight when her name slipped past his lips again so naturally, and she willingly allowed herself to be embraced by him. 'Don't make the mistake of underestimating me. You say you have learned a lot from me but you can't have enjoyed the experience as much as I have. At first, I looked upon you as a challenge. A lonely young lady afraid to open her mouth for fear of earning ridicule. I saw your potential but you have surpassed my most optimistic expectations. You are like a flower that has blossomed beneath my nurturing. I take all the credit for that, you know,' he continued, his capable hands sliding to her back and holding her more firmly against him, 'and I never walk away from what I create.'

Anne felt dazed, disorientated, euphoric, and barely able to believe this was happening. She wasn't altogether sure what *was* happening. She had absolutely no idea what he meant by her being his creation, nor did she much care. All she wanted was to continue being held by him, to feel the warmth and strength from his body seeping into her own. This was where she was supposed to be. He made her feel safe and protected, as though a great weight had been lifted from her shoulders. She screwed her eyes tightly closed, willing him to kiss her.

To her intense disappointment, he did not.

'Come,' he said instead, his voice gravelly and rough, almost dismissive. Her eyes flew open and she sent him an enquiring look, wondering what she had done to cause such an abrupt change in him. 'We ought to get back to the house before we are missed.'

* * *

Joshua found Mr and Mrs Darcy together in the drawing room. He paused in the doorway to observe them, heads close together, laughing at something one of them had just said. Darcy reached out a hand and gently touched his wife's face, his eyes soft, adoring. She leaned her cheek into his palm and sent him an enticing smile that prompted Darcy to groan, lower his head, and cover her lips with his own.

The intimacy of the snatched moment reinforced Joshua's long-held opinion that Darcy had found his soul mate, a woman who would be the making of his intelligent yet rigidly correct cousin. With her irreverent attitude and lively wit, Eliza's character was diametrically opposed to Darcy's and could only have a beneficial effect upon his mercurial temper. Watching them together now, he wondered if she knew how much influence she wielded over him. He suspected that she did, and Joshua was glad. Darcy took life far too seriously and deserved to put his own happiness ahead of duty.

Joshua hesitated on the threshold, feeling like the intruder that he was, wondering if he ought to leave them alone. Unfortunately, his business was too urgent to brook delay. He needed the benefit of his cousin's advice and was unlikely to find a better opportunity for a quiet word.

He cleared his throat and walked into the room.

'Colonel Fitzwilliam.' Mrs Darcy offered him a warm smile. 'You look as though you have lost a guinea and found a farthing. Pray sit down and tell us what bothers you.'

'It is not quite as serious as that, ma'am,' he replied, smiling as he sat across from them.

'You have made yourself scarce all day, Fitzwilliam,' Darcy said, a cynical twist to his lips. 'If I didn't know better, I would say you were avoiding our aunt.'

Joshua grunted. 'The very idea.'

'I believe the colonel has been to pay a call on our neighbours,' Mrs Darcy said, her eyes sparkling with lively interest.

'Yes, and I was rather taken aback by what I learned from Mrs Sheffield. The fact of the matter is that I am unsure what to do about it and badly in need of your advice, Darcy.'

Mrs Darcy stood. 'Then I will leave you gentlemen to talk.'

'No, don't go.' Joshua grimaced. 'If you can spare the time, Mrs Darcy, I would appreciate a lady's point of view.'

'I have all the time in the world for you, Colonel.' She resumed her seat. 'Besides, you have made me curious. It is most unlike you to appear so unsure of yourself.'

Succinctly, Joshua outlined all Mrs Sheffield had told him and all he had subsequently learned from Asquith.

'It sounds to me as though Percival Sheffield is definitely trying to bamboozle your Mrs Sheffield out of her inheritance,' Darcy said after a moment's contemplation.

'There is no doubt in my mind about that,' Joshua agreed. 'The question is, how do I prove it?'

'If Asquith is to be believed—'

'You doubt his word?' Mrs Darcy asked, looking rather shocked.

'It's not that I doubt him precisely. It is more that he seems a little too good to be true.'

'He is in the same position as Wickham was as a young man,' Darcy said. 'The favoured son of an employee who has enjoyed his master's largesse. Unlike Wickham, Asquith appears to have made the most of that opportunity.'

'He certainly knows how to behave in society,' Mrs Darcy added. 'His manners are faultless.'

'True enough, but he had the temerity to suggest Mrs Sheffield might know more about her husband's death than she said, or that she might even have arranged it.'

Darcy chuckled, something Joshua had seldom heard him do before his marriage. 'You are not looking at the broader picture, Fitzwilliam, because you support Mrs Sheffield's cause.'

'Quite so, but—'

'Were that not the case.' Darcy paused, idly plucking at the arm of the settee he occupied. 'Think like the soldier you are. Would you not suspect her too if you had all the facts at your disposal?'

Joshua stood up. 'I came to you for sound advice,' he said hotly. 'But if all you can do is cast aspersions on an innocent lady's character, then I have obviously wasted my time.'

'Sit down, Fitzwilliam.' Joshua scowled at his cousin and was slow to react. 'I am merely playing devil's advocate—'

'He does that a lot,' Mrs Darcy said with a wicked smile that lightened the tension in the room.

'All I am saying,' Darcy continued, 'is that in Asquith's position, I might have had my suspicions, too.'

'Hmm, well I still think Asquith is not all he appears to be.' Joshua crossed his arms in a defensive pose, wondering why he was so determined to think ill of Asquith. 'However, that is nothing to me. What is important is finding a way to disprove Sheffield's claim.'

'Will you allow me to think about it?' Darcy asked. 'It would not be wise to rush into anything.'

'By all means.'

'It will be difficult to do anything with Sheffield in Buckinghamshire and his solicitor in London,' Mrs Darcy remarked. 'It seems to me they are the main characters in this real-life drama playing out alongside Mr Asquith's fictional one, and we will never get at the truth at arm's length.'

'True,' Darcy replied. 'But even to oblige my cousin and forward his matrimonial ambitions, we are not going to London.'

'Who said anything about matrimony?' Joshua asked.

Both Darcys sent him wry smiles, but before either of them could speak, Lady Catherine joined them, bringing the conversation to a premature end.

'Oh, there you are, Fitzwilliam. I thought you must be with Anne,' she said accusingly. 'I cannot find her anywhere.'

'Is she not in the ballroom, practising her lines?' Joshua asked politely.

'No one is in the ballroom. I just checked.' Lady Catherine settled herself in the chair closest to the fire. 'Anne is not in her room either, but her maid says her pelisse is gone.'

'Then presumably she is walking in the grounds,' Darcy said calmly.

Lady Catherine seemed scandalised by such a reasonable suggestion. 'In this weather?'

'It isn't cold,' Mrs Darcy pointed out. 'In fact, it is now a rather bracing late summer's day. The girls have been indoors for two entire days. I expect they felt the need for fresh air and exercise. I know I do.'

'We are not all fortunate enough to share your robust health, Mrs Darcy.'

'Anne seems much stronger these days,' Darcy remarked.

'She thinks she is but I know better. Besides, I would not see her set herself back with rash behaviour. It is bad enough, all this play acting.' Lady Catherine shook her head, her expression disapproving. 'I am still unsure why I permitted it. It will sap her strength.'

'She appears to be enjoying herself enormously,' Darcy remarked.

'Bah, life is not all about pleasure.'

'I shall ring for tea,' Mrs Darcy said diplomatically.

Before she could do so, Simpson entered the room and waited for Darcy to acknowledge his presence. 'What is it, Simpson?'

'Mr Collins is here, sir.'

'Mr Collins?' Lady Catherine looked astonished. 'My Mr Collins? What on earth could possibly bring him all this way?'

'You had best show him in, Simpson,' Darcy said with a glance at his wife. 'And then we shall find out.'

'Have some tea sent up please, Simpson,' Mrs Darcy said.

'At once, ma'am.'

The butler left the room, returning almost immediately. 'Mr Collins, sir,' he said, standing back and allowing the clergyman into the room.

Mr Collins was much as Joshua remembered him – red of face, thin-lipped, full of self-importance. He bowed low to Lady Catherine, and then to Darcy and Joshua.

'Cousin Elizabeth,' he said to Mrs Darcy. 'I trust you will excuse my unexpected arrival. I can assure you that nothing other than the most urgent business would have brought me here uninvited. Indeed, I must apologise for my dishevelled appearance since I have been on the road these past three days.'

'What can possibly be so urgent that you could not commit it to an express letter, Mr Collins?' Lady Catherine asked.

'Well, ma'am, it is... er, very delicate. Perhaps your ladyship would be kind enough to grant me an audience in private.'

Heavens, Joshua thought, trying hard to maintain his countenance. The damned man makes Lady Catherine sound like the pope.

'Nonsense, man,' Lady Catherine replied briskly. 'Whatever you have to say can be said in front of my relations.' Her gaze lingered on Mrs Darcy, as though she still couldn't decide if she qualified as a relation and was considering asking her to leave her own drawing room. Common sense prevailed and she remained silent on the point.

'Please take a seat, Mr Collins, and recover your breath.'

Mrs Darcy looked as though she too found the situation amusing. Joshua had heard rumours that Collins once aspired to marry Eliza Bennet. The rejection of his suit wounded his pride and he transferred his imaginary affections to Eliza's friend Charlotte Lucas with astonishing speed. This time his proposal met with success, presumably because Miss Lucas must have given up hope of attracting a husband, and the prospect of becoming an old maid did not sit well with her. Lady Catherine, it transpired, had deemed it time for Hunsford's clergyman to find himself a wife. Mr Collins would die rather than return home to Kent and disappoint his patroness, so everyone was satisfied with the arrangement.

'Tea will be here directly,' Mrs Darcy said when her uninvited guest settled himself in a chair. 'When you are refreshed there will be ample opportunity for you to explain your reasons for coming to Pemberley.'

'Thank you, Cousin Elizabeth. I confess that refreshment would be welcome. I cannot seem to dislodge the dust of the road from my throat.'

'How did you leave Charlotte?' Mrs Darcy asked.

'In the best of health, I thank you. She is much occupied with our daughter, of course, but sends you her most affectionate best wishes. Naturally she is also taken up with the affairs of the parish, as becomes the wife of a clergyman, and I...'

Joshua only half-listened to Mr Collins's monologue about life in Hunsford and the important role he and his dear wife played in it. He knew from experience that Collins was perfectly capable of conducting a conversation entirely on his own and saw no reason to listen to it. However, he had no intention of removing himself from the drawing room since he too was curious as to the reason for Collins's arrival at Pemberley.

Only when tea was finished and Collins had talked non-stop throughout it, his obsequiousness already starting to grate on Joshua's nerves, did Darcy remind him he had urgent news for Lady Catherine.

'Thank you for reminding me, Mr Darcy.' He shook his head. 'As though I could forget about this unfortunate business.'

'What unfortunate business, Mr Collins? Pray out with it,' Lady Catherine said irascibly. 'You know how much I dislike procrastination.'

'That was not my intention, Lady Catherine, I do assure you.' Looking exceptionally sombre, Collins cleared his throat, grasped his lapels, and finally had the goodness to explain himself. 'Your ladyship will recall I was not impressed with Mr Asquith and advised your ladyship against exposing Miss de Bourgh to his company. Such a delicate young lady should be protected at all costs.'

More to the point, Joshua thought, Collins disliked another man having Lady Catherine's ear. He probably felt as though his influence at Rosings had diminished with the arrival of such a well-educated, charismatic young man as Asquith. Even so, Joshua's interest was piqued, especially given his own reservations about that gentleman.

'This is about Asquith?' Darcy asked.

'Indeed it is, Mr Darcy. I take no pleasure in being proven right in my advice to you, Lady Catherine. But you see, a lady called at the vicarage, having been directed there in search of Mr Asquith.'

'A lady?' Lady Catherine frowned. 'What lady?'

'A Miss Miranda Glover, my lady.'

Lady Catherine appeared startled, and rather discomposed. 'One of Sir Marius's daughters?'

'Apparently so.'

'What on earth brings her to England?'

'Was she travelling alone?' Mrs Darcy asked at the same time as Lady Catherine posed her question.

Collins paused, presumably getting to the point at last. Even by his long-winded ways, Joshua thought he had dragged this matter out to its lengthiest extreme because he enjoyed being the harbinger of bad tidings. Better yet, he enjoyed being proven right, which he obviously thought he was.

'She came in search of Mr Asquith.' Collins tried to look disapproving but failed to achieve that ambition. Instead, he appeared smug and very self-satisfied. 'She said they were engaged to be married but Mr Asquith ran away to England and deserted her.'

13

Lizzy felt as shocked as everyone else appeared to be at this startling revelation. No one spoke, or knew quite what to do, until Lady Catherine broke the silence.

'I don't believe a word of it,' she said forcibly. 'There must be some other explanation. I am never wrong about people. Besides, I trust Sir Marius's judgement implicitly. He recommended Mr Asquith to me and would hardly have done so if he had jilted one of his daughters.'

'Perhaps he sent the recommendation before he became aware of the broken engagement?' Colonel Fitzwilliam suggested. 'Asquith has not been in England long enough for another letter from Sir Marius to reach you, ma'am. You know as well as I do that letters from such far-flung places as Jamaica can take months to arrive.'

'That is of course a possibility,' Lady Catherine conceded grudgingly.

'You didn't answer Mrs Darcy's question, Collins,' Will said. 'Was the lady travelling alone?'

'She travelled to England with her father.'

Lady Catherine gasped, and her face lost all colour. Lizzy became quite concerned about her. Will filled a glass with water and handed it to his aunt, who looked as though she was about to swoon. How curious. Lady Catherine was the last person on this earth whom Lizzy would ever have considered capable of swooning. She would look upon it as a weakness, a character flaw, and Lady Catherine did not hold with weaknesses or flaws. Lizzy was now truly intrigued. Could it be Lady Catherine had some sort of dark secret in her past that was to do with Sir Marius? That would explain the peculiar situation with Mr Asquith being taken on to tutor Anne, and Lady Catherine's disinclination to think badly of him.

'Sir Marius is in England?' Lady Catherine asked faintly.

'Apparently he had business in England, and his daughter, suffering as she was, persuaded him to bring her along for a change of scenery and society,' Mr Collins replied.

'Sir Marius never comes to England.' Lady Catherine appeared to recover a little of her customary fortitude. She straightened her spine as she asserted the fact, as if by so doing she would make it a reality. 'Did you actually see him, Mr Collins?'

'No, my lady. Miss Glover was accompanied by her maid. Sir Marius had business in Dover, and she took the opportunity to travel on to Hunsford in the hope of seeing Mr Asquith. I am unsure if Sir Marius knew she planned to do so. In fact, I am persuaded he could not have done. After all, I am sure he would not wish his daughter to face Mr Asquith and all the awkwardness that meeting would engender alone.' Mr Collins shook his head, adopting a scandalised expression. 'No young lady ought to be exposed to such a tawdry situation.'

'That all sounds rather questionable,' Will said, sharing a glance with Lizzy, who was thinking exactly the same thing.

'And easily resolved. Ring the bell, Darcy, and summon

Asquith,' Lady Catherine said. 'We will have this out with him this moment. If there is a grain of truth in Miss Glover's claim, or the slightest stain attaching to Asquith's character, then of course he must not be allowed anywhere near Anne ever again.'

Lizzy glanced at Mr Collins, noticed that his smug expression had now taken up permanent residence on his countenance, and disliked him more than ever as a consequence. No matter what Colonel Fitzwilliam thought, Lizzy was convinced Mr Asquith was not a cad or a fortune hunter. At the very least they ought not to jump to conclusions until he had been given an opportunity to explain himself.

'We ought to leave you to conduct this interview alone,' Lizzy said, standing. 'I would not have Mr Asquith embarrassed or feel as though this is some sort of inquisition.'

'Nonsense.' Lady Catherine sniffed. 'You all know the particulars, and I see no occasion to think of his finer feelings, especially if he is culpable. It would be as well if you heard what Asquith has to say for himself.'

'Very well.'

But the situation did not sit comfortably with Lizzy. It would be extremely embarrassing for Mr Asquith to have to account for his conduct in front of such a large audience, especially if he was innocent, which Lizzy was inclined to believe was the case. She was usually a good judge of character and had taken to Mr Asquith upon first acquaintance. Then again, she had taken to Wickham, and look how that had turned out.

Lizzy wanted to leave the room but also wished to stay. She had a feeling Mr Asquith might be in need of a supporter. Mr Collins and the colonel were both disposed to think badly of him, albeit for differing reasons. Lady Catherine liked Mr Asquith but regretted employing him because Anne was so taken with him that she had developed a rebellious streak. Only Lizzy and Will were truly neutral, prepared to give the young man the benefit of the doubt.

Simpson answered the bell and despatched a footman in search of Mr Asquith. An uneasy silence descended upon the drawing room as its occupants waited for him to respond to the summons.

'I simply refuse to believe Mr Asquith capable of such base behaviour,' Lady Catherine said after several minutes during which everyone had appeared to be lost in thought.

'I agree with you, ma'am,' Lizzy said. 'He seems far too honourable.'

'Forgive me, Cousin Elizabeth, but as a well brought up lady you cannot be expected to know how certain men behave when given sufficient license.'

Of all the pompous, self-opinionated... Will squeezed her hand, as though understanding the nature of the thoughts running through her head. 'And you must forgive me, Mr Collins, if I assure you that I understand far better than you could possibly imagine.'

Mr Collins looked as though he wished to argue the point. One glance at Will and he wisely held his tongue. That, in Lizzy's knowledge of the man, was a rarity.

'You wished to see me, Lady Catherine,' Mr Asquith said as he strode into the room. 'Oh, excuse me, I did not realise you were not alone. And Mr Collins. It is a surprise and a pleasure to see you here.'

Mr Collins mumbled what for him was a very short and exceedingly ungracious response. Mr Asquith's congenial expression faltered.

'Has something happened?' he asked. 'You all look exceedingly grave.'

'Mr Asquith,' Lady Catherine said with asperity. 'Mr Collins felt it necessary to come to Pemberley in person because he has received a visit from a most unexpected quarter.'

'Someone known to me, I assume, which would account for your wish to speak with me.'

'Quite so.' Lady Catherine paused. 'Miss Miranda Glover.'

Lizzy watched Mr Asquith carefully when this disclosure was made and noticed the profound effect the mention of that lady's name had upon him. His eyes widened, his jaw slackened, and his manner became rather agitated.

'Miranda is in England?'

'Apparently so.' Lady Catherine fixed her daughter's tutor with a steely gaze. 'You know the lady.'

'She is one of Sir Marius's daughters. I know all of his children. In fact, I taught many of them, especially the younger girls, including Miranda, since they did not go away to school.'

'Mr Asquith, you know me well enough to appreciate I prefer plain speaking and so I shall come straight to the point.' But Lady Catherine paused, as though unwilling to do so. 'Miss Glover left her father in Dover and travelled to Hunsford in search of you. She told Mr Collins you and she were engaged to be married and that you deserted her.' Lady Catherine's lips tightened. 'There, what do you have to say to that?'

Mr Asquith didn't immediately respond. Instead, he paced the length of the room, hands clasped behind his back, muttering something unintelligible. For the first time, Lizzy doubted him. If it was untrue, why did he not immediately refute Miss Glover's claim?

'You must accept my word, Lady Catherine,' he eventually said, turning to face his employer with an expression of complete sincerity, 'that Miranda and I were never engaged.'

'Then why would she suggest otherwise, and come all the way to England in search of you?'

'That I cannot tell you, nor am I prepared to discuss the matter further. If you require proof that I speak the truth, then I must refer you to Sir Marius. Only he can explain why his daughter has acted in the way that she has.'

He is protecting the lady's reputation, Lizzy thought, feeling vindicated for having placed her faith in him.

Lady Catherine made an unladylike scoffing sound. 'I am asking *you*.'

'I hesitate to appear disobliging, but I cannot prove what I know to be the truth, and so will not reveal the circumstances that led to Miranda's claim. If being a man of honour is sufficient grounds for you to dismiss me from my post, then there is nothing I can do to prevent you.'

'Lady Catherine,' Mr Collins said when his benefactress did not immediately do precisely that. 'I beg you to consider Miss de Bourgh's situation. You cannot take the risk—'

'Be quiet, Mr Collins. If I require your opinion I will ask for it.'

Lizzy could understand Lady Catherine's dilemma and felt a certain sympathy for her. Ordinarily she would not give Mr Asquith the benefit of the doubt, not when the possible corruption of her daughter's morals was at stake. Besides, Anne was almost of age and certainly beyond the point where continued education was strictly necessary. Lizzy knew that was not why Mr Asquith had been hired. He had replaced Anne's former female companion, but he could hardly be described as a young lady's companion. There was no actual way to describe his true purpose, which was to broaden Anne's mind in a way that Mrs Jenkinson could never have accomplished.

Lady Catherine clearly thought highly of Sir Marius, and of Mr Asquith too, and was not prepared to act without definitive proof of the latter's duplicity. Even so, it was obvious she took exception to his refusal to explain himself. Not many people had the courage to stand up to Lady Catherine when she demanded to know something.

'If I dismiss you, I shall not give you a character and you will find it impossible to gain suitable employment without one.'

'I understand that, but unfortunately I am still unable to oblige you, ma'am.'

'If Sir Marius is in Dover, a letter will quickly find its way to him,' Lizzy said.

'But what of the meantime?' Mr Collins asked. 'Miss de Bourgh's education.'

'I will permit you to continue mentoring Anne,' Lady Catherine said after a moment's contemplation. 'For now. But I am most displeased by this development, and I intend to get to the bottom of things. If you are not being honest with me, Mr Asquith, you will soon be found out and it will be the worse for you.'

'I understand.'

He also appeared to understand he was being dismissed. With a bow for Lady Catherine, and another for Lizzy, he left the room, closing the door quietly behind him.

Anne was tired after her active day but lay on her bed, unable to sleep. She picked up a novel Mr Asquith had recommended she read, anxious to finish it so she could discuss it with him. Their tastes in literature were so similar, just as they were in many other respects. Mama would not approve of the book but Anne found it enlightening and informative. Did Mr Asquith ask her to read it for any particular reason other than that he thought she might enjoy it? The heroine was in a remarkably similar situation to Anne, burdened by a rich inheritance she had no particular wish to have. Unlike Anne, she was beautiful and sure of herself, determined to marry for love rather than allow her Papa to choose the right man for her.

Anne marked her place, thinking it surely could be no coincidence that Mr Asquith had recommended the book. Not that she could absorb very much of what she read in her current confused state of mind. Her head was still full of her walk in the garden with Mr Asquith, the things he had said and done, his use of her name, and his abrupt change of mood just when things were getting interesting. She had felt as though she had turned a corner in her mind at that moment. She was no longer a sickly child, but a grown woman with opinions of her own, and thoughts she was entitled to keep to herself.

She wished she had someone she could talk to about it, to help her understand, but in spite of her growing closeness to Georgiana and Kitty, she would not risk discussing it with them. They would probably tell her she was imagining things, and if that was the case, she would vastly prefer to remain ignorant of the fact so she could continue with her wild visualisations. Besides, they had no more experience in such matters than she did and probably wouldn't be able to offer much helpful advice.

Anne heard light footsteps approaching her room. She recognised her mother's rapid tread, hid the book beneath her pillow, and closed her eyes. Mama burst into the room without knocking.

'Anne, are you awake?'

'Yes, Mama.' She leaned up on one elbow and rubbed non-existent sleep from her eyes. 'What is it? You look distressed. Has something happened?'

'Where have you been? I have been looking for you all over.'

'I was painting scenery with Georgiana and Kitty, and then I took the air with Mr Asquith.'

Mama looked scandalised. 'Alone?'

'Yes, the others wanted to rest.'

'Anne, we have talked about this. It is not seemly for you to be with Mr Asquith unchaperoned, not under any circumstances.'

'I fail to see why not. He is a perfect gentleman. Besides, no one saw us.'

'He is the son of a plantation manager and you are an innocent heiress who might be seen by some as ripe for the plucking.'

'Mama!'

'Don't pretend not to understand me. More importantly, never lose sight of that fact.'

'As if I could,' Anne replied, almost to herself.

'Did you say something?'

'No, nothing.'

Mama seated herself in the window embrasure. 'What of Fitzwilliam? Has he spoken with you yet?'

'No, he has not.'

'Probably because you are never to be found. Instead of spending your time play-acting and taking illicit walks, you ought to make yourself available. The man cannot address you if he can't find you.'

Anne considered the colonel had had ample opportunities to express himself but knew it would do her no good to say so. 'You are blaming me because he has no interest in me?'

'Don't be so impertinent.' Mama looked down her nose in the disapproving manner she had perfected to terrorise her servants. 'If this new-found manner of speaking back to me is the result of Mr Asquith's influence then I made a grave error in engaging him.'

'I disagree.' Anne surprised herself at finding the courage to refute her mother's assertion. It was so unjust that she couldn't allow it to pass unchallenged.

'You look pale and fagged out,' Mama said, examining Anne's face closely and not appearing to like what she saw. 'You think you are capable of doing the same things as Georgiana and Miss Bennet, but that is patently not the case.'

'Again, I must disagree with you, Mama. I am having a perfectly splendid time and don't feel the least bit short of breath or unwell in any way. I no longer cough hardly at all, either. I believe that with maturity I have outgrown my illnesses.'

'Nonsense, one does not outgrow such weaknesses. They remain with one for life. You do not have a strong constitution, Anne, and you cannot manage the same things as other young ladies. The sooner you accept that, the happier your life will be.'

Anne knew it was an argument she would never win and so didn't risk angering her mother by attempting to persuade her otherwise.

'Go down half an hour early this evening and situate yourself in the conservatory. I shall tell Colonel Fitzwilliam you will be there and that he can expect to speak with you without interruption.' Mama exhaled. 'If he cannot contrive a simple conversation alone with you then I shall just have to arrange it for him I suppose. I have had quite enough of this shilly-shallying. Besides, if things are settled between you and the colonel, then the other matter does not signify.'

Sadness gripped Anne's heart. She should not have allowed herself to take hope from Colonel Fitzwilliam's indifference, only to have those hopes dashed. 'What if the colonel does not wish to speak with me?'

'Don't be ridiculous. Of course he wishes to. He is very fond of you.'

Of course he is. 'And more so of Rosings.'

Mama tutted. 'Stop acting as if you were the only child who ever had to make a sacrifice for the sake of her family's honour. You have been behaving most peculiarly since we arrived here and I feel as though I no longer know you. That being the case, I must have your assurance that we are in agreement and you will oblige me in this matter.'

Anne swallowed down a burst of anger, wanting to tell her mother she was no longer a child, and resented being told what to do and whom to marry. No one had ever asked her opinion before, certainly not her mother, who would not have listened even if Anne had found the courage to challenge one of her decisions. But now, suddenly Anne had grown tired of being invisible. Her anger gave way to incredulity when she realised that with maturity she had also developed a rebellious streak. Whether she would find the courage to put it to use remained to be seen.

Her mother tapped her fingers impatiently on the window ledge as she waited for Anne to give her the assurance she sought. Anne was conflicted, unsure if she could casually commit herself to a lifetime beside a man whom she respected but did not love. Then the implication behind her mother's words struck home and Anne's curiosity was piqued. 'Did you make sacrifices, Mama?'

'Never mind that.' Anne could tell from her mother's set expression that no further revelations would be forthcoming. How vexatious. She knew precious little about her mother's life when she had been Anne's age. Could it be that she had been disappointed in love? 'Of course Colonel Fitzwilliam will be tempted by Rosings. It would be unrealistic to think otherwise. We cannot change what we were born to be, Anne, much as we might sometimes wish that we could.'

'Do you ever wish that, Mama?'

'We are not discussing me. I made the best of my life and you must do the same. You will be perfectly comfortable as Mrs Fitzwilliam. In fact, you will continue to live in the only home you have ever known and nothing will be very different.'

Anne opened her mouth to protest, and then closed it again. She had learned enough from the books she had read, such as the one beneath her pillow, to know things would be very different indeed. That was partly what worried her.

'What other matter, Mama?'

Mama was gazing out of the window, seemingly lost in a reverie. Her head snapped around at the sound of Anne's voice. 'I beg your pardon?'

'You said that if things were settled between myself and the colonel then the other matter would not signify.'

'Mr Collins is here.'

'Oh.' That was all Anne needed. Mr Collins seemed to think that being Hunsford's clergyman gave him the right to interfere in her affairs. 'Was he expected?'

'He came with alarming news.'

Anne gaped at her mother when she related the reason for Mr Collins's visit.

'It cannot be,' she said faintly. 'The Mr Asquith I know would never act so dishonourably.'

'Perhaps not, but if you fix your future with the colonel then I will have no further need of his services and it will not matter anyway.'

'Yes, I understand that much.' *Oh, I understand better than you could possibly imagine.* 'But you must give him a character, otherwise he will starve.'

Mama adopted a haughty, stubborn expression. 'I must do no such thing.'

'Mama, be reasonable. What explanation did Mr Asquith give for this lady's claim?'

'He said it was untrue but he could not explain why.'

'Well, there you are then.' Anne struggled to hide her relief. 'He would not tell an outright lie.'

Mama huffed. 'Which just goes to show how little you understand the world. A young man in need of employment will do or say many things in order not to lose his position.'

'Not Mr Asquith,' Anne replied stubbornly.

'Mr Asquith, Mr Asquith.' Mama threw her hands in the air. 'I must have been out of my senses when I engaged him. You seem to think of no one else. You certainly think nothing at all of the sacrifices I have made to get you to this point. I did not expect any thanks, but I do expect your obedience.' Mama stood up and brushed down her skirts. 'I shall ring for your maid. Wear your best gown and be in the conservatory to receive the colonel's address within the hour.'

And with that, Mama swept regally from the room.

Anne watched the door close behind her, feeling close to despair. There could be no turning back now. The colonel would not ignore such a direct order from her mother and Anne would have no choice but to accept him. Unlike the heroine in the novel still buried beneath her pillow, she did not have the strength of will to stand up to her mama and reach out to grasp happiness. Besides, even if Mr Asquith offered for her, she would not accept him for the simple reason that he couldn't possibly return her feelings. One-sided love could never prosper.

She sat perfectly still as her maid helped her out of her afternoon gown. Poor Mr Asquith. Whatever the circumstances behind this woman's claim, she was absolutely sure he could not have jilted her. Anne might accept he was lost to her, but her soft heart melted at the thought of him being unable to find alternative employment because there was a question mark against his character. She loved him with a passion that surprised her, and there was one thing she could do for him to prove it, even though he would never know it. She would marry the colonel, do whatever her mother asked of her, but only if her Mama promised to give Mr Asquith a glowing reference.

* * *

'What did you make of all that?' Will asked Lizzy as they made their way up to their chambers to change for dinner.

'I believe Mr Asquith,' Lizzy replied without hesitation. 'He made no promise to the young lady, I am sure of that, but is too gentlemanly to explain what really happened.'

'I agree. If Sir Marius were still in Jamaica and a letter had to be sent to him there to apply for the truth, then I might think differently. But Asquith knows he is in this country and that verification of his innocence can be obtained in a matter of days. I can see no profit in being untruthful under such circumstances.'

'I admire the way he stood up to Lady Catherine with such polite determination. It shows an honourable disposition that does him credit.'

'Do I need to worry about him?' Will asked with a mock scowl as he opened the door to Lizzy's chamber and stood back so she could precede him through it.

'Well,' Lizzy replied playfully, plucking her lower lip with her forefinger as she pretended to consider the question. 'You must agree he is remarkably good looking.'

'Wench!' Will lifted her from the floor and closed his arms tightly around her waist. 'Have you no shame?'

Lizzy laughed. 'Apparently not, but just because I can appreciate Mr Asquith's handsome face, it does not mean I fail to appreciate yours also.'

Will kissed the end of her nose and sat her on the edge of her bed. 'Said not a moment too soon.'

'Ah, but I am safe from your punishments in my current condition so I can say whatever I please.'

Will harrumphed. 'You say precisely what you please anyway.'

'Which is one of the traits you admire about me.'

'I wish I could deny it, but you know me too well.' Will sat beside her and took her hand, running his fingers gently down the length of hers. 'Why do parties here at Pemberley never proceed smoothly?'

Lizzy rested her head against the breadth of his shoulder, wondering if she would ever get tired of using it as a pillow. 'Where would be the amusement in that?'

'We never did get around to offering Fitzwilliam any advice about his situation with Mrs Sheffield.'

'I have some thoughts on that.'

Will rolled his eyes. 'Somehow that doesn't surprise me.' He fell back onto her bed and pulled her with him. 'And I suppose I had better hear what you have in mind, much as I would prefer to occupy our time with more pleasurable pursuits.'

Lizzy lightly punched his chest. 'There is no reason why we should not do both.'

'Other than that you need to rest, none whatsoever.'

'I knew you would be like this,' Lizzy complained. 'Overprotective and domineering.'

Will's throaty, suggestive chuckle sent shivers of anticipation tingling down her spine. 'You like me best when I am at my most domineering. You have said so more than once.'

'Hmm, it depends upon the circumstances.'

'Name your circumstances, Lizzy, my love.' His expression turned passionately, ardently sincere. He was no longer teasing her, and his dark eyes smouldered with intense emotion, stealing her breath away as his face hovered mere inches from hers and his lips brushed gently against hers. 'You must know I would give you the moon itself, if it was mine to give. Everything I have is yours. Everything I am is because of you.'

'Oh, Will, I love you so very much, especially when you turn poetic.' She leaned in, taking her turn to steal a kiss. 'But as far as your cousin is concerned, I think we should invite the odious-sounding Sheffield to Lambton, or rather Mrs Sheffield should.'

'Go on,' Will said, stroking her hair.

'She ought to write to him, say she has had a chance to reflect since her solicitor's visit, and that they ought to discuss the matter face to face. She will not invite him to Briar Hall, of course. I am sure she can think of a good reason not to do so.'

Will chuckled. 'I am equally sure Fitzwilliam wouldn't sleep a wink if she did. So why have him come to Derbyshire?'

'Because he doesn't know Mrs Sheffield has allies here, of course. He must be aware that she seldom shares her affairs with Lord Briar for fear of oversetting her sister, who does not enjoy a strong constitution. That being the case, he will assume she is ready to capitulate.'

'But she has no intention of giving up what is rightfully hers.'

'Nor would I ask her to, but if Sheffield puts up at the inn in Lambton I dare say he will while away his spare time in the tap room.' Lizzy sent her husband a mischievous smile. 'There is no telling whom he might encounter in that establishment. Perhaps even a military man who does not at all relish the idea of being leg-shackled to an heiress.'

Will scowled. 'I see what you are thinking, and it is very clever. Fitzwilliam befriends Sheffield and complains about being obliged to marry his cousin when he is in love with another lady.'

'Well, that part is certainly true.'

Will flexed a brow. 'You think Fitzwilliam is as far gone as that.'

Lizzy shook her head in faux despair. 'You men are blind when it comes to such matters. I have seldom seen any man more love-struck.'

'Oh dear. Poor Lady Catherine.'

'Hang Lady Catherine,' Lizzy replied impatiently. 'Now, where was I? Oh yes, I understand Sheffield to be a handsome man, popular with the ladies and very sure of himself in that arena. He is also unquestionably greedy. If he thinks there might be an opportunity to meet this elusive heiress and make himself agreeable to her, he will be obligated to the colonel. Naturally, the colonel will ask his new friend what business brings him to the district. They will start talking about Jamaica and it will all come out. Fitzwilliam can then say his plan won't work because in order to pursue Anne, Sheffield will have to give up his claim to Mrs Sheffield's estate. If they have this conversation when Sheffield has consumed enough brandy to loosen his tongue, I dare say he will admit he has no legitimate claim to the estate anyway. Men like him can never resist bragging, especially when they are in their cups. Needless to say, Colonel Fitzwilliam will have someone else situated in the tap room, close enough to overhear the conversation and bear witness to it if necessary.'

'It's ingenious, Lizzy, but for one snag.'

'Oh, did I overlook something?'

'Something rather important as it happens. This could endanger Anne.'

'Not if we don't allow Sheffield to set foot on Pemberley, or Anne to leave it.'

'Even so.' Will shuddered. 'I dread to think what Lady Catherine would have to say if she got wind of the scheme.'

'You underestimate your cousin's newfound determination. Anne has no wish to marry Fitzwilliam. Her affections are engaged elsewhere.'

Will sighed. 'Perhaps, but Anne marrying Asquith was always going to be out of the question, even before these accusations against his character came to light.'

'Maybe so, but she lives in dread of the colonel paying her his addresses. If he is otherwise engaged in pursuit of Mrs Sheffield and if he manages to restore her estate to her, I feel persuaded it isn't Anne who will benefit from his attentions.'

'Leaving Anne free to persuade her mother to let her follow her heart.'

'Precisely.'

'She will never succeed in that ambition,' Will said.

'Oh, I am not so very sure about that. Lady Catherine has a weak spot when it comes to anything to do with Sir Marius.' Lizzy wrinkled a brow. 'I would give much to understand why. Anyway, it must be so, otherwise she would never have given Asquith the benefit of the doubt and permitted him to remain in his post.'

'Yes, that was rather peculiar.' Will lapsed into thought, idly twisting one of Lizzy's many escaped curls around his forefinger as he did so. 'I will put the proposal to Fitzwilliam later and let him decide. If we are to do this, time is of the essence. Lady Catherine won't stay here much longer, nor can Fitzwilliam avoid addressing Anne indefinitely.'

'Or not doing so and have Lady Catherine leave Pemberley in a high dudgeon.'

'Quite so. But apart from all that, I have one condition of my own.'

'What is it?'

'That Anne must be made aware of the plan and decide for herself if it goes ahead or not.'

Lizzy grinned. 'In that case, it is as good as agreed. Miss de Bourgh is hungry for adventure, and even if there is an outside chance of her procuring Mr Asquith as a result, she will grasp it with both hands. You just see if I am not right.'

'Talking of occupying one's hands, Mrs Darcy.'

Lizzy treated her husband to a flirtatious smile. 'Yes, what did you have in mind?'

Will spent the next half an hour allowing his actions to answer that question for him.

14

Joshua was dressing for dinner when Darcy knocked at his door.

'Mrs Darcy is nothing if not inventive when it comes to righting wrongs,' he said by way of greeting.

'Really?' Joshua dismissed Cox and gave his cousin his full attention. 'You refer, I presume, to Mrs Sheffield's problems.'

'Yes, she has made a proposal that is both daring and a little irresponsible. My initial reaction was to dismiss it out of hand. Then I decided you ought to hear it first.'

Joshua listened with growing astonishment as Darcy related his wife's suggestion.

'I see what you mean about inventiveness,' Joshua said when Darcy ran out of words.

'But the dangers. It could easily fail. We don't know enough about the man's character to be sure he would give himself away. And then of course there is a risk to Anne, to say nothing of Lady Catherine's reaction were she to find out that we had involved her.'

'Only Mrs Sheffield will know if her brother-in-law is likely to fall for the ruse,' Joshua replied thoughtfully. 'I must consult her as a matter of urgency.'

Darcy flashed a half-smile. 'Naturally you must.'

'As to Anne, I have just received a not-so-subtle message from our aunt to say she will be in the conservatory a half-hour before dinner.'

'So you will speak with her?'

'Yes, but not on the subject Lady Catherine expects me to.' Joshua flexed his jaw. 'I know there are many risks and uncertainties connecting to Mrs Darcy's plan, but I have been racking my brains all the afternoon and can't think of an alternative that is half as likely to work. But whether Anne will agree—'

'Lizzy thinks she will jump at the opportunity. She firmly believes that Anne has matured since being influenced by Asquith, and I tend to agree with my wife. Asquith has encouraged Anne to think for herself and express her opinions freely. That, as we both know, is something she has never done before.'

'Yes, that is certainly true. Georgiana and Miss Bennet must take part of the credit too. It must be pleasant for Anne to mix with other young ladies and be accepted by them.'

'According to Lizzy, who has a happy knack for discovering such things, Anne has never had companions of her own age before. Lady Catherine thought the local children were either beneath Anne's notice, or that Anne was too frail to join in their rough and tumbles.'

Joshua shook his head, feeling guilty that neither he nor Darcy had noticed these things on any of their visits to Rosings and attempted to do something to rectify the situation. He must shoulder his share of the guilt for simply accepting that Anne was weak and assuming she had nothing of consequence to say for herself.

'Anne has no wish to marry me and I don't see why she should be forced into a union when we both know it would be for all the wrong reasons. It is time we discussed the matter between ourselves and decided on a plan.'

'I know you are keen to help Mrs Sheffield,' Darcy said, his expression sombre. 'But if Anne even hesitates to go along with the scheme, I need your assurance that you will not put undue pressure on her.'

Joshua scowled. 'What sort of cad do you take me for?'

'Sorry, Fitzwilliam.' Darcy slapped his shoulder. 'I intended no insult. I merely needed to be sure we understood one another.'

'Absolutely.' Joshua straightened his cuffs, optimism filtering through his earlier feelings of ineffectiveness. 'But now, if you will excuse me, I have an engagement with our cousin. One which I am suddenly very anxious to keep.'

Darcy chuckled. 'Then don't let me detain you.'

Anne was already in the conservatory when Joshua arrived. He watched her from the open doorway before she realised he was there. She stared out of the window without appearing to take in the view, her expression remote as she repeatedly pleated the fabric of her skirt between her fingers. She looked nervous and upset, as though her life was about to come to an end. Joshua felt for her excessively. Being an heiress and having Lady Catherine for a mother could not be easy burdens to bear, especially for such a delicate creature as Anne. In spite of the fact that she had almost come of age, she was still a child in so many respects and Joshua couldn't understand Lady Catherine's determination to marry her off when she was still so unworldly wise. Unless...

A disquieting thought occurred to him. Could Lady Catherine herself be unwell? She certainly appeared to be her usual robust, disapproving, autocratic self. But now that he thought about it, Joshua realised she was less outspoken than usual, spent a lot of time alone in her chamber, and when she was in company she often seemed to drift off into a reverie and make no attempt to dominate the conversation. That was not at all like his aunt, and Joshua wondered why he had only just noticed the changes in her. She normally had opinions on every imaginable subject and wasn't slow to voice them. Perhaps being at Pemberley and being forced to give way to Mrs Darcy was the reason for her unnatural reticence.

In spite of everything, Joshua felt great affection for his aunt and hoped there was nothing more to the changes in her attitude than sullenness at having been gainsaid. But if so, why the great rush to see Anne married when it must be obvious, even to Lady Catherine, that Anne was nowhere near ready for marriage? Anne's spirit had been suppressed for too long and she needed to live a little before settling into marriage.

At least Joshua came with a scheme that, if she was willing, would help to restore the balance. His plan would require her to have the courage to go against her mother's wishes, and would give her a taste of adventure. Of course, it would also set her mind at rest about being obliged to marry Joshua.

'Anne, I hope I have not kept you waiting.'

She started at the sound of his voice. 'No, not at all.' She spoke distractedly and didn't turn to look at him. 'I was deep in thought and did not realise you had come.'

'What were you thinking about so intently?' he asked.

'Oh, nothing of consequence.'

Realising what an intrusive question that must appear to be, Joshua didn't persist with it. 'May I sit?' he asked instead.

'Please do.'

'I think you know why I am here.'

She lowered her eyes. 'Yes, of course.'

'Anne, look at me.' Slowly, she lifted her eyes and turned her head in his direction. She looked pale and afraid. 'There, that was not so very difficult, was it?'

'You must forgive me, Colonel. I am a little nervous.'

'And distressed, because you don't wish to receive my address but your mother has insisted.'

'Oh no... well, yes.' She bit her lip, her anxiety giving way to animation Joshua had never seen light up her narrow face before. 'I am sorry, Colonel, I didn't mean to make light of this situation. I realise it is as awkward for you as it is for me.' She sighed. 'It all seems so very... well, cold and formal, I suppose. Although I know that is often how these things are arranged.'

'Supposing then that we decided not to marry?'

She gasped, and this time Joshua didn't need to request her full attention. He most assuredly had it. 'How can that be? My mother, she—'

'I hold you in great respect, Anne, and I am considerably attached to Rosings. But I don't think those are strong enough foundations upon which to build a successful marriage, do you?'

'I feel exactly the same way about you, Colonel,' she replied breathlessly. 'But it does no good. Mama is quite determined, you see.'

'I am not afraid of Lady Catherine.'

Anne wrinkled her nose. 'Unfortunately I am, although not as much as I used to be.' She fixed Joshua with a curious gaze. 'Since we appear to be speaking plainly, how can you afford to pass up on Rosings?'

'I have fixed my interest elsewhere, as I think you have.' She lowered her eyes again but remained silent. Joshua wondered if she found his admission insulting. After all, he had just admitted that he preferred another lady to her. Even so, as she had just pointed out, this was definitely a time for plain speaking. Besides, she was in a similar position to him. 'Nothing has been agreed between myself and the lady in question and probably never will be, but I cannot bring myself to marry for money when my heart is not in it. That would not be honourable or fair to you.'

'You certainly do believe in plain speaking, Colonel,' she replied with a nervous little laugh.

'Whereas you find the prospect of marrying the man your mother tells you to appealing?'

She shook her head. 'What would you have me say, Colonel?'

'Plain speaking, remember.'

'Yes, all right. I enjoy your company but I do not think we would suit.'

'Quite so. I can see we understand one another perfectly.' Anne's uncontrived smile seemed too wide for her face. 'But Mama will be beside herself if you don't do as she asks and will probably blame me for not encouraging you.'

'I will not allow any blame to be directed upon you.' Joshua matched her smile. 'But I do have a suggestion to put to you.'

'By all means.'

'Firstly, we ought not to tell her quite yet that we have decided against matrimony.'

'She will want to know what passed between us.'

'Tell her we have agreed to go for a drive in the morning and get to know one another better.'

'We have known one another for years.'

'Not in the manner your mother has in mind. Any young lady on the brink of matrimony is entitled to be courted.'

'But you don't intend to court me, Colonel.' She lifted her shoulders. 'You have already admitted as much. And so why—'

'Instead of courtship I require your help.'

She elevated her brows. 'My help? How can I possibly be of help to you?'

'The lady I have fixed my interest on has a problem, but with your permission, I think we might have devised a way to resolve it for her.'

'Mrs Sheffield?'

It was Joshua's turn to flex both brows. 'What makes you suppose I refer to that lady?'

Anne laughed. 'Colonel, I saw the way you looked at her when she dined here the other night and I was seated beside you. Your manners were perfectly correct and I cannot claim you neglected me in any way. However, I saw how frequently you glanced across the table at Mrs Sheffield and how you didn't seem to be able to look away again. I have never seen such a look of total adoration on your face before.'

And I thought she was not worldly wise. 'Oh dear, it seems I have given myself away.'

'Don't worry. I am sure no one else noticed. I was seated beside you so I was bound to see. Everyone else was far too busy trying to be witty and amusing to take much interest in you.' Joshua was too astonished by her powers of observation to respond. He had definitely underestimated his quiet cousin. She was far more intelligent than he had ever supposed and had hidden depths that even her mother could not know about. 'I tend to be overlooked in company, you see, and so I occupy my time by watching the reactions of others. It can be a very productive pastime.'

'Clearly. And since you have guessed my secret, I might as well explain Mrs Sheffield's problem to you, together with Mrs Darcy's suggested resolution of it. First, I will require your word that even if you do not agree to help, you will not reveal any of this to anyone. Not to your maid and especially not to your mother.'

'You have it,' Anne replied, clearly intrigued. 'I would certainly never confide in my maid. She reports everything I say directly back to my mother. I always suspected as much and so one day I gave her a quite erroneous account of my day's activities, which my mother lost no time in upbraiding me for.'

'A lesson in discretion well learned,' Joshua said, doing what he could to conceal his anger at the extent of Lady Catherine's determination to control all aspects of her daughter's life. Had Joshua decided to marry Anne, she would doubtless have attempted to subject his own life to the same degree of scrutiny, and Joshua would never permit that to happen.

'Quite so.'

Joshua spent the next ten minutes explaining Mrs Sheffield's difficulty, together with Mrs Darcy's plan to resolve it. She listened without once interrupting, a series of unreadable expressions passing across her face as she did so.

'Certainly you may use my name, Colonel,' she said without hesitation when he came to the end of his narration. 'If it helps you to achieve your heart's desire, it will be my pleasure to have assisted you in some small way.'

'Thank you, but as to achieving my heart's desire, as you put it, I have no way of knowing if that will be possible even if we are successful, which is far from certain. I have not declared myself and most likely will not do so for fear Mrs Sheffield might feel compelled to accept me out of some sense of misplaced gratitude. Besides, she is a beautiful woman and can do far better than me.'

'You underestimate your attraction, Colonel. Besides, has it occurred to you that her feelings might mirror your own?'

Joshua couldn't conceal his surprise. 'Whatever makes you say that?'

'Oh, nothing in particular.' She sent him a teasing, almost flirtatious smile. 'It is just that I noticed she was observing you across the table just as often as you were looking at her, and I am sure it wasn't the cut of your coat that engaged her attention.'

'Good God!' Joshua exclaimed, astonishment taking precedence over good manners.

'You sound surprised.' Anne's eyes gleamed with mischief. 'Surely you do not plan to make me say what a fine figure you cut, with your charming and elegant manners? Why should a lady such as Mrs Sheffield not enjoy what she sees?'

'Hmm, yes.' Joshua coughed behind his hand. 'Er, thank you.'

Anne laughed at his discomfiture and Joshua eventually joined in. He had certainly not started this interview with any thought of being the one to feel embarrassed.

'As to your own situation, if we go ahead with this plan there is no danger to you, Anne,' he said, regaining his composure, 'provided you remain here at Pemberley. Sheffield won't be able to get anywhere near you but he will learn all about you from anyone he talks to in Lambton. You know very well that everyone in the village knows everything that happens at Pemberley. I am sure it is much the same with Rosings and Hunsford. Anyway, that ought to be enough to convince him I speak the truth, especially if I have my man spread rumours about our impending nuptials.'

'Yes, I dare say.' She smiled. 'I must say, Mr Sheffield sounds most disagreeable.'

'Not precisely the word I would choose to describe the bounder, but I shall not offend your sensibilities by using a more appropriate one.'

'Oh, I do wish you would, Colonel. No one ever says anything inappropriate within my hearing. How am I supposed to learn anything interesting if everyone treats me so delicately?'

Joshua threw back his head and laughed, making no attempt to hide his relief at her ready capitulation and lively curiosity. 'Ask Asquith. I have already led you quite far enough astray.'

'I have asked him, repeatedly.' Anne tossed her head. 'But he has a way of distracting me with some interesting fact or other, and manages not to answer me without giving offence. It is most vexing.'

Mrs Darcy had been right about her, Joshua thought. She had matured and was hungry for adventure and rebellion. But he needed to be absolutely sure she understood.

'Do you wish to spend the night considering the matter? You can give me your answer in the morning.'

'Not at all. I am quite determined you should bring the odious Mr Sheffield down to size. However, I should like to explain our plan to Mr Asquith. I know you swore me to secrecy, but he knows Sheffield and might be able to suggest other ways to lure him in.'

'Hmm, that is true. I have already discussed Mrs Sheffield's problems with him, and he might have thought of some way to help her. Although I suppose he has other concerns of his own now.'

'Mr Collins's accusations, you mean?' Joshua nodded. 'Well, I am sure there is nothing to them, but it is typical of Mr Collins to come charging up to Derbyshire like an avenging... I hesitate to say "angel", because a less likely looking angel I have yet to encounter.' Anne pulled a disgruntled face and blew air through her lips. 'He so likes to interfere, and he never did approve of Mr Asquith. I believe he is jealous because Mr Asquith has displaced him at Rosings. I like Mrs Collins very much and cannot imagine what made her marry Mr Collins, although I suppose, like me, she was pressured by her family for fear of her being left on the shelf and becoming a burden to her siblings.'

Joshua was vastly entertained by this new, talkative side of Anne's character and would happily have listened to her prattling on. However, time was not on their side.

'Very well, by all means tell Mr Asquith of our plan. And tomorrow you and I, in the spirit of a couple on the verge of engagement, will drive out together. No one will object. In fact, your mother will encourage the outing. She need not know that we are heading for Briar Hall to acquaint Mrs Sheffield of our plan.'

'Oh, will I not be in the way?'

'Not in the least. Besides, when she hears what you are prepared to do to help her, I feel sure she will wish to thank you in person.'

'She has nothing to thank me for.' Anne smiled. 'I cannot remember a time when I felt more useful. I am sorry for Mama, of course. She genuinely does have my best interests at heart and thinks she knows what is best for me, and for Rosings too, of course. Still, since you do not wish to marry me there is nothing she can do about it.'

'Anne, you must not think—'

'Shush, I am just teasing you.'

His cousin Anne, having the confidence to tease? Who would have thought it?

'We do not have much time to make our arrangements. In less than a week's time you perform your play, and by then I am sure your mother will expect us to do more than spend our afternoons out driving.'

'Hmm, yes, I see what you mean.' Anne furrowed her brow. 'Providing she doesn't get suspicious, she will be happy to remain at Pemberley for at least another week, expecting us to become better acquainted and resigned to our fate. She will be very angry when we admit the truth but there is no help for that.'

'It is I who will do the disappointing. No blame will attach to you.'

'Is a week long enough for Mr Sheffield to come up here and for this matter to be settled?'

'Oh yes. He is in London at present according to Mrs Sheffield's solicitor, and not in Buckinghamshire. If he doesn't mind the discomfort of long days on the road, which I am sure he will not if he thinks there is profit in it for him, he can be here within three days.'

'Well in that case, I shall enjoy seeing him get his just deserts.'

'If our plan works we shall all enjoy that experience, and you will have the satisfaction of knowing that you helped to bring it about.' Joshua took her small hand, kissed the back of it and pulled her to her feet. 'I am so glad we understand one another. Now come, let us join the others before we are missed.'

A hum of polite conversation filled the drawing room. It seemed to Joshua as though it stalled when he and Anne entered the room. All heads certainly turned their way, some displaying more interest than others. Lady Catherine descended upon them, and Joshua diplomatically left mother and daughter alone, confident that Anne would play her part in this real-life drama at least as well as she reputedly did in Asquith's production. The Darcys were in conversation with Jane Bingley but joined Joshua a short time later.

'You and Anne look very pleased with yourselves, Colonel,' Mrs Darcy said. 'Are we to wish you joy?'

'No, ma'am, but I certainly owe you my thanks.'

'She agreed then,' Darcy surmised.

'With alacrity. She is so pleased not to be forced into marriage with me that she will do just about anything.'

'Fitzwilliam!'

'Sorry, Darcy. You looked so severe for a moment that I couldn't resist shamming it.'

'Anne has matured beyond imagination and is more than ready for a little adventure,' Darcy said, taking Joshua's joke in good part.

'I hope you have given her leave to inform Mr Asquith of your plans,' Mrs Darcy said. 'He looks ready to cut his own throat at present. After he has cut yours, of course.'

'Yes, he will soon learn the truth, but Lady Catherine must

never know. Anne is telling her now that we have agreed to take some time to get to know one another. I shall drive her over to Briar Hall in the morning and meet with Mrs Sheffield.'

'Will you just look at Mr Collins strutting about my drawing room like a peacock in full plume.' Mrs Darcy looked as disgusted as she sounded. 'He has taken great pleasure in casting doubt over Mr Asquith's character which is not very Christian of him. I believe he has grown even more pompous since we last met, and I did not think that was possible.' She sighed. 'Poor Charlotte.'

'Come, my dear, I believe Simpson is about to announce dinner,' Darcy said. 'Where shall you seat Mr Collins?'

'As far away from me as possible.'

'Have him take Lady Catherine in,' Joshua suggested. 'He will butter her up for the entire meal, which will work wonders for her pride.'

'Oh, I think you and Anne already managed that when you walked into this room wearing identical smiles,' Mrs Darcy replied, wandering off to organise her guests.

15

'Am I to wish you joy, Miss de Bourgh?'

Mr Asquith posed the question early the following morning at a time when he and Anne had fallen into the habit of spending an hour discussing literature before rehearsals commenced. He looked so crestfallen that Anne's soft heart went out to him. He had been unnaturally quiet and withdrawn the previous evening, she had noticed. Mr Collins on the other hand had been his usually verbose self, dominating the conversation until Mr Darcy had expressed his disapproval, cutting him with a look. Anne wanted to ask Mr Collins when he planned to leave, but now that he was here, he appeared to be in no hurry to quit Pemberley. God forbid that he expected to return to Hunsford in their carriage.

'Are you asking me if I have accepted Colonel Fitzwilliam's proposal?'

He fixed her with an intent gaze. 'Have you?'

Anne took pity on him and, laughing, she shook her head. She knew his only concern was for his lucrative position, even if a tiny part of her wanted to believe he was disappointed for more personal reasons. They had grown so very close recently that he probably understood her better than anyone else on earth, including her mother. Be that as it may, she reminded herself not to be so fanciful and returned her attention to Mr Asquith.

'The colonel and I have decided we would not suit.'

'He does not wish to marry you?' Mr Asquith's jaw dropped open. 'He actually told you so?'

She bit her lip to prevent herself from laughing at his expression – a mixture of surprise, disbelief and, dare she hope, a little relief too? 'Has it occurred to you, Mr Asquith, that it might be I who do not wish to marry him?'

'I know you were not keen on the match, but I thought... well, I thought—' He stood up and ran a hand through his hair. 'Forgive me. I did not think you would deliberately go against your mother's wishes.'

'Sometimes I surprise myself,' she replied playfully.

'You were closeted together for so long, and then both smiling when you finally entered the drawing room last night. Lady Catherine has been in a very light-hearted mood ever since. I just assumed everything had been settled between you.' His words ground to a momentary halt. 'It is not my business of course, but if you wish to tell me what happened I would be happy to listen. I know you did not wish to marry the colonel, but if he did actually reject you and not the other way around, do you not feel insulted? If that is the case, I would call him out for his incivility were it my place to do so.'

'That would be very rash, Mr Asquith. He is after all a trained soldier.'

'You think me incapable of protecting your honour?' he asked passionately. 'I can assure you that Colonel Fitzwilliam does not frighten me.'

'I do not in the least doubt you.' Anne's heart swelled at his obvious determination to protect her. It was a new and very agreeable feeling. 'However, such drastic action will not be necessary.'

'I have never seen you like this before. So self-assured, so carefree. I understand you are relieved, but Lady Catherine... why is she so buoyed if the match is not to go ahead?'

Anne recalled her mother pulling her aside when the ladies left the table the previous evening, demanding to know what had happened. When Anne had explained they had decided to spend a week getting to know one another better, she appeared satisfied.

'I should have thought you knew one another well enough as it is,' she'd replied. 'But still, I suppose there is no harm in delaying matters by a week. I know you don't wish to do this, Anne, and that you need time to adjust. Even so, you will thank me in the end when you realise I have done you a favour by choosing a man with whom you will be able to live in great harmony.'

And yet your first choice for me was Mr Darcy. 'I dare say I will, Mama.'

Anne had crossed her fingers behind her back as she'd spoken and escaped to join the rest of the ladies as soon as she could. They'd all looked at her with varying degrees of curiosity but were too polite to cross-question her on her lengthy interlude with Colonel Fitzwilliam.

'The colonel and I have reached a rather unique understanding and he has given me his permission to confide in you,' she told Mr Asquith. 'Before I do so, I need hardly tell you that what I have to say is absolutely confidential.'

Mr Asquith settled himself more comfortably in his chair and crossed one leg elegantly over its twin. He was like a large cat, she thought. He probably was not aware that he appeared sleek, sophisticated, glorious in his male splendour, and ever so slightly dangerous, which only added to his appeal. What she would give to be able to express so much self-confidence in her movement and gestures. 'Now I am really intrigued.'

'It has to do with Mrs Sheffield.'

Mr Asquith frowned. 'He spoke to you about his feelings for another lady?'

'Oh yes, we had a very free and frank discussion. It was highly illuminating.'

His frown intensified. 'I think you had best tell me everything.'

Anne did so, watching Mr Asquith's face for any sign he might disapprove or decide to warn Lady Catherine. When she ran out of words, she looked at him expectantly.

'I am very glad you will not have to marry a man whom you do not love.'

'Oh, I will have to do that, Mr Asquith. I have merely been granted a stay of execution. Better yet, the colonel and I now understand one another perfectly.'

'I cannot believe he is prepared to put you in the path of danger, however indirectly. It is too rash of him.'

'He asked my permission and would not have done so if I had not agreed. I feel very sorry for Mrs Sheffield and intend to help her in any way I can. I hope you are not going to say you know what is best for me and inform my mother.' Anne squared her shoulders and narrowed her eyes at him. It was a habit of Kitty's that Anne thought very expressive. She had been waiting for a suitable opportunity to try it out for herself. It felt wonderful to behave as she saw fit, with reference to no one's standards but her own. 'I have had quite enough of other people trying to live my life for me. I thought you were my friend and that I could trust you.'

'As you can.' His voice softened, and the deep vertical lines around his nose dissipated as the grip of winter left his eyes. 'My concern is entirely for your welfare.'

'And your position,' she said before she could stop herself.

He shrugged his broad shoulders. 'My position is at best tenuous.'

'I spoke with Mama about you last night. Remember, she thinks I am to accept Colonel Fitzwilliam and that she will no longer need your services. I made her promise to give you a glowing character.'

Mr Asquith sent her a devastating smile. 'In the middle of all the things that are happening in your life, you spared a moment to think of me?'

'Certainly I did. You have taught me a very great deal and I would not see you turned away with no means of making a living. Anyway, I happened to hear Mama asking Mr Collins if he knew where Sir Marius is lodging. Naturally Mr Collins did know, being so eager to engineer your downfall. Apparently he asked Miss Miranda's coachman for that information and ensured the young lady was put safely on the road back to Dover. Not that the coachman needed his interference but Mr Collins does so like to make himself useful. Anyway, I believe Mama intends to apply to Sir Marius and the truth will come out, proving your innocence and enabling her to give you a character with a clear conscience.'

'You are remarkable,' he said softly. 'I have offered you no explanation for Miranda's extraordinary claim and yet you have complete faith in my innocence.'

'That is because I understand you well enough to believe you incapable of jilting a lady,' Anne replied, firm conviction in her tone. 'I imagine you are protecting her reputation in some way because I know you to be an honourable man. I am guided by my instincts in this matter.' She paused, somehow finding the courage to meet his gaze. She seemed to have a plethora of courage these days and wondered where it had been hiding itself all these years.

'I have spent enough time in your company these past months to know that you have the highest standards of conduct.'

'I rejoice in your faith in me. Few other people in this establishment feel the same way. They all have their doubts, thinking there must be some truth in Miranda's claim even if they don't actually come out and say so. The shadow of false accusation will dog me for a long time to come.'

'Only if people do not know you for who you really are, and that would be their loss.'

Anne felt a deep oneness with her handsome tutor that broke through the boundaries of rank separating them. Mr Asquith held her gaze for a prolonged moment, an elusive warmth in his dark eyes that caused her body to react with a series of deliciously disturbing tremors. She enjoyed them for a fleeting moment before shaking her head to clear it. She was being fanciful again, reading more into their relationship than existed, and it really would not do. One way or another, Mr Asquith's days as her tutor were numbered and she must train herself to face life without him in it.

'Colonel Fitzwilliam is driving me over to Briar Hall before today's rehearsals, so that we can explain the plan to Mrs Sheffield. If she is in agreement then we will require your help to bring it about.'

'I am entirely at your disposal.'

'After today, Colonel Fitzwilliam will wish to call upon Mrs Sheffield daily. Obviously he can't be seen to be doing that and courting me. Even Mama might notice something amiss. And so we thought he could drive me to the end of the lane, you could meet me there and we could... well, read or something until the colonel returns to collect me.'

Mr Asquith laughed. 'The colonel is a good strategist.'

'Naturally. How could he be a colonel otherwise?'

'Many far less capable men rise to that rank. However, as to his plan, I think I could tolerate your company.'

'Excellent.' Anne canted her head. 'Do you think Mrs Sheffield will get her property back?'

'If you are asking me whether I think Sheffield is making a false claim, then the answer is that I do. As to his admitting to it... well, that is something else. The man is crafty as a fox and will not be easy to deceive.'

'What do you think of Mrs Sheffield?'

Mr Asquith hesitated for so long that Anne thought he would not answer her question. 'I did wonder if she had anything to do with the fire that destroyed their plantation and killed her husband.'

Anne gasped. 'Surely not?'

'No, you are probably right, but at the time everything was in confusion and everyone was suspect. She hated Jamaica, her husband was a cold, brutal man, and she was clearly unhappy in her marriage. The fire meant she was free of him and she could return to England.'

'Just as my instincts tell me you are not guilty of jilting Miranda Glover, they also tell me Mrs Sheffield had nothing to do with the tragedy you just described.' Anne smiled at Mr Asquith. 'Your problem, if you don't mind me saying so, is not that you don't possess integrity, but that you have too much of it. You are a man of principal and honour and your standards are if anything too rigid. There is always another explanation, you know.'

'My goodness. What happened to the shy young lady who didn't have two words to say for herself when I first met her?'

'She grew up.'

'I noticed,' Mr Asquith replied softly.

The room fell so quiet it felt to Anne as though the air had been sucked out of it. This time her breathing difficulties had nothing to do with her supposedly weak chest and everything to do with the disturbingly poised specimen of male beauty sharing the room with her. There was a tangible excitement between them now which Anne didn't entirely understand. It had been brought about by them being partners in deception, she supposed. The problem was if Mr Asquith's part in it was discovered, he really would lose his position. Anne should have thought about that instead of insisting upon involving him because... well, because she was selfish and wanted an excuse to spend more time alone with him.

He fascinated and compelled her in a manner she had never imagined possible. Her every conscious thought was of him. His was the last face she imagined before closing her eyes at night, and the first that sprang to mind when she opened them again in the morning. She was being unreasonable expecting him to compromise his standards, knowing he had little choice but to do as she asked. He was an honourable man, and she had asked him to behave in a manner that wouldn't sit comfortably with his conscience. She opened her mouth to say as much but no words emerged.

'I know what you are thinking,' he said, reaching out to touch her cheek gently. 'But you must not concern yourself on my account. I am perfectly willing to be of service to you.'

* * *

'Do you think anyone suspects?' Joshua asked the following morning as he drove Darcy's curricle, with Anne seated beside him, down Pemberley's long driveway.

'Mama was put out that we had not made an immediate commitment but I knew that would be the case. After complaining at length about needless delays—'

'Why is she in such a tearing hurry to have the matter settled, I wonder.'

'That I could not say, but I agree with you. She does seem extraordinarily anxious to marry me off.'

'Lady Catherine does enjoy having everything in her life in proper order.'

'And everyone in it doing what she wants,' Anne added with a wry smile. 'Anyway, she accepted the situation and didn't ask any awkward questions that required an outright lie. I mean, it is not as though you have actually asked me to marry you and so I could not have rejected your suit.'

Joshua laughed, agreeing that her logic was irrefutable. 'That is true. But what of Asquith?'

'I spoke with him this morning and he is perfectly willing to play his part.'

'Are you still absolutely sure, Anne? I shall not hold it against you if you have had a change of heart this morning. I realise I am asking a lot of you.'

'I promised to help and wouldn't think of reneging on that promise.' Determination underscored her words, reassuring Joshua of her willingness to play her part. 'I cannot remember a time when I enjoyed myself more.' She put up her parasol when the sun broke through the light cover of cloud. 'Quite apart from anything else, we cannot allow Mrs Sheffield's property to be taken from her without at least trying to prevent it.'

'I can tell you are resolved and so nothing remains except for me to offer you my heartfelt thanks.'

'Oh, there is absolutely no need for that. If you think about it, we are being of service to one another in our different ways.'

Once again Joshua could find no fault with her logic and they made the rest of the journey in companionable silence. Anne looked quite pretty today in a crisp muslin gown, devoid of all the shawls and additional layers she once would have considered indispensable. Or rather, layers that would have been insisted upon by those who concerned themselves about her health.

Upon arrival at Briar Hall, they learned that Lady Briar was not at home and they were received by Mrs Sheffield alone. She appeared surprised and confused by Anne's presence but hid it well. Without the need to make polite conversation with Lady Briar, Joshua wasted no time in apprising Mrs Sheffield of the reason for their visit, which he did the moment refreshments had been served and the footman who delivered them had withdrawn.

'Well,' Mrs Sheffield said, looking exceedingly shocked after hearing him out in silence. 'I am unsure what to say.'

'Do you think it will work?'

'Possibly, but I would not think of asking Miss de Bourgh to risk her reputation, and—'

'Oh, don't spare a thought for me,' Anne replied, flapping a hand. 'I shall remain at Pemberley and your odious brother-in-law will not get within a mile of me.'

'Yes, but what if word reaches Lady Catherine?'

'I cannot see how it would.'

'Servants talk.'

'Yes, that's true,' Joshua replied. 'But I will charge my man with ensuring that nothing untoward is mentioned within the hearing of Lady Catherine's retainers.'

'Is that possible?' Mrs Sheffield asked in a dubious tone.

'No offence, Anne, but if half of what my man tells me is true, no one below stairs at Pemberley thinks much of your mother's maid, or yours. Or your coachman either, for that matter. Apparently they have inflated opinions of their own worth.'

Anne nodded. 'You know my feelings about my maid, so I am not surprised to hear it.'

'Prejudices below stairs can, in my experience, be even more brutal than those held in smart drawing rooms.' Joshua grinned. 'No, I think we can safely assume that Lady Catherine will hear nothing of our plans from the servants' hall.'

Mrs Sheffield stood up, obliging Joshua to do the same thing. She paced the length of the room, her gown swishing about her ankles as she rested her chin in her hand and thought the matter through. 'I am perfectly sure that Percival would come rushing up here, given the slightest encouragement from me.'

'Yes,' Joshua replied, almost snarling the word in a fit of jealous pique. Just the thought of another man desiring Celia Sheffield sent him into a murderous rage. 'I dare say he would. The question is… would he be sufficiently tempted by the prospect of a vulnerable heiress such as Anne to become indiscreet about his claims on your property?'

'With respect to Miss de Bourgh, unquestionably. It's just the sort of challenge he would enjoy. Percival has never been backward in putting himself forward in an effort to have a lady notice him. As to revealing the true nature of his claim on my estate… well, that is another matter entirely. I cannot say for sure.'

'Greed has a way of loosening tongues,' Joshua replied. 'And I can be very persuasive when I wish to be.'

Their gazes clashed, and Mrs Sheffield's lips quirked. 'I am sure you can.'

'Well, there you are then. Tell me, would he expect to be welcomed here to Briar Hall?'

'Oh no. Lord Briar detested my husband and made no secret of the fact that he disliked Percival even more. My sister feels the same way, and Lord Briar would never let him sleep beneath his roof for fear of oversetting my sister and me.'

'I am very glad to hear it. Briar is obviously a man of taste and good sense. My main concern is that if you summon him here with the intention of speaking with him, that meeting must take place somewhere.'

'I am sure he will be permitted to call here, if I advise Lord Briar in advance. That way he can ensure my sister is out of the way and that I have a servant with me all the time. He will want to know why I have invited him, of course.' She pondered upon that for a moment. 'Hmm, I will have to indulge in a small untruth, I suppose, since I do not wish him to know of your involvement, Colonel, and especially not of yours, Miss de Bourgh. No matter, I am sure I shall think of a plausible reason to have invited him that will satisfy Lord Briar.'

'Then if we are agreed, perhaps you ought to write your letter now,' Joshua suggested. 'I will ensure it is sent immediately by express. If you were to say that your plans are not settled and you intend to leave Derbyshire very soon, it will hasten his arrival.'

'Before I commit pen to paper,' Mrs Sheffield replied, resuming her seat and fixing Anne with an inquisitive glance, 'I would very much like to know how you came to be drawn into this, Miss de Bourgh.'

Joshua felt almost surplus to requirements as the two ladies fell into a conversation that excluded him. One of those ladies he was expected to marry, and the other he would very much like to wed but would never be in a position to propose to. They were so very different in appearance, experience and every other possible way. And yet they chatted together now in a companionable manner as though they had known one another for years. Anne was quite open about her disinclination to marry Joshua and explained how relieved she had felt when she discovered he was of a similar mind.

'I wish I had possessed the strength to defy my parents when they insisted I marry Albert,' Mrs Sheffield said wistfully. 'How different my life might have proven to be if I had.'

'I can accept no credit for strength of character,' Anne replied.

'If the colonel had proposed marriage I would have accepted him, simply because... well, I clearly don't need to explain to you the pressure that was brought to bear upon me. I swear, if I hear one more time that I have a duty, I shall scream. However, I am very glad he did not... propose, that is. We now understand each other perfectly and are the very best of friends.'

'You are proving your friendship by offering to help me.' She shot a glance Joshua's way. 'Now if I could only decide what motivates the colonel.'

Joshua, elegantly draped across one corner of a settee, merely raised a brow and sent her a teasing smile. Mrs Sheffield cocked a brow in return, almost as though she was issuing some sort of challenge, and returned her attention to Anne. Leaning forward, she patted her hand. 'I want you to know that however matters turn out, you will always have my eternal gratitude. I cannot remember the last time anyone helped me without wanting something in return.'

'That is something else we have in common then.'

'I hope that I too can be your friend,' Mrs Sheffield said.

Anne smiled. 'I would like that very much.'

'Your letter, Mrs Sheffield,' Joshua said softly.

'Yes, of course. Pray, excuse me. It will take but a moment.'

'I suggest you say you have reserved a room for him at the inn in Lambton for three days' time and that he should let you know by return if he intends to make use of it. That way we shall know his intentions and it will give us time to prepare.'

'A good suggestion.'

She disappeared, and as good as her word, she returned a short time later with a letter in her hand.

'Here is what I have written. Tell me if you approve, Colonel.'

Dear Percival,

I was disturbed and overset to receive a visit from Albert's solicitor earlier this week. I had no idea there was a partnership agreement between you and Albert, or a will in existence that gifted our estate to you. As you can imagine, this news came as a great shock and has caused me considerable worry. I cannot believe Albert meant to leave me destitute and can only hope a resolution can be reached that will satisfy us both. We ought to speak face to face, to avoid further misunderstanding. Involving solicitors always complicates things.

I leave Derbyshire in a week's time for a prolonged stay with relations in Scotland. Could I prevail upon you to travel north at the earliest opportunity? I have reserved a room for you at the inn in Lambton for three nights' time. Please advise me by return if you plan to make use of it.

Yours etc.

'Perfect,' Joshua said, sending her an approving smile. 'I suspect he will find the prospect of meeting with you too tempting to resist.' In Sheffield's place, Joshua certainly would have. 'You have made it sound as though you are confused by the whole affair and on the point of capitulation, which is exactly the right way to tempt him. He is anxious to get his hands on your property and cannot do so until the matter of ownership is established beyond question. Seal the letter if you please, and I will arrange to have it sent.'

'This is all very well,' Mrs Sheffield replied, affixing her seal and handing the letter to Joshua, 'but what am I to say to him when we actually meet?'

'If you will allow it, I shall call on you tomorrow afternoon when I am supposed to be driving Anne, and we will be at leisure to discuss the matter then.'

'I look forward to it. But what of you, Miss de Bourgh? How will you occupy your time?'

Anne blushed. 'Don't worry about me. The colonel and I have arranged matters.'

'Ah, I see.' Instead of ringing the bell, Mrs Sheffield conducted them to the door herself. 'I am very greatly indebted to you both,' she said as they took their leave.

16

Three days later, Lizzy and Will snatched a few minutes alone in the small salon. Lizzy was reclining in her favourite position, which meant her head rested in her husband's lap and his hands stroked her hair. Their guests were all gainfully occupied and they did not anticipate being disturbed.

'What's troubling you, Will?' Lizzy asked. 'You keep scowling and so I know there must something.'

'Other than my allowing my cousin Anne to take part in a dangerous deception, you mean?'

'You are not allowing her to do anything. Anne is perfectly capable of making up her own mind. In fact, I have seldom seen her more animated. She is enjoying herself for once and you ought to take credit for that.'

'Even so, I would never have given permission for Georgiana to become involved in anything so rash. I now have grave reservations about Anne doing so. What if something were to go wrong?'

'Even if it does, it won't involve Anne because she will be safe and well protected here at Pemberley.'

'Which is the only reason I did agree to the scheme.'

'Stop brooding, my dear. It will do you no good.' Lizzy smiled up at her husband. 'Anne is being adequately rewarded for lending her name to the plot by spending an hour or more every afternoon in Mr Asquith's company, unchaperoned, when she is supposed to be driving with the colonel.'

'Which gives me something else to be concerned about.'

'I think that is the least of your worries. I am perfectly convinced that Mr Asquith is a man of the highest integrity.'

'I agree with you. But Lady Catherine would not approve.'

'Of course she would not. When does she ever approve of people enjoying themselves?'

Will conceded the point with an abrupt nod.

'Besides,' Lizzy added. 'We know Mrs Sheffield's brother-in-law will be in Lambton tomorrow and so the afternoon liaisons will no longer be necessary.'

'After which Fitzwilliam telling Lady Catherine he and Anne have decided not to marry can no longer be put off.'

'She will get over her disappointment and you have nothing to chastise yourself about. You had no part in that decision.'

'True, but it is Lady Catherine whom I am worried about, since you ask. I have never seen her beset by such a prolonged fit of the blue devils before. Ever since Collins arrived—'

'That would be enough to cast anyone into despair.'

'My aunt is one of the few people who likes and approves of the man. After all, she did appoint him to the living in Hunsford.'

Lizzy snorted. 'She only likes him because he hangs on her every word, treating them more reverently than the gospel he reads from his pulpit on a Sunday.'

'That is undeniable, but ever since he arrived with tales of Asquith's nefarious wrong doings, we have hardly seen my aunt except at meal times. She spends all her time in her chamber and doesn't even find anything to dissatisfy her in the way you manage

Pemberley.' Will shook his head. 'I am worried she might be unwell, seriously unwell, which would account for her desire to see Anne married.'

Lizzy sat up and gave Will her complete attention. Lady Catherine could be, and usually was, domineering and overbearing, but she was still Will's aunt and he was fond of her in his way. 'I cannot see anything different about her. She looks as strong and well to me as she did when we met in Kent. She is perhaps a little less forthright than I have grown to expect, but then she is not in her own home and knows you will never permit her to usurp my position here.'

'Even so, something is not right about her.'

'If you want my opinion, I think it has to do with Sir Marius.' Lizzy flashed a playful smile. 'She knew him years ago. I do not know how close they were, but I do think it accounts for her willingness to employ Mr Asquith.'

'How do you know this?'

'Anne told me. It came out in a conversation between mother and daughter. I also happen to know that Lady Catherine has written to him – I saw her letter on the table in the hall waiting to be posted. Presumably she wants to know the truth about Mr Collins's allegations, and I think she is nervous about the prospect of meeting Sir Marius again.'

'Good God!' Will looked shocked rigid. 'Could that be all it is?'

'Why not? She pretends to have no time for romantic love, but perhaps that is because she was once disappointed.'

'But all these years later. To still feel—'

'If we were separated for twenty years, would that change your feelings for me?'

Will's eyes glowed like molten lava as he gently covered her lips with his own. 'What a question. You know very well I would never allow that situation to occur. If we were parted for any reason, I would come after you, throw you over my shoulder and carry you back to Pemberley if necessary.' His lips worked their way down her neck, nipping and kissing until she was in a fervour of need. 'Nothing will ever keep me away from you, Lizzy. Never doubt it for a moment.'

Much as she would enjoy it if Will finished what he had started, now was neither the time nor the place. 'Perhaps Lady Catherine felt the same way about Sir Marius,' she said, shuffling so there was a little, a very little, distance between their bodies and Will was obliged to stop nibbling her neck. 'It would be lovely if that was the case. Everyone deserves to be happy, even your curmudgeonly aunt.'

'You have a romantic soul, Mrs Darcy.'

'Whose fault is that, Mr Darcy?'

'Anyway,' Will continued, 'Lady Catherine isn't likely to see Sir Marius again. All she has done is write to him and for all we know she could have been doing that for years.'

'But equally, she very well might not have done either. You know how disciplined she is.'

Will shook his head. 'I find it difficult to imagine my aunt suffering from lovesickness.'

'Whereas I think it the most natural thing in the world.'

A burst of laughter and chattering voices warned Lizzy her precious time alone with Will was about to come to an end.

'It sounds as though the morning's rehearsal is over,' Will said.

'So it does.' Lizzy sighed. 'Poor Jane. Since Lady Catherine has stopped offering her services as chaperone, my sister has to sit in on all the rehearsals. She says she doesn't mind, but it hardly seems fair.'

'What isn't fair?'

'Oh, Jane, we were talking about you having to supervise the actors, simply because you're the only one entrusted with the play's ending.'

Jane smiled good-naturedly as she took a seat. 'I don't mind in the least. In fact, I enjoy being useful. Mr Asquith is wonderful at getting the girls to perform. Kitty isn't shy, we all know that, but he has managed to get Georgiana and even Anne to throw themselves fully into their parts. It actually might turn out quite well.'

'If enthusiasm equates to success,' Will said, 'then they are sure to please. I have never seen any of the girls half so taken up with an occupation before.'

'Not that their enthusiasm could have anything to do with the involvement of a certain major, captain and tutor,' Lizzy remarked playfully.

'Lizzy, how could you suggest such a thing?' Jane asked, laughing.

'I cannot begin to imagine where that idea came from. Anyway, Jane, I am glad you feel useful. Personally, I still can't get used to the fact that we now qualify as chaperones. It only seems like yesterday that we were the ones whose reputations were being guarded.'

'Very true.' Jane glanced down at her expanding waistline and smiled. 'How quickly times change.'

They were joined by the girls, who threw themselves into chairs, still all talking at the same time about the play.

'I hear rehearsals progress well,' Lizzy said, smiling at the three animated faces.

'I think so,' Georgiana replied. 'Mr Asquith doesn't need to correct us quite so often, at any rate.'

'And I remembered all my lines today,' Kitty added. 'Who would have thought it?'

'Not you, obviously,' Lizzy replied, 'since this time yesterday you despaired of ever knowing them all.'

'Yes, it does seem extraordinary but I expect I shall forget them all when the time comes to perform for you all and I am beset by nerves.'

'Nonsense,' Anne said. 'You are a natural.'

Will shook his head, but smiled as he stood up and left the ladies to their chatter, presumably going off in search of male company.

'Mr Collins tried to intrude on our rehearsals again,' Kitty said. 'He seems to think he can order Mr Asquith about, but he soon discovered he was in the wrong.'

'Mr Asquith was very polite, but firm,' Anne added, her eyes glowing with pride. 'Mr Collins soon realised he had met his match and took himself off somewhere or other.'

'He has been pacing about in the garden for the last hour,' Lizzy said. 'I noticed that even the gardeners try to keep their distance from him.'

'Oh dear,' Jane said. 'I do feel rather sorry for him.'

'Of course you do, Jane, but I do not. No one invited him here. Besides, I should have thought he would be needed back in Hunsford, but he shows no inclination to leave.'

'He is very thick-skinned when it suits him to be,' Anne said.

'Kitty and I are finishing up the scenery this afternoon,' Georgiana said, 'while Anne goes driving with Colonel Fitzwilliam.'

Anne caught Lizzy's eye, blushed and said nothing.

'Come along, girls.' Lizzy stood up. 'It is almost time for luncheon. I am sure you are all sharp set after your busy morning.'

'Yes, I'm starved,' Kitty said.

Jane and Lizzy ushered the girls ahead of them and made their way to the dining room. Will's mood had rubbed off on her and Lizzy now felt unsettled. Tomorrow would see the arrival of Mrs Sheffield's brother-in-law and her plan to catch him out would be put into action by the colonel. Lizzy was gripped with a sudden desperate desire to call it all off. She had a peculiar feeling that they had overlooked something.

Something important that could have catastrophic consequences for them all. And if that happened, the blame would be entirely hers.

* * *

Celia Sheffield was waiting for Joshua in the woods adjoining Briar Hall, a location they were using as a meeting place for the third consecutive day. It was a convenient distance for Celia to walk, and the chances of their being seen there together were virtually non-existent. Joshua halted the curricle, secured the reins and allowed the horse to crop at the sparse grass. He then jumped down from the box seat and joined Celia, raising his hat by way of greeting. He took her hand, kissed the back of it and saw no reason to release it again. Instead, he tucked it in the crook of his arm, a perfectly natural place for it to remain.

'I hope you haven't been waiting for long,' he said, smiling down at the top of her straw bonnet.

'I arrived early.' She shrugged. 'I was restless. Anxious to see you.'

'I would be delighted about that if I could bring myself to believe it was my company you desired.'

She looked up at him and blinked in evident surprise. 'Why ever would it not be?'

'You cannot fool me, Celia. I know just how anxious you must be feeling. Sheffield will arrive in Lambton this afternoon and tomorrow you will have to face him. It would be peculiar if you didn't want to talk about it to the only person who knows the truth.'

'You are quite wrong, Colonel.'

'I thought we had agreed upon Joshua.'

'Yes, so we had. I'm sorry.' She shook herself. 'I probably am more anxious than I realised.'

'I shall visit Lambton Inn this evening and make Sheffield's acquaintance.'

She shuddered. 'How nice for you.'

'I don't anticipate enjoying the experience but I want to get a measure of the man as soon as possible.'

'He is sure to be found in the tap room,' Celia said, not for the first time. 'He has a strong head for liquor so it won't be easy to get him intoxicated.'

She had told him that several times as well. Joshua patted the hand trapped on his arm and sent her a reassuring smile. 'Just worry about what you will say to him when he calls on you tomorrow morning.'

'We have discussed that endlessly.'

'Even so, oblige me. I need to be sure that in your anxiety you have not forgotten anything.'

'Very well. I shall pretend not to understand the new will and ask to see it. I feel sure he will have a copy with him. He will assume I am incapable of grasping the particulars and take pleasure in explaining them to me, odious man! I shall act confused, tell him I need time to think, but that I am not at all sure I accept the document as being genuine.'

'Be careful not to anger him.'

'Oh, I shall assure him that I don't blame him for believing it is legally enforceable, at which point he will probably suggest we occupy the estate together.' Celia shuddered, causing Joshua acute concern.

'Come,' he said, leading her to a fallen tree and seating himself on it. After a moment's hesitation, he pulled her onto his lap and enfolded her in his arms, waiting for a protest that didn't materialise. 'You are cold?'

'No.' She rested her head on his shoulder and sighed. 'I just want tomorrow to be over with. I am being weak and foolish. I know there is nothing he can do to harm me in Briar Hall, or to coerce me to return to Buckinghamshire with him, but still... everything about him reminds me of Albert, you see, and I would infinitely prefer to forget that period in my life.'

During his previous meetings with Celia, Joshua had called upon all his military discipline not to overstep the mark. Using her given name and inviting her to use his was as far as he had allowed himself to go. He had sat her on his knee purely to infuse some of his strength into her and to protect her skirts from the splintered tree trunk. Of course he had. But seeing a fat tear trickling down her cheek, noticing just how badly she was trembling, cut through his crumbling resolve. His arms tightened around her and he placed a finger beneath her chin, tilting it upwards until she could no longer hide beneath the brim of her bonnet. She looked so pale, so vulnerable, so scared, that his heart melted and the desire to comfort her overrode common sense.

With a smothered oath, he lowered his head and captured her lips in a slow, incendiary kiss that promised so much more than he could allow himself to give her. It would certainly expose a great deal more of his feelings for her than was strictly necessary, which was not a sensible idea. Far from chastising him for his forwardness, she responded with enthusiasm, which was almost Joshua's undoing. His tongue tickled the corner of her mouth as his lips played against hers with possessive intent.

Ye gods, she would be the death of him yet!

Powerless to help himself when gripped by the fierce, burning desire that had grown stronger with every meeting between them, Joshua deepened the kiss, pulling Celia firmly against him as it turned unashamedly carnal. Their breathing quickly grew ragged and uneven as Joshua's control slipped. The reward he had been dreaming of claiming since first meeting Mrs Sheffield was within a hair's breadth of becoming a reality and yet he could not allow that to happen. Not now, certainly not here in the open air.

Not ever.

When Celia groaned around their fused lips and settled herself more firmly against his burgeoning desire, the extent of which she could not fail to notice, it actually brought Joshua to his senses. He broke the kiss and released his hold on her.

'I am sorry,' he said, not meeting her gaze. 'I should not have done that.'

'I disagree.' It was the last thing he had expected her to say and it caused Joshua to look at her aghast. 'There is no need to look so shocked,' she said, musical laughter accompanying her words, all signs of her earlier distress eradicated. 'I know you only intended to reassure, but I am tired of being reassured and so I pretended to be upset.' She bit her lower lip, presumably to prevent the renewed laughter he could see in her eyes from escaping. 'It worked better than I could have anticipated.'

'You wanted me to kiss you.'

'I hope you are not this slow when you are in command of your men, Colonel, or the enemy would run rings around you.'

'I want you very much,' he said softly. 'I didn't think you could possibly doubt it, but I will not take advantage of your reliance upon me, and there's an end to the matter.'

'I am not being fair to you, am I?'

'We need to get through the next few days, deal with Sheffield, and then we will be at leisure to discuss anything you wish.'

'It is not what I wish that concerns me. I know my own mind.'

Joshua wanted to ask her what she meant by that comment but refrained for fear that her answer would not be what he wished to hear. Once she had her property restored to her and no longer felt obligated to Joshua, she would feel very differently than she did at that moment. He had nothing to offer her, he reminded himself bleakly, other than his undying love and a colonel's pay. Marrying for money, which he had always known he would have to do, hadn't seemed so bad because he had never anticipated actually falling quite so violently in love with the lady he chose. Now that it had happened, he was unprepared to fall back on her fortune in order to support them both. It seemed ungentlemanly, especially given that the fortune in question had been amassed through the exploitation of slaves.

Dear God, what had he got himself into?

* * *

Anne sat beside Mr Asquith on a bench in a pretty part of Pemberley Park, a good distance away from the house. She had a poetry book open on her lap but wasn't reading aloud from it as she had done the two previous days. Instead, she looked up from it and smiled.

'What do you find so amusing, Anne?' Mr Asquith asked.

'Mr Collins.'

'Collins?' He elevated his brows. 'I thought you disliked the man.'

'I do, more than you could possibly know. He came here to cause you harm, and took considerable pleasure from doing so, yet calls himself a man of God.'

'Many worse crimes have been committed over the centuries in the name of God.'

'I know that, and since we are talking in ecclesiastical terms, Mr Collins is my personal cross to bear.'

'And yet he has managed to make you laugh.'

'I am laughing *at* him, not *with* him; there is a difference.'

'Certainly there is.'

'I overheard him telling Mama this morning that I ought not to be allowed to drive out with Colonel Fitzwilliam alone and that he would be happy to bear us company just to ensure the proprieties were observed.' Her smile widened. 'Only imagine if he could see the two of us now. He would probably have apoplexy.'

'And would have a legitimate reason to claim he had been right about my character all along.'

'But we are not doing anything wrong.'

'We are alone.'

'Yes, but quite innocently.' Anne bit her lip to prevent herself from adding the word 'unfortunately'. She had rather hoped that Mr Asquith – Pierce, as he had invited her to address him in private – would use the opportunity to... well, to do something to show his true feelings for her. Perhaps he had. By behaving in a gentlemanly fashion, he had made it clear that he did not return her rather transparent regard.

'Even so.' Pierce scowled, presumably because he didn't seem to find Mr Collins's clumsy attempts to interfere in her life amusing. 'I trust Lady Catherine told him to mind his own business.'

'Oh, but I am his business, or so he thinks.' Anne continued to smile, until Pierce reluctantly did the same thing. 'The problem is that no one at Pemberley wants anything to do with him, as he discovered when he tried to intrude on our rehearsals.'

'He would be best advised to take himself back to Hunsford where he has a legitimate excuse to interfere in his parishioners' lives.'

'He will not leave here until he is sure Mama intends to dismiss you.' Anne's smile widened. 'I don't think Mr Collins likes you very much, Pierce.'

'The feeling, I can assure you, is entirely mutual.' He fixed her with a penetrating gaze.

'You should smile more often, by the way. It suits you.'

Perversely, his words caused Anne's smile to fade abruptly. 'A few more days and I will have little to smile about. When Mama learns Colonel Fitzwilliam and I have decided not to marry, she will be furious with me. She will say it is all my fault, that I did not make myself agreeable enough.' She felt tears welling but impatiently brushed them aside. 'She will most assuredly take you away from me as a punishment, simply because she knows I enjoy your society.'

'Hush now. Don't get upset on my account.' He gently brushed an escaped tear from her cheek. 'I am a survivor.'

'That is not what I meant.'

'I know you did not.' Pierce stood and half turned away from her, probably embarrassed by her immaturity. 'Let us worry about the here and now and leave the future to take care of itself.'

In other words, he is anxious to leave me, Anne thought desolately. 'What shall you do?' she asked.

'Find another position,' he said, not looking at her. 'What else can I do?'

17

'You had best be off to Lambton, Cox,' Joshua told his valet later that afternoon. 'Even if Sheffield hired a saddle horse from Newcastle instead of springing for a private carriage to complete his journey, he ought to have arrived in the village by now.'

'Right you are, sir. I shall see you there later.'

'That you will.' Joshua flexed his jaw. 'You know what you have to say?'

Cox nodded. 'That I do, sir.'

'Keep your wits about you. By all accounts, Sheffield is nobody's fool.'

Joshua stared out of the window for a long time after Cox had left, wondering if there was the remotest possibility of this plan actually working. They intended to play on a greedy man's rapacious nature, along with his arrogant assumption that no female on the planet could help but fall for his looks and charm – especially one as sheltered and innocent as they planned to make Anne sound.

The difficulty was that Sheffield appeared to have developed a genuine attachment to Celia, damn his eyes. If she gave him the remotest encouragement during their meeting the following day, albeit unintentional – the product of her nerves – Sheffield might just decide he would prefer to settle for less blunt if it meant he could have Celia. Joshua groaned in frustration. If the man was that far gone, nothing they did to try to gull him into indiscretion would have the desired effect.

Joshua forced himself to give Cox an hour's head start, filling the interminable wait by pacing the length of his chamber, deep in thought about his meeting with Celia earlier. Even if he did manage to get the better of Sheffield, he had come to the agonising yet incontrovertible decision that he would definitely not ask her to marry him. The only way he could show how much he loved her was by restoring her property to her and setting her free of all commitment to him.

He tightly compressed his lips as he withstood the debilitating pain brought on by his decision. Her desire to be kissed by him that afternoon implied that she enjoyed his society. She definitely hadn't kissed him solely out of a sense of gratitude, but that was neither here nor there. Mrs Celia Sheffield deserved time and solitude in which to consider her future, without Joshua around to muddy her thinking. He would leave here as soon as this matter was resolved, and of course after he had weathered the storm that would rage when he told Lady Catherine he would not be marrying Anne.

With a heavy heart, Joshua slid his arms into his greatcoat and left the house by the side door that led to the mews, anxious not to draw attention to himself. If he encountered Lady Catherine, she would most likely demand to know where he was going, and why. Fortunately, that situation did not arise, and minutes later he was cantering his horse down the drive in the direction of Lambton.

He left his mount in the care of the head groom at Lambton Inn, a man he knew well, and pushed open the door to the taproom. As he would expect at this hour, he found it crowded to capacity with thirsty men eager to wash away the dust from a day's work with a tankard of ale or two. The noise of a dozen different conversations filled the air, as did smoke from a fire fuelled by peat that was obviously still damp. The odour of unwashed bodies and spilt ale barely registered with Joshua as he scanned the crowd, looking for Cox. He panicked when it occurred to him that a man of Sheffield's ilk may prefer not to share the taproom with farm labourers, gardeners from the Pemberley estate, market traders and assorted locals. If he had chosen to hire a private room instead, Joshua's plan would not even get off the ground. He released a long breath when he observed Cox at a corner table with a man who could only be Sheffield.

Joshua caught the landlord's attention and ordered a tankard of ale. Then he stood to one side of the room for a moment, watching Sheffield, sizing him up carefully. It was impossible to tell how tall he was since he was seated. Even to someone as predisposed as Joshua was to dislike him, he had to concede the man was blessed with more than his fair share of good looks. Long fair hair fell across a face with features that attractively complemented one another – no crooked nose or jutting jaw to spoil the picture. He was dressed elegantly in the latest style, even if his boots still showed signs of dust from the road. It was obvious he felt perfectly at his ease in this environment as he banged his empty tankard on the table to attract the attention of the barmaid. He was served quickly. Millie had received instructions from Cox, and a healthy tip, to ensure the ale flowed. She flashed a flirtatious smile as she placed a full tankard in front of Sheffield and then bustled away to serve others.

'Hello, Fitzwilliam. I did not know you planned to come into Lambton this evening.' Cox waved to Joshua, just as they had agreed he would. 'I thought you preferred to drown your sorrows with Darcy's expensive brandy.'

'Needed to get away from Pemberley,' Joshua replied, pulling out a chair next to Cox and seating himself.

'This is the friend I was telling you about,' Cox said to Sheffield. 'Sheffield, meet Fitzwilliam, the luckiest man on earth with a face like a badger's arse to prove it.' Cox laughed at his own joke and slapped Joshua's shoulder. 'Sheffield here has just arrived from London.'

Joshua grunted and kept his attention focused on his ale.

'Sorry about my friend's lack of manners,' Cox said. 'You'd think that marrying one of the richest heiresses in the country would be cause for celebration.' Cox chuckled. 'As you can see, Fitzwilliam is in raptures at the prospect.'

Joshua shot his valet an evil look that caused Cox to laugh even harder.

'I've only been here for an hour,' Sheffield said, 'but all I hear mention of is the great Pemberley. Is that where you're staying?'

Cox nodded. 'Darcy is Fitzwilliam's cousin. I'm here for moral support.'

Joshua snorted. 'Nothing moral about you.'

'I aim to please.'

'I hear there is a Miss Darcy. Is she your intended, Fitzwilliam?'

'Miss Anne de Bourgh is the lady in question,' Cox replied, because Joshua was concentrating on his brooding expression, and on his ale. 'She is ten times more consequential than Miss Darcy.' Cox took a sip of his ale, warming to his theme. 'Imagine an estate at least as grand as Pemberley, run by a widow who has just one child set to inherit the lot.' He paused for effect. 'A daughter.'

'Is that what you're in such a funk about, Fitzwilliam?' Sheffield asked, looking incredulous. 'What great good fortune. It sounds like manna from heaven to me. Every man in the land would give his right arm to be in your boots, I shouldn't wonder.'

'Any man with half a brain would agree with you, Sheffield, except, it seems, for the would-be bridegroom.'

'And why is that?' Sheffield's tankard was empty again. Glancing up, Joshua noticed that his eyes were glazing over. Good. Millie had obviously remembered Cox's instructions and put a tot of rum into each of Sheffield's tankards. He would never notice the addition against the strong spicy taste of the famous local ale. 'I say, this ale is just the thing. Damned odd aftertaste, but it grows on a man.' He banged his tankard down, and once again Millie replenished it in double-quick time, saving a saucy wink for Cox as she turned away.

'My lunatic of a friend has taken a fancy to another lady,' Cox said, rolling his eyes. 'Claims to be in love, whatever that is supposed to mean.'

'What is this heiress like?' Sheffield asked, his expression calculating.

Joshua continued glaring morosely at the table, and again it was Cox who answered him. 'Small, quiet as a church mouse, biddable, not bad looking but shy and unworldly. Spent most of her childhood fighting illness so she ain't seen much of life beyond Kent.'

Sheffield, now definitely the worse for drink, leaned back in his chair and stared at the soot-blackened beams above his head. 'Let me see if I understand you a'right. You have the chance to become master of a vast valuable estate, Fitzwilliam, with just a sickly wife and her compliant mother in your way.' A bark of a laugh escaped Joshua at the thought of Lady Catherine ever being compliant, but he quickly turned it into a cough. 'Are you out of your senses, man? You can buy a dozen other women once you've married into that sort of money.'

'That's what I keep trying to tell him but it don't do me no good.' Cox pulled a disgruntled face. 'He's got it bad for this lady of his.'

'Must be quite a stunner,' Sheffield remarked.

'She would never agree to be my mistress,' Joshua said, addressing the comment to his ale. 'Anyway, she deserves better than that.'

'We always want what we can't have.' Sheffield took another long swig of his rum-laced ale and smacked his lips together in appreciation. 'I'll tell you what. I will do you a good turn and change places with you.' He chuckled to show he was joking but Joshua could tell the idea had taken root. 'Far be it from me to stand in the way of true love. Besides, it sounds to me like your Miss de Bourgh is ripe for the plucking.'

'Reads lots of romantic fiction, so she does,' Cox replied, 'and expects to be swept off her feet with grand romantic gestures. A good-looking man like you could probably melt her precious little heart in no time flat, but it wouldn't be any use. Her mama has quite made up her mind that only Fitzwilliam will do.'

Sheffield belched. 'Changing the minds of mamas is something I excel at, along with avoiding irate husbands, of course.' He chuckled. 'Whoops, bit indiscreet there.'

'You haven't told us what brings you to this part of the world,' Cox said.

'Ah, I have come to see my late brother's wife. He made a fortune in Jamaica, bought an estate here and left it to me. Problem is his lovely wife didn't know it and ain't too happy about the way things have turned out. I reckon she'll soon see sense though 'cause she sent for me.' Sheffield's lecherous grin caused Joshua to clench his fists beneath the table. It was the only way he could be sure of not planting the man a facer for his insolence. 'I think her and me could make ourselves very cosy back in Buckinghamshire.'

'Dare say you could,' Cox replied. 'Shame about that. Perhaps you could have done Don Juan here a favour and taken Miss de Bourgh off his hands, but it won't serve, not if you already have a love nest set up elsewhere. What you do after you tie the knot is another matter, but Lady Catherine would check up on you if you turned her daughter's head, and the slightest whiff of scandal would give her the excuse to cut off all relations.'

'What are you talking about, Cox?' Joshua asked, slamming down his tankard. 'I might not want to marry Anne but you can't just try and palm her off onto a stranger.'

'Just trying to be of service.'

'Hmm.' Joshua staggered to his feet, giving every impression of being in his cups when in fact he was icily sober. 'We had best get back to Pemberley. It's almost dinner time.'

'So it is.' Cox stood up and shook Sheffield's hand. Joshua couldn't bring himself to do the same. 'Nice meeting you, Sheffield, and good luck with your business. We might meet again if you're here for a while. Fitzwilliam seems to find his way in here most nights to drown his sorrows and someone has to make sure he gets back to Pemberley in one piece.'

Joshua and Cox walked away, leaving Sheffield in a pensive frame of mind.

'Well done, Cox,' Joshua said when they reached the mews and reclaimed their horses. 'You sowed the seed perfectly.'

'What will happen now?'

'Sheffield will ask more questions about Pemberley and Lady Catherine. Everyone here will tell him the same thing. That Rosings is as grand as Pemberley and he will discover that everything we told him is true. You know how every tiny detail connected to the Darcy family is the equivalent of folklore around these parts. He had his eye on Millie, and she will certainly set him straight.'

They mounted up and trotted down the village street side by side. It was a fine evening. A lot of people were out for a stroll, smiling indulgently at children with energy to burn who enjoyed a rough and tumble at the side of the road. Fitzwilliam acknowledged one or two people he recognised as they made their way back.

'All we can hope for now,' Joshua added, 'is that Mrs Sheffield plays her part right.'

The next morning, Joshua waited impatiently for Celia to join him in their usual place. When their appointed time came and went, and there was no sign of her, he became anxious that something had gone wrong. Perhaps Sheffield had somehow coerced her into parting with her property. He was at the point of making his way to Briar Hall, no longer caring if he exposed himself to Sheffield, when she ran breathlessly into the clearing. She was bareheaded, her face flushed and her eyes huge and luminous. To Joshua she had never looked lovelier, but he could see she was distressed, and his resolve not to touch her in an inappropriate manner did not survive the first minute. He opened his arms and she flung herself into them.

'Sorry, he was late arriving.'

'That is probably my fault. We managed to get him intoxicated.'

'Ah, that explains it. He didn't look quite as debonair as usual.'

'Was it so very bad?' he asked, brushing his lips across the top of her head when he felt her entire body tremble.

'I hate being in the same room as that man,' she cried passionately. 'I always feel the need to wash after speaking with him. There is just something predatory about him that makes me shudder. He reminds me of a wild animal on the prowl.'

'A very apt description.'

Joshua forced himself to release his hold on her. 'Tell me what he said and how you responded. I need to know it all.'

'I asked to see the will and he had the original in his coat pocket. I got the impression he always carries it with him.'

'Which is exceedingly foolish of him but typical of his arrogance.'

'He was at his most charming and persuasive, suggesting there was no reason why we shouldn't share the property.' Celia tossed her head and sniffed. 'He made it clear without actually saying so that that was not all he expected to share.'

Joshua was filled with a murderous rage but quelled it with difficulty. As a soldier, he knew very well that rational decisions could not be made when one allowed passion to overcome reason. 'I hope you told him you planned to have the will authenticated.'

'Certainly I did and he wasn't at all pleased to hear it. He said it could take months, all but implying he didn't have months to wait.'

'You think he has pressing debts?'

She wrinkled her nose. 'He usually does. He enjoys playing cards but doesn't always win. Anyway, he was not impressed by my procrastination and went to a lot of trouble to try and talk me around. I told him I had no desire to share my house with him and that his attempts to try and take it from me had caused me to lose all respect for him. Not that I had any in the first place, but still.'

'You did well.' He broke his resolve for a second time by reaching out and gently touching her face. 'But now it is over. You can leave the rest to me and need never see him again.'

'What happened at the inn last night?'

They walked together, her hand on his arm as he told her.

'Cox and I will return this evening and I have every expectation of getting him to admit the will is a forgery. He is desperate for easy money, will have asked about Anne and found out what I told him, or rather what Cox told him about her situation, is true.' Joshua allowed himself a prolonged glance at her lovely profile, dying a little inside when he recalled his decision not to press her into matrimony. To walk away and leave her to live her life on her own terms would be like tearing out his own heart with a blunt spoon. But he would do it because it was the right – the honourable – thing to do. He should never have allowed himself to get carried away by thoughts of what could never be. 'I have met men like him before. He will not be able to resist.'

She sighed. 'You make it all sound so straightforward.'

'There isn't any reason why it should not be.' Joshua patted her hand. 'Anyway, tonight will tell.'

'And will you let me know as soon as you possibly can? I shall be in a fervour of expectation.'

'I promise to send word immediately.'

'Will you not come yourself?'

Joshua avoided making an answer, unwilling to commit himself to a promise he could not afford to keep. His resolve was not that strong. He escorted her back to the house but declined her invitation to go inside. He had no wish to explain his presence to Lady Briar. He had every wish to prolong his time with Celia but what would be the point? His mind was made up. He raised her hand to his lips, kissed the back of it and bade her adieu. He sensed her confused gaze boring into his back as he strode away to the position where he had left his horse. He resisted the urge to look back. He couldn't allow her to see his expression, which he suspected was as bleak and desolate as his empty heart.

Joshua had just spent the last moments he would allow himself to be alone with the only woman he would ever love.

* * *

Joshua and Cox arrived earlier at the Lambton Inn that evening and Sheffield wasn't yet in the tap room. Millie sent Cox a cheerful wink, implying Sheffield had asked all the questions they had predicted and received the right answers. Confident Sheffield would appear, they took their tankards to a table by the window and waited. They heard booted feet clumping down the wooden stairs a short time later and Sheffield came into view. Joshua pretended not to see him and continued to stare into his ale.

'Let him come to us,' he told Cox.

Sure enough, he did precisely that. Raising a hand in greeting, he pulled out a chair at their table without being invited to do so.

'Evening,' Sheffield said, looking and sounding a little less chipper than he had the previous day. 'Mind if I join you?'

Joshua merely shrugged. Cox was more forthcoming. 'By all means,' he said. 'How did your business go today?'

Sheffield grunted. 'Damned woman thinks she can lead me a merry dance and get away with it. Why the devil can't women just do as they're told and leave the thinking to us men, as they are supposed to?'

'See,' Cox said. 'I told you Sheffield and Miss de Bourgh would be a perfect match. She would never dare to answer back.'

'Miss de Bourgh, Miss de Bourgh,' Joshua growled, scowling at the world in general. 'I came here to get away from the sound of her name for an hour or two.'

'Is she really that biddable?' Sheffield asked.

'Oh aye. Brought up to be seen and not heard,' Cox replied. 'You would think, what with her being such a grand heiress, she would be high and mighty, but the truth is she hardly opens her mouth.'

'She sounds too good to be true.' Sheffield shook his head. 'You're a few farthings short of a guinea, Fitzwilliam, and don't know when you're well off.'

'His latest plan, if you can believe it, is to propose to his lady love and ask her to live on a colonel's pay,' Cox said, looking totally disgusted. 'She would be a damned fool to even consider it. She can do much better than that but Fitzwilliam won't listen to a word I tell him.'

'Money ain't everything,' Joshua replied.

Cox rolled his eyes but made no comment.

'It is when you don't have any,' Sheffield said. 'You can take my word for that.'

'Darcy will give me a helping hand,' Joshua mumbled.

'Are you really serious about passing the heiress up?' Sheffield said, tucking into his second tankard of ale in ten minutes.

Joshua shrugged.

'You can take it from me that he is,' Cox said. 'I know him when he makes up his mind about something. Wild horses couldn't change it.'

'Then I don't suppose you could arrange for me to accidentally meet the lady? I might be able to help you out by turning her head.'

'Hardly.'

'It is possible, I suppose,' Cox said in a pensive tone. 'Nothing to stop you inviting Sheffield to Pemberley for dinner, Fitzwilliam. I'm sure Mrs Darcy won't mind. You know how fond she is of you, for some obscure reason.'

'It will never work,' Joshua said. 'Miss de Bourgh would never go against her mother's wishes.'

'Care to take a wager on that?' Sheffield asked smugly, proving Celia's point about his penchant for gambling. 'I have a way with the ladies. Besides, if I do manage to pull it off I'd make it worth your while, Fitzwilliam. Give you enough for you to keep your lady in style.'

'You don't have much of a way with the lady you came up here to deal with, by all accounts.' Sheffield scowled at Joshua's words but said nothing. 'Talking of which, you can't even think about pursuing Miss de Bourgh if you're in dispute over this other property. Lady Catherine would cut her daughter off without a penny if she thought you were a party to any questionable transactions, especially if there's a lady involved.'

Sheffield was quiet for a long time. Joshua's nerves were on edge, but he forced himself to remain quiet and let the man sup his ale while he thought things through. Cox opened his mouth to break the silence but Joshua kicked his shin and he quickly closed it again.

'Perdition, Mrs Sheffield has left me with no choice.' Sheffield's expression filled with rage. 'I don't have time on my side, or I would—'

'But if you have genuine claim to the property, why would you give that up on the off chance that you might be able to woo Miss de Bourgh? I assume you have debts, who doesn't? But I dare say your creditors would be prepared to wait if they knew you have expectations.' Cox scratched his chin. 'This sudden desire to pursue a lady you've never met sounds a bit tenuous to me.'

'Stupidest idea I ever heard,' Joshua grumbled.

'Damned strong, this ale.' Millie's rum measures were obviously generous this evening and Sheffield was already slurring his words. 'Truth to tell, I don't actually have a legitimate claim to the estate.' Joshua tensed. There – he'd said it, just like that. Cox had heard him. So too had Millie, who loitered directly behind their table. 'My brother intended to change his will but didn't get around to doing so before he died. Didn't seem right that the cold bitch he was married to should get it all when I had toiled hard to get us to the point we were at. I'll admit I cut a few corners to get us there, but taking chances is what I do best. My brother was cut from a different cloth and never would have had the nerve to do what I did. Come to that, he never would have had anything if it weren't for me driving him on and keeping a steady nerve when all he could do was bleat about what might go wrong.' Sheffield leaned back in his chair and scratched his thigh. 'The way I see it, God helps them as helps themselves. Anyway, Albert ain't no great loss, truth to tell. He died trying to save some damned useless slaves.' He rolled his eyes in disgust. 'What a fool!'

'If he was such a lost cause, how did he become a plantation owner rather than you?' Joshua asked.

'Ah, well now, that was merely an accident of birth. He got all the help to get started simply because he was older than me and our father's favourite.' Sheffield focused a glower on his tankard which was again almost empty. 'He was also better at routine than me, I'll give him that. Order, method and prudence were his bywords. Me? I like to get something started, which I did by pointing out the opportunities in Jamaica to Albert. He never would have taken the plunge if I hadn't been there to hold his hand. So the man owed me. No question about it.' He ground his jaw. 'And I aim to collect, one way or another.'

The man was deranged, which made him dangerous and unpredictable. A cold chill worked its way through Joshua's body. He relaxed when he reminded himself that they had caught him out. He had condemned himself with his own words, and there was no further damage he could do to Celia or her property.

'Sounds as though you deserve something,' Cox agreed.

And he's about to get it, Joshua thought with satisfaction. Unfortunately for him, it would not be what he expected.

'Damned right I do,' Sheffield slurred.

'How did you come by a will?' Cox asked.

'I had someone in Jamaica forge it for me, along with a partnership agreement. It looks genuine and I figured she would believe it was. It fooled my brother's own solicitor, but the damned woman just won't lie down and accept it.' Sheffield jutted his chin. 'I really didn't think she would make so much fuss, and truth be told, I'm too hard pressed to wait on the off chance that she might feed me a few crumbs.' He sat forward and leaned both forearms on the table, suddenly appearing disconcertingly alert and sober. 'So, when can I meet the lovely Miss de Bourgh?'

'That won't be possible,' Joshua said, standing and pulling himself up to his full height.

'Hey, just a minute.' Sheffield's momentary confusion gave way to anger. 'What is all this? You said—'

Cox stood also. 'No, I believe the suggestion came from you.'

'Did you just hear this man admit to trying to gull Mrs Sheffield?' Joshua asked.

'Yes, sir,' Cox replied without hesitation. 'I heard him clear as day.'

'So did I,' Millie said cheerfully from behind them.

'What is all this? Why should you care?'

'The game's up, Sheffield.' Joshua's harsh tone rang with the authority that usually had everyone scurrying to carry out his orders. 'Now, here is what will happen. Firstly, you will write a letter confirming you are making no further claim upon Mrs Sheffield's estate.'

'The devil I will!'

'When you have done that you will leave Derbyshire immediately. You will go nowhere near Mrs Sheffield or her property ever again. If you do, I'll have you taken in charge to account for the crime you just admitted to in front of witnesses.'

'Mrs Sheffield.' A slow grin of comprehension spread across Sheffield's face. 'She's the woman you've fallen for, ain't she? That's why you set me up like this. Well, you're wasting your time. She's as cold as ice. My brother told me as much more than once. She's just used you to get the better of me, but you'll get nothing from her in return.'

The urge to strike the man grew more compelling by the minute. 'Unlike you, I do not help a lady in expectation of receiving anything in return.'

Sheffield stood up on unsteady legs and glowered at Joshua. 'This ain't over,' he said belligerently.

Before Joshua realised what he intended to do, Sheffield roared and aimed a roundhouse punch to his gut. Joshua turned sideways and deflected the worst of it, but it still hurt like the devil. Ignoring the pain, he drew back his arm and finally had the satisfaction of doing what he had been itching to do these past two days. His clenched fist connected squarely with Sheffield's face. He thought of Celia Sheffield and the pain this man had caused her, the future he ached to have with her but could not, and he put all the force of his disappointment behind the punch.

Sheffield was knocked clean off his feet and landed on a stool, which splintered beneath his weight. He cried out as blood spurted and bones cracked. Joshua had obviously broken his nose.

Sheffield's features would never be quite as regular again.

A rough cheer went up from the watching crowd. Anyone connected with Pemberley was a firm favourite in this inn. Sheffield was an outsider. By throwing the first punch, the locals would know Sheffield had crossed Joshua in some way and he would get no sympathy from them.

Joshua leaned over the prostrate man, felt inside his coat and extracted the original copy of the will.

'Hey, that's mine.'

'I don't think so.' Joshua turned to a couple of the inn's servants. 'Help him pack and get him back on the road tonight,' he said, slipping them each a few coins. 'Cox, stay behind, make sure he writes that letter and then ensure that he leaves.'

18

'Well, ladies and gentlemen, you have exceeded my expectations and there is nothing more we can do to improve. You are all to be congratulated.' Mr Asquith's smile embraced all the actors, but Anne chose to believe his praise was exclusively for her. 'Everything is in readiness for tonight's performance. I would suggest we give ourselves the remainder of the day to rest and prepare ourselves.'

A general murmur of assent greeted this suggestion.

'I shall never be able to settle to anything,' Georgiana said. 'I am far too nervous, even though I know it is only our family and neighbours we shall be performing for and they are bound to be kind.'

Kitty nodded. 'I know they are predisposed to like us but still the prospect terrifies me.'

'Perhaps a brisk walk before luncheon will calm us all down,' Major Halstead suggested. 'It is a fine day and a shame to remain indoors.'

'I a-agree,' Captain Turner said.

'Very well.' Georgiana shared a brief glance with Kitty. 'Will you join us, Anne?'

'Thank you, but no.'

When applied to, Mrs Bingley also declined. Anne couldn't blame her. Lizzy's good-natured sister had sat through endless rehearsals in her capacity as chaperone when she probably had any number of other occupations vying for her attention.

'Take a servant with you instead, Kitty,' she said.

The walking party went off to fetch outdoor clothing, leaving Anne alone with Mr Asquith and Mrs Bingley. Unsure what to do with herself, the decision was made for her when Mr Asquith passed her a book, holding her gaze significantly as he did so.

'I believe you expressed an interest in this novel, Miss de Bourgh. I happened to find a copy of it in Mr Darcy's library.'

Anne blinked. She did not recall discussing this particular tome with Pierce. She opened her mouth to express her surprise, looked down, and abruptly closed it again in an effort to stifle a gasp. There was a piece of paper jutting from between the pages. He was trying to gain her attention and had gone to considerable trouble to do so. Why could he not have simply waited until they had a moment alone to say whatever it was he wished to say? Anne was perplexed and had no idea what to make of the situation.

'If you will excuse me, ladies,' he said, turning to leave the room.

'Certainly, Mr Asquith,' Mrs Bingley replied. 'You are to be congratulated upon working miracles with the players, but you must be exhausted. I am sure you would welcome a respite yourself.'

'I do have plans for the rest of the morning,' he said cryptically as he opened the door for them both, offering them another of the glamorous smiles as he stood back and waited for them to pass through it.

Anne didn't think she would ever tire of his smile. Her heart lurched when she recalled that she would very soon have to. She sighed, absently waving as Mrs Bingley excused herself and disappeared in the direction of her chamber.

Anne noticed Colonel Fitzwilliam lingering in the open doorway to the billiards room and gave him a little wave, to which he responded before returning to his game. His efforts to expose Mrs Sheffield's brother-in-law for the fiend he was had been successful. Anne was very glad for the colonel's sake, but she also knew that after tonight's play they would have to inform Mama they had decided against marrying. Anne's stomach roiled in harmony with her already thumping heart as she anticipated that interview. Mama would be furious to have her hopes disappointed for a second time and Mr Asquith, regardless of what Sir Marius might say to vindicate his conduct towards his daughter, would bear the brunt of her displeasure. Anne knew it and so did Mr Asquith. *Pierce*, she mentally amended. She really must get accustomed to using his name as he had asked her to do now more than once.

Alone, Anne extracted the piece of paper from between the pages of the book he had given her and slowly unfolded it. It was covered by a few brief lines of Mr Asquith's – Pierce's – elegant hand.

> *Anne, please meet me beside Pegaz in half an hour. We have urgent matters to discuss and require absolute privacy in which to do so. PA*

Anne hugged the note to her breast – the first personal missive she had received from Pierce, and very possibly the last. Fearful of creasing it because she knew she would never throw it away, Anne smoothed out the paper as she ascended the stairs. Naturally she would keep the engagement. She couldn't refuse him anything. Besides, her curiosity was piqued. What could he possibly wish to talk to her about that necessitated absolute secrecy? Panic gripped her when she realised she would have to find her own way to the centre of the maze. Alone. She couldn't possibly.

Except, of course, she could. The old helpless Anne had briefly reared her head, but Anne pushed her feeble objections aside. There were few things the new Miss de Bourgh would not attempt, especially if there was the remotest possibility of earning Pierce's approval through her actions.

She had never been invited to partake in an assignation before, if that was what this was, and she had a great desire to learn what would happen if... no, *when*, she reached their rendezvous. *Just keep turning right*, she reminded herself as she snatched up a flimsy shawl and ran from her room without even bothering with a bonnet, anxious to avoid her maid who would ask awkward questions about where she intended to go. She didn't need to concern herself about Mama. Strangely, she had gone off in her carriage that morning and was driven away from Pemberley without telling anyone where she was going.

Anne cut across the lawns at a brisk pace and reached the entrance to the maze without, as far as she could tell, being seen by anyone, not even a gardener. Taking a deep breath, she plunged between the tall beech hedges, which without Pierce's comforting presence seemed especially sinister and forbidding. Anne jumped at every sound, saw things that didn't exist in the shadowy hollows between the hedges. She swallowed down her anxiety and concentrated on turning right at each opportunity, determined to prove to Pierce that this simple task was well within her capabilities. She chose not to think what might happen if she took a wrong turn and became lost in the maze. The alarm would eventually be raised, she supposed, Pierce would have to admit what he had asked her to do, and his fate would then definitely be sealed.

She could not permit that to happen, but her resolve was almost immediately tested when she came upon a confusing crossroads that brought her to halting indecision. Knowing she must always turn right ought to have made it easy, but alone and nervous, she discovered it was anything but. She convinced herself that the narrow right-hand turn confronting her now was too insignificant to be an actual turn and so walked straight past it. Pierce's warning the last time they had done this together echoed through her mind, stopping her before she had advanced ten paces. *Never be tempted to deviate, and have the courage of your convictions.*

She turned back and took the narrow path, breathing a sigh of relief when it widened almost immediately. Pierce knew these traps waited to fool the unwary but had faith in her ability to find her way alone. That was another milestone in her life. She had never before been allowed to be alone, much less attempt anything this complicated unaided. It would simply have been assumed she lacked the ability, and before Pierce came into her life, she would not have questioned that conclusion. This newfound freedom was liberating and she would repay Pierce's faith in her by not getting lost.

She absolutely would.

Surely it had not taken this long to find their way out of the labyrinth on the last occasion? Once again Anne was filled with doubts. Perhaps this was not such a good idea. But Pierce was waiting at the end of it and she would walk barefoot over hot coals to reach his side, such was her total fixation with the man. Perhaps being with Pierce when they did this before and trusting his navigational skills, or because there was absolutely nothing he could not do and do well, she had not noticed the passing of time. Time always seemed to move at twice its usual rate when she was with her *inamorato*, and there was never enough of it to discuss with him all the things that were in her head – things that he always had answers to, no matter how complex or obscure the question.

Anne felt desolate when she contemplated being parted from Pierce, as she knew she would be, but also in a perverse sort of way, she counted herself fortunate. She now knew the blissful agony of being totally and completely in love with a man even if that love was entirely one-sided. Many ladies never got to experience that joyful state at all and so Anne would make the most of the time remaining to her with Pierce and then settle down with the husband her mother chose for her without complaint.

She was confident she could do that because no one – not Mama, not the man she would choose for her husband – no one could take away her precious memories. It didn't matter who Mama chose to become master of Rosings because it was not his face she would see in the familiar rooms. Images of the only face she cared about were locked away within the safe capacity of her heart where no one could reach them except her.

Her mental perambulations made her forget about getting lost and she continued to walk on, more confidently now, turning right without having to think about it. It was with a small gasp of triumph that she unexpectedly emerged into the clearing with the statue of Pegaz dominating it. Pierce was already there, a lock of dark hair falling across his brow as he concentrated on the sketch he was working on, presumably of Pegaz. Her heart lightened. He had recalled her wish to capture the statue's likeness and had thoughtfully lured her here for that purpose.

He looked up when a twig snapped beneath her foot, put his pad aside and stood up, sending her an enticing smile.

'You found your way. I knew you would manage it.'

Anne felt tongue-tied and shy. She had always been that way in the past, but it was a situation that seldom happened when she was with Pierce because they always seemed to have so much to say to one another.

'Yes, I just kept turning right,' she replied, glancing at her feet because her heart was overflowing and she knew that if she looked at him she would give herself away.

'I am sorry if my invitation appeared mysterious but I was anxious to see you and knew if we met anywhere else, Mr Collins would most likely find us.'

Anne managed a brief smile. 'Undoubtedly.'

'Come and sit down.'

He held out a hand and Anne slipped hers into it. The moment she felt his warm skin against her ungloved hand, his long fingers curling around her palm, her nervousness left her and she was able to meet his eye.

'Are you drawing Pegaz?' she asked.

'No.'

He seemed distracted and unsure of himself, which was highly unusual.

'Then what?'

He put the pad aside and didn't answer her. 'Colonel Fitzwilliam was successful,' he said, staring at a point somewhere beyond the silent statue.

'Yes, and I am glad for it.'

'You realise what that means?'

'Of course.' Anne clutched her hands together in her lap and shivered. 'We will perform the play tonight and then tomorrow the colonel and I must face Mama's wrath.'

Pierce stood up and paced up and down in an obvious state of agitation. Anne wanted to reassure him and opened her mouth to do so, but closed it without speaking. She was unable to find the right words. There was little she could say that would make him feel any better about his future other than that her mother would give him a character. But would she? Now that she had wilfully disobeyed her, Anne was unsure if she would keep her word, and she was unwilling to offer assurances she wasn't in a position to keep. Fidgeting, she waited for him to speak again.

'My timing is deplorable, I know that perfectly well.' He stopped directly in front of her and ran a hand through his hair. The thick, sleek locks fell directly back into place again, gleaming, unruffled. 'I am asking the impossible but I cannot seem to help asking it anyway. If, as I suspect, I am to be disappointed, I would prefer to know it now.'

To Anne's utter astonishment, he fell to one knee in front of her and took her hand. 'Will you do me the honour of becoming my wife, Anne?' he asked, his gorgeous eyes filled with uncertainty.

He looked up at her with a convincing display of adoration. Anne was too shocked and too angry with him to make any response. In spite of her best efforts to conceal them, he must have picked up on her feelings for him and was exploiting them to his own advantage. His cruelty took her breath away. She had not thought him so hard-hearted. It was not her he wanted of course, but Rosings.

Rosings, always Rosings.

She shook her head and brushed away an errant tear. She had no wish to cry or to demonstrate any form of weakness before him. She was not her mother's daughter for nothing, and she took refuge behind a haughty expression and her fierce personal pride. Instead of weeping, she needed an outlet for her pent-up rage, and since he had put her in this mood with his total disregard for her feelings, he had no one to blame but himself if she took him severely to task.

'I know it is asking a great deal of you,' he said passionately, 'to give up everything you have been raised from the cradle to consider your own, but if I have learned nothing else in this world, at least I know that happiness is a rare and precious commodity.' Still grasping her hand, he implored her with his eyes. 'You have blossomed in the time I have known you from a shy, delicate creature into a woman in your own right with growing confidence, an enquiring mind, and lively spirit. With the restoration of your health has come a translucent beauty that is as compelling as it is precious. You have stolen my heart, Anne. Even though we are poles apart in our situations in life, I feel we are also soul mates. Can you not feel it too?' He did not pause to allow her to respond. 'I have never felt this way before and know I never will again. I cannot think what it is about you, but you have captured my heart.'

Anne knew precisely what it was. Rosings, she thought cynically He might dress it up with pretty words and protestations of undying love, but Anne knew better. No one who looked like Pierce would choose her above prettier, more confident ladies of his own volition.

Anger had filtered out his words and it took her a moment to appreciate what he had actually said.

'What do you mean, give up everything I have been raised to consider my own?' she asked suspiciously.

He blinked, looking as surprised as she felt. Anne had to admire his acting skills. He ought to be performing, instead of merely directing their production. If he did so, their success would be guaranteed. 'Why, Rosings, of course,' he said. 'And your mother's guidance and advice.'

'Rosings.' Anne shook her head, totally bewildered. 'I'm sorry, did I hear you right? Are you saying you don't want me for Rosings?' Her mouth fell open in a most unladylike manner. 'I do not have the pleasure of understanding you. If you don't hanker after the estate then what other reason could you possibly have—'

'Oh, sweet love.' He gently cupped her chin with the fingers of one hand. 'I cannot bear to see how all this expectation has sapped your self-belief.'

'You make no sense, Pierce,' she replied, not daring to believe what she thought he was trying to tell her.

'Then, at the risk of earning your derision, let me make myself clear. I would be lying if I said the proposition of Rosings was not attractive, but I am a realist, my love. Your mama requires you to marry a gentleman, not a plantation manager's son with barely three farthings to his name. She tolerates me as your tutor following Miranda's slur on my character, but I have lost her trust and doubt whether it will be so easy to regain it. Even if I could achieve that ambition, she would never give her permission for you to marry me.'

'No, I am perfectly sure she would not.'

'You will soon be of age, free to do as you please. I realise I am asking you to forego your mother's love as well as your birthright, and you will be reduced to living on what a school teacher can provide for you, but I have fallen in love with you.' He grasped her shoulders and fixed her with an intent look. 'You, Anne. Not Rosings, not your wealth and consequence, but you – the real you. The lovely creature I have watched emerge like a butterfly from a chrysalis these past weeks.'

'Yes!' she cried joyously. 'Yes, yes, a thousand times yes.'

His arms closed around her and he expelled a long, expressive sigh. 'I did not mean for you to give me an answer immediately, my dear. I am asking a very great deal of you. You will have to give up your fortune and most likely never know your mother again. Such considerations are not to be taken lightly.'

'I care nothing for my fortune. I should be very sorry if my mother put pride before my happiness.' She paused, tilted her head back and met Pierce's gaze. 'But if she forces me to choose between her and you, then I could not hesitate.'

'Your bravery leaves me speechless with admiration.'

Pierce lowered his head and kissed her deep and long, his arms holding her in a tight prison she had no wish to escape from as delicious sensations cascaded through her body. When he broke the kiss and they pulled apart, they were both breathing deeply, and Anne already felt the loss of the warmth that made her feel safe and protected in a manner she had never considered possible. It was all she needed. More than enough to ensure her happiness.

'I must make one stipulation,' she said breathlessly, almost unable to speak since she seemed incapable of not smiling.

'Name it,' he said, gently tucking a stray curl behind her ear.

'I do not require false compliments.'

He looked bemused. 'Whatever can you mean?'

'You spoke earlier of my beauty.' She laughed, wondering why the entire world was not laughing with her. Everyone deserved to be as deliriously happy as she was at that moment. She put disappointing her mother and the serious arguments that would ensue temporarily to the back of her mind and concentrated on enjoying the moment. 'I have never been beautiful, nor will I ever be. I know that very well, but if you like me the way I am then that is enough for me.'

Once again, Pierce shook his head. 'Come and see this.' He led her to the bench and picked up his discarded sketch. 'You asked me what I was drawing when you arrived.'

Anne looked at his picture and gasped. It was a very flattering, very well executed likeness of herself. 'I do not look a bit like that.'

'You mistake the matter. When we are alone and you feel as though you can be yourself, when you ask me a particular question about some point in literature or other that has been perplexing you, that is exactly how you look. Your eyes widen, your lips... well, we will not talk about your lips or I will be compelled to kiss you again. And once I start that I might never stop.'

'I feel numb with happiness,' she said simply. 'Never in my wildest dreams—'

'We have a lot of hurdles to clear before we can be together. First of all, your mother will be angry with you and the colonel. Then she will almost certainly dismiss me. Even if Sir Marius convinces her that I am not the rogue she takes me for, she will separate us as a punishment.'

'Yes, I know.'

'There are six months before you come of age. I wanted to speak to you today because I don't know how much more time we have together before I am cast out. Your mother will start looking for another husband for you immediately. If you are serious in your love for me, which, by the way, you have not put into words, then we ought to make plans for our future together while we have the chance.'

She laughed, stood on her toes and placed a gentle kiss on his lips. 'How could you ever doubt my feelings? I love you, Pierce. If I did not, I would not find the courage to stand up to Mama. But I will stand up to her. Never doubt it. No man she tries to push on me will find favour.' She smiled up at him. 'Only you, my love. Always you.'

'I shall take myself off once I lose my position. Hard as it will be to be apart from you, I shall endeavour to find something else and I will be at Rosings on the morning of your twenty-first birthday, ready to take you away with me.'

'We could always elope.'

He looked scandalised. 'We most certainly could not. I will not marry you in a tawdry ceremony over the anvil, as though I was ashamed of you. We will marry before God and a parson in a church of your choosing.'

'Whatever you say,' Anne replied, biting her lip because all the smiling surely was not ladylike.

His arm closed around her and she knew he meant it. It was all she needed to know to withstand the pressure she would receive from her mother.

Even so, six months suddenly seemed more like an eternity.

19

Lizzy heartily wished Mr Collins back in Hunsford, a place to which he seemed in no particular hurry to transport himself. One additional guest in a property as vast as Pemberley ought not to make any difference, and nor would it if that guest was anyone other than Mr Collins. He had a happy knack of tracking her down wherever she happened to be and insisting upon bearing her company. She tolerated him and his long-winded speeches because he was her relation and because she would not wish him upon the others.

She was aware that he had strongly advised Lady Catherine against allowing Anne to participate in the play. Lizzy had heard him repeatedly saying Anne was not strong enough; and anyway, such behaviour was beneath her dignity. The same did not appear to apply to Georgiana or Kitty, or perhaps he simply didn't dare to caution Will against Georgie taking part.

When his advice was not heeded by Lady Catherine, he looked in on the rehearsals to – as he put it – ensure the spiritual and moral wellbeing of the young ladies. He told anyone who would listen that as a man of the cloth, he was the only person at

Pemberley qualified to undertake that duty. He explained at tedious length that he was happy to bear that responsibility, mindless of the inconvenience. Mr Asquith, much to Lizzy's satisfaction, refused him entry to the rehearsal room.

Mr Collins now had nothing to do with himself. Lizzy fell over him at every turn and could no longer call her house her own. She repeatedly reminded herself that by his remaining at Pemberley, her friend Charlotte was given a respite from his company. For that reason, she managed to remain civil and polite. But this morning, after something especially trifling that Mr Collins had chosen to advise her against, she could tolerate him no more. Unless she found a way to distract him, she would most likely say something she would later regret. Will, Fitzwilliam and Mr Bingley had taken refuge in the billiards room, Jane was resting, glad to be relieved of her chaperone duties, most of the young people were out walking and Lizzy was stuck with Mr Collins. Again.

That did not seem fair.

She was unsure about Mr Collins's attitude to the game of billiards, although she was confident he would enlighten her, given the remotest encouragement. Such encouragement was not forthcoming. Instead, she told him the gentlemen needed him to make up the numbers. Lizzy watched him bustle away, muttering something about billiards being a perfectly acceptable pastime for gentlemen of quality, provided of course that no wagers were struck and play did not take place on the Sabbath. She suppressed a smile, anticipating the revenge Will would exact later in the privacy of their chambers.

Giddy with relief, Lizzy headed for the gardens, looking forward to a long, solitary stroll. She had not been outside for more than five minutes before she noticed Anne and Mr Asquith approaching from the direction of the maze. Surely they had not been... Lizzy grinned, thinking from the looks of them that they very likely had. Anne appeared flushed yet radiant. Mr Asquith seemed quietly pleased about something. They were in deep conversation, heads close together, and were almost upon Lizzy before they noticed her.

'Mrs Darcy.' Mr Asquith's head jerked away from Anne's. 'Forgive me. I did not see you there.'

'We have been exploring the maze,' Anne explained, blushing crimson.

'Have you indeed. I hope you did not get lost in it.' Although Lizzy rather thought Anne would enjoy getting lost with Mr Asquith, and he with her.

'Pray excuse me, Mrs Darcy,' Mr Asquith said. 'I have a few matters to attend to regarding tonight's performance.'

'By all means.' Lizzy turned towards Anne and together they watched Mr Asquith until he disappeared into the house. 'Walk with me, Anne, unless exploring mazes has exhausted you.'

'Not in the least. I would enjoy taking a walk. Besides, I was hoping to catch you alone.'

'Without Mr Collins dogging my footsteps, you mean.' Lizzy rolled her eyes. 'I am seriously considering taking up full-time residence in my private sitting room. It is about the only place in the house where he cannot intrude.'

Anne laughed. 'He can be rather tenacious.'

'That is not the word I would use to describe him but I shall not offend your ears by using a different one.' She linked arms with Anne and together they crossed the lawns at a slow pace, taking a track that bordered the trees at the far end of the reflecting ponds. 'Now, what did you wish to speak with me about?' Lizzy laughed. 'As if I couldn't guess.'

Anne canted her head, looking embarrassed. 'Am I so very transparent?'

'You are violently in love, and it shows.' Anne gasped but Lizzy waved a hand to prevent her from interrupting. 'Your complexion glows, your eyes sparkle, and you cannot seem to stop smiling. I feel persuaded that Colonel Fitzwilliam has not inspired such a change in you. That does not leave many other candidates.'

'Yes, Colonel Fitzwilliam plans to tell Mama of our decision not to marry after the play, probably tomorrow morning.'

'And when does Mr Asquith plan to speak with her?'

Anne winced. 'What does it matter? Mama will never agree to the union.'

'No, I dare say she will not.' Lizzy felt terribly sorry for Anne. She had changed from a timid mouse into a lively, independent woman with character and determination. Lizzy didn't doubt that she would marry Asquith as soon as she was of age, regardless of her mother's feelings, forfeiting her fortune for the man she adored. Even so, it could not be an easy decision to have to make, choosing between one's mother – no matter how dictatorial – and one's heart's desire. 'Presumably the liaison in the maze was arranged by Mr Asquith so he could propose.'

Anne's permanent smile widened. 'Yes.' She gave her head a defiant toss. 'And I have accepted him.'

'I am delighted to hear it. I hope you will be very happy.'

'You approve?' Anne looked both surprised and relieved. 'I hoped you might but I thought you would caution me against giving up Rosings. I am perfectly sure I shall have to, and everyone will think I am out of my senses. But to tell you the truth, it feels as though a great weight has been lifted from my shoulders. I know Mr Asquith wants me for myself and not for Rosings, you see, because he is aware Mama will disinherit me and he doesn't care. Well, of course he would much prefer to be master of Rosings, but he is sensible enough to know that cannot be.'

Lizzy smiled. It was the longest speech she had ever heard Anne make. Being in love, and defiant, had made her loquacious.

'You never know.'

'Oh, I know. Believe me, I know only too well. Mama hates to be defied. She will never tolerate it from me.'

'Yes, there is that.'

'Mr Asquith declared himself now because he is convinced he will be dismissed the moment Mama learns the colonel and I do not plan to wed. He wanted to know how I felt, but can you believe this?' Anne stopped walking and turned to face Lizzy, her eyes glowing with animation. 'He really thought I would reject his suit. How silly!'

'I am very glad you had the good sense not to do so. Mr Asquith is a fine young man and worth fighting for. I am sure you will be very happy.'

'Yes, I am sure of that too, although I expect I shall feel guilty about Mama for a long time. She will be very lonely in that big house without me, but she would never admit it.'

'Will Mr Asquith start looking for a new position?'

'Yes, he plans to do so.'

'Then I shall have a word with Mr Darcy. He has a lot of influence around these parts, and if anyone is in need of a tutor then I am sure he will be happy to recommend Mr Asquith.'

'Oh, thank you. That is very kind. I should like to be close to Pemberley.' Anne looked startled. 'Who would have imagined me ever saying that?'

'Times and circumstances change.'

'That is certainly true. Speaking of which, please make sure any positions on offer allow for a wife to remain with her husband. I do not intend to cross swords with Mama only to be separated from Mr Asquith.'

Lizzy laughed. 'As if I could overlook anything so important.'

They strolled along the treeline, enjoying the array of colours above their heads. With the arrival of autumn, the leaves had started to turn glorious shades of red, russet and brown. Because they were both looking up, they did not see a man emerge from the tree line until they almost bumped into him.

'Miss de Bourgh?' the man asked, sweeping off his hat and executing an elegant bow.

Fear trickled down Lizzy's spine. She had never met this man but knew at once who he must be. His nose was swollen and crooked as though it had recently been broken. She recalled seeing scratches on Colonel Fitzwilliam's knuckles last night. It did not take a genius to put the two things together. This was Percival Sheffield and he had sneaked onto the Pemberley estate to extract revenge in some way.

Before Lizzy could turn and call for help, Anne spoke.

'Yes, I am Anne de Bourgh. Who are you and what do you want of me?'

'Anne, run!'

Anne turned to look at Lizzy with a quizzical expression, but didn't move. 'Why?'

Perdition, Anne. Just run! You are in danger! Anne still didn't move. What to do? With seconds to react, Lizzy could do nothing more than thrust herself between Anne and Sheffield.

'Leave this property at once,' she said. 'You are trespassing.'

'Gladly, but I won't be leaving alone. Stand aside.'

Lizzy spread her arms in a futile attempt to hide Anne from his view, as if by not seeing her, he would forget she was there. 'Certainly not.'

'Very well then. Have it your way.'

Sheffield gave Lizzy a vicious shove, causing her to lose her balance. She gave a startled cry as she fell heavily to the ground, badly winded. Her head swirled, and her first thought was for the baby she carried. *Please God, don't let it be harmed.* She was conscious of Anne crouching beside her, her brow creased with concern. Lizzy wanted to shake her, tell her to flee while she still could, but it was too late now to do anything. She watched, helpless, as Sheffield bent down, scooped Anne from the ground, threw her over his shoulder, and disappeared into the trees.

* * *

Joshua caught Darcy's eye across the table. This was purgatory, attempting a serious game of billiards with Collins, who could barely strike the ball cleanly. Joshua could see that Darcy had reached the end of his patience. Following his example, he replaced his cue in the rack. Bingley did so too, claiming the need to check on his wife. Darcy disappeared in the direction of the estate office and Joshua made a hasty exit also, leaving Collins standing beside the table looking rather stupid, with a cue still in his hand.

Joshua strode away from the room, mentally rehearsing what he planned to say to Lady Catherine when the time came, and encountered Asquith crossing the vestibule.

'A perfectly good game of billiards was brought to an end by Collins,' he explained by way of greeting.

Asquith expressed sympathy. 'Does he even know how to play?'

'Barely. His cueing was so uncoordinated that we feared for Darcy's baize and brought the game to an early end.'

Asquith chuckled. 'Very wise.'

He glanced out the window, smiling at the sight of Mrs Darcy and Anne arm in arm on the farthest edge of the lawn. His smile turned into a frown when it occurred to him that something wasn't quite right. The ladies were talking to a man who approached them from the trees. At first, Joshua thought it must be one of the estate's keepers, but he soon realised his mistake when the rogue knocked Mrs Darcy violently to the ground.

'Asquith, look!'

Asquith took in the scene in a second, and both men headed for the door at a run. Joshua paused to tell a footman to summon Darcy from the estate office. They raced across the expanse of grass, not wasting breath by speaking. Joshua groaned as they got closer and he recognised the man. It was Sheffield. Damnation, Cox had put him on the London coach but he had obviously got off at the first stop and doubled back, bent on revenge. Deuce take it, Joshua should have considered that possibility.

They reached Mrs Darcy, who was attempting to sit up.

'I think it was Sheffield. He took Anne,' she said, gasping. 'Someone has to stop him.'

'Stay with Mrs Darcy, Asquith.'

'No, you stay. I shall get Anne back.' Asquith's tone brooked no argument. 'Which is the most likely direction for him to have taken?'

'There's a path directly through the woods to the perimeter of the estate,' Joshua replied. 'He probably has a horse tethered there. Go! I shall send others after you as soon as they get here.'

'You go too, Colonel. You know the estate. I shall be fine.'

Asquith disappeared. Much as Joshua would have liked to go with him, he could not leave Mrs Darcy. She was in a delicate condition, and Darcy would crucify him when he saw her like this, pale and trembling. And so he should. This was all Joshua's fault. He had been told Sheffield was devious and intelligent, but he had not given those factors suitable consideration. When a man loses all expectation, he can become desperate, rather like a cornered wild animal.

Darcy came racing across the lawn, several footmen in his wake.

'Lizzy!' he cried, crouching down and cradling his wife's head. 'Are you hurt?'

* * *

Anne could not believe her own stupidity. This oaf had no business being on the Pemberley estate, springing out of the woods and accosting them. She ought to have heeded Lizzy's warning and taken to her heels instead of standing there like a fool. But even if she had reacted quicker and understood the danger, she still would not have done that and left Lizzy to face this brute alone. She was in a delicate condition and could not run. Lord above, the man knocked her down! If she or the baby were hurt, Mr Darcy's fury would know no bounds.

Don't think about that now, she told herself. There was nothing she could do to help Lizzy. Instead, she concentrated on her own situation. Her head bumped repeatedly against the man's back as he clutched her legs and moved through the trees at a rapid pace. She was unable to kick him because he had too tight a hold on her calves. The impudent brute! But she refused to be kidnapped without making a fight of it. She tried wriggling around. If Sheffield – for she realised now that was who he must be – was inconvenienced by her movement, it didn't slow him down. She didn't weigh very much and he appeared to be discouragingly strong.

Even so, there must be something she could do to help herself, or at least delay him until reinforcements arrived.

'Where are you taking me?'

'Be quiet or it will be the worse for you.'

Nothing could be worse than this. This had proven to be the very best morning of her entire life and also the very worst. She had accepted a proposal of marriage from a man who had demonstrated his absolute love for her in the most romantic fashion imaginable, and then was careless enough to allow herself to be kidnapped by a desperate fiend. She had once thought her life dull and tedious. At that particular moment, she would not complain about a little tedium.

He would have a horse somewhere, she thought. She could not allow him to get her on its back and take her off the estate. If that happened, she might never be found. Either way, her reputation would be in tatters. In some respects, that might work in her favour. If she was looked upon as having been compromised it would be social suicide. All her money and position would be insufficient to restore her to society's good graces, and Mama could hardly object to her marrying Mr Asquith. Even so, she would infinitely prefer to be rescued before Mama returned from her mysterious outing, then she need know nothing about it.

Her hopes improved when her abductor turned off the path and took a narrow fork, reminding her of her earlier journey through the maze. Was that only an hour or so ago? Clearly he meant to hide her on the estate until the search went wider. Anne tugged one of the yellow ribbons from her hair and dropped it at the juncture of the main path and the fork Sheffield had taken. It would be impossible for her pursuers to miss. Impossible for Sheffield to miss as well if he happened to look back. Fortunately that did not happen. He seemed too intent upon reaching his destination before anyone caught up with him. He must know he wouldn't have much of a head start.

They reached a ramshackle building. Anne thought it was probably an abandoned woodsman's cottage. Even from her undignified upside down position over Sheffield's shoulder she could see the roof had collapsed and the entire structure looked on the point of falling in on itself. This man had chosen well, especially given what little time he must have had to reconnoitre. But for her ribbon, she doubted whether anyone would think to look in this direction.

Sheffield ducked his head as he carried her through the

crooked doorway and threw her, none too gently, onto some foul-smelling sacking. She sent him a murderous glare as she rubbed her sore limbs, but he didn't appear to notice. Satisfied that she was uninjured, Anne took a good look around the place, intent upon escape. It exuded an aroma of damp and decay and had only one way in and out through the doorway Sheffield was blocking with his bulk. The walls were of flimsy timber and looked as though a strong male shoulder would be able to knock them down. A male shoulder. That was the problem. One as feeble as her own would never do the job.

She looked up at her abductor, adopting one of her mother's most aloof expressions.

'What is the meaning of this outrage?' she asked imperiously, astonished to discover that she was furious rather than afraid.

'Blame your friend Fitzwilliam.' Sheffield spoke with difficulty, his voice nasal thanks to his broken nose. 'He took what was mine and I'm returning the favour.'

'If you think you will get away with this then you are deluded.'

'I got you this far, didn't I?'

'And they will find you.'

'Nah, they'll go straight for the perimeter. I didn't have long to plan this. Thanks to Fitzwilliam, I knew you was likely to leave here tomorrow, once your loving Mama realised the two of you ain't set on marrying. Still, Percival Sheffield don't need long to make plans. I have an accomplice who will collect us at nightfall and take us somewhere safe. That will give Mama time to get really worried. Then, when I make my demands tomorrow, she will fall over herself to pay me. From what I hear, she will hardly notice the loss.'

'You seem to forget, they know who you are. It is hard to disguise oneself with a broken nose.'

Sheffield snarled at her. 'I shall be long gone, back to Jamaica, by the time they think to hunt me down. Besides, they won't want to make a fuss for fear of damaging your precious reputation.'

Yes, very likely, but Anne remained silent rather than giving the odious man the satisfaction of knowing he was right.

* * *

'Is Mrs Darcy all right?' Asquith asked when Joshua and two footmen caught up with him.

Joshua's lips tightened. 'She says she is. Darcy is not so sure. Any sign of Sheffield?'

'Not so far, but he must have taken this path.'

'Make haste,' Joshua said. 'There is no profit in stealth. We must stop him taking her off the estate at all costs.'

Asquith led the way, moving fast but keeping a close eye on the ground. It had rained heavily a few days ago and footprints made by a man bearing the weight of a young lady over his shoulder, damn his impudence, had sunk into the loamy leaf mould. Joshua continuously glanced ahead but saw no movement, heard no unnatural sounds. Why wasn't Anne screaming as loud as she could? She must know they would be immediately on her trail. Although perhaps she did not. She and Mrs Darcy had been some distance from the house and it was pure chance that Asquith and Joshua happened to observe the abduction.

'If anything happens to Miss de Bourgh, if Sheffield harms so much as one hair on her head, I will not be held responsible for my actions,' Asquith muttered, his expression murderous.

Ah, so that was the way things were. Joshua slapped his shoulder. 'Fear not, Asquith, she is too important to him to risk harming her.'

'That had damned well better be the case. I am responsible for her welfare, but instead of putting her interests first, I agreed to go along with your plan, indirectly placing her in danger.' He ground his jaw. 'Worse yet, I was not there to protect her when she needed me the most.' He shook his head in disgust. 'I am a miserable failure, a sorry excuse for a man.'

'Don't waste time on regrets,' Fitzwilliam replied. 'Besides, Anne herself agreed to go along with the scheme. I doubt anything you said would have stopped her.'

'I could have told Lady Catherine.'

'For which Anne would never have forgiven you.' Although part of Joshua now wished he had done so anyway.

'Here, what is this?'

Asquith stopped abruptly, and Fitzwilliam almost cannoned into his back. He held a finger to his lips, advising caution.

'This is the ribbon Anne had in her hair earlier,' he whispered, glancing further along the main path. 'The footsteps end here. They only go one way, which is towards Pemberley, so Sheffield must have taken this path to try and fool us. Miss de Bourgh kept her wits about her. I told her leaving signs was a good way not to get lost in a maze. Do we know what's down here?'

'There used to be a woodsman's cottage, but it was abandoned years ago when I was still a boy,' Joshua whispered back.

'A perfect hiding place,' Asquith said softly. 'We never would have thought to look there without Miss de Bourgh's quick thinking.'

'How did he find it?' Joshua mused. 'He hasn't had much time.'

'He must have an accomplice, someone he met at the inn, who worked here at one time and holds a grudge. I can't think how else he can have done it. He would not risk trying to get back to the perimeter in case we caught up with him. Besides, being mounted on a horse in broad daylight with an unwilling lady would attract attention.'

'Right, this is what we ought to do.' Joshua took control because he was a soldier accustomed to strategic planning. 'There are four of us against one, but we don't know if Sheffield is armed. If he is, you can be sure he will hurt Miss de Bourgh if that's what it takes to get away. He won't be expecting us to find him, but he will still be alert.'

'What do you have in mind, sir?' Asquith asked.

'A ruse,' Joshua replied. 'He knows me and wants to revenge himself against me. I suggest I walk right up to the door, without using any stealth. I will tell him others are searching farther into the woods, but I plan to take Anne back from him then and there. Of course he will decline that invitation.'

'And in the meantime we will have crept to all sides of the building,' Asquith said. 'While you two argue, we swoop in and get Anne.'

'Precisely, but only when I give you the signal. Are we ready?'

Everyone nodded, and Joshua, his expression grim and resolute, strode purposefully up the path.

Anne thought Sheffield had probably been a handsome man before the colonel broke his nose, but there was also a petulance about him. He was the sort of man who assumed life owed him a living simply because he had been blessed with good looks. His indolent nature and what she had been told about his disinclination for honest work implied he traded on his looks and charm to get what he wanted. Anne could well understand why Mrs Sheffield wanted nothing to do with him. Unfortunately, Anne currently had a great deal to do with him and was powerless to stop him from harming her if that was his intention. She didn't think he would actually kill her. If he did that, his financial expectations would die with her. She suppressed a shudder when she considered there were worse things he could do to her.

He stared at her, his expression cruel and calculating, unnerving her, but she refused to show any reaction whatsoever. She occupied her mind by wondering instead if she and Lizzy had been missed yet. Most likely not, but she refused to be discouraged. The hour for luncheon was approaching, if it had not already arrived, and the alarm would be raised when they didn't appear. Pierce knew they were walking together and she was sure they had been seen at one point by at least one gardener. Her ribbon would be found and then... and then what? Sheffield would not let her go without putting up a fight, would he?

She received an answer to her unspoken questions when she heard someone approaching – someone who was making no effort to do so quietly. Sheffield tensed, but Anne's heart lifted.

'What the devil?' Sheffield peered through the doorway and an evil grin spread across his face. 'Morning, Colonel. You should not have come, but I am very glad you did. You and I have unfinished business.'

'I am hardly likely to let you kidnap my cousin and do nothing about it.'

Anne wanted to cry with relief when the colonel peered past Sheffield's shoulder to ensure she was unharmed. She had never been more pleased to see anyone in her life. She smiled at him and nodded once, which appeared to satisfy him.

'The way I see it, you'll do nothing about it now 'cause you have to get past me to get to her, and I won't let you catch me unawares a second time.'

'You are still on Pemberley land, Sheffield, and you will not be allowed to leave it with Miss de Bourgh. If you try to harm her in any way then you will lose your only bargaining tool and swing for your crime.'

'It might almost be worth hurting her,' he snarled, 'because I know you will be blamed for pulling her into your scheme.'

'I volunteered,' Anne said sweetly.

Sheffield turned to glance briefly at her. His eyes widened, and she took satisfaction from having shocked him. 'You knew what they were doing?'

Anne shrugged. 'The colonel would not do something like that without my permission. Unlike you, he is a gentleman.'

'So, Sheffield, what is it to be?'

Anne's sight of the colonel was impaired by Sheffield's body, but she was sure her rescuer had his hands behind his back, making some sort of signal with them. She understood the colonel's plan now, or thought she did. He was taunting Sheffield into fighting with him, aware that Sheffield couldn't fight and keep her from running. In his haste to abduct her, he had overlooked the very obvious need for rope to restrain her. Perhaps he was not so intelligent after all. What self-respecting kidnapper went about his business without a way to keep his captive subdued?

She would not like to see Colonel Fitzwilliam come to any harm if it came down to a fight of course, but she was fairly sure he would be able to overcome Sheffield. Sheffield clearly thought the same thing because instead of standing to face the colonel, he moved back into the hut, pulled Anne to her feet, and thrust her in front of him, a dagger at her throat.

'Very brave,' the colonel said in an indolent tone. 'Hiding behind a lady's petticoats.'

'A change of plan,' Sheffield replied. 'Miss de Bourgh and I are leaving the estate, and if you attempt to prevent us then she will suffer the consequences.'

A crystalline stillness filled the hovel, broken only by the sound of Sheffield's rapid breathing and the beating of Anne's heart. She felt the cold steel of the dagger nicking the skin at her throat, sensed a wild desperation about Sheffield's behaviour, and thought he might actually be sufficiently deranged to kill her. Truly afraid now, she implored the colonel with her eyes to do something to help her. She dared not move her head for fear of the dagger actually penetrating her skin. The colonel nodded just once and definitely made a signal behind his back this time. Now that she was standing in front of Sheffield, she saw it quite plainly.

The next second a thunderous noise came from the back of the small hut. The crumbling wooden wall crashed in, and Pierce stood there, glowering at Sheffield, magnificent in his anger. Sheffield himself had turned to see what was happening, loosening his hold on Anne just enough for her to dip beneath his arms and flee straight into the colonel's arms. He swept her from the ground, and they watched Pierce as he floored Sheffield with two massive punches, adding more damage to his nose and, unless Anne was mistaken, relieving him of several teeth.

'It's all over,' the colonel said. 'Are you all right?'

She nodded. 'Yes. He didn't actually hurt me, just scared me half to death.'

'That is as well for him,' Pierce said, taking her from the colonel and swinging her effortlessly into his arms. 'Come along. I shall take you back to the house while the colonel deals with the mess here.'

20

'Are you absolutely sure that you are both all right?' Will asked for the tenth time, sitting beside Lizzy in the small salon and holding her hand, mindless of the fact that Anne, Mr Asquith and the colonel were also in the room. 'You look fearsome pale.'

'Yes,' Lizzy replied. 'Please stop fussing.'

'The doctor has been sent for,' Will said. 'I want his reassurance. I do not trust you to tell me the truth.'

'I am so very sorry this happened,' the colonel said. 'I underestimated Sheffield.'

'Well, he is locked safely away in the cellars for the time being,' Will replied, scowling, 'until we decide what to do with him.'

Lizzy blinked. 'Surely he must answer for his crimes?'

'Not if we wish to protect Anne's reputation and keep this business secret from Lady Catherine,' Will said.

'Ah, yes.' Lizzy nodded. 'I had not considered that.'

'It is fortunate Mama is not here today,' Anne said. 'I have a great curiosity to know where she has gone but would infinitely prefer her not to know what happened.'

'Then it is fortunate you found a reason to send Mr Collins into

Lambton,' Lizzy said to her husband. 'He knew something was not quite right and I wouldn't put it past him to listen at doors.'

'Especially if he thought he might overhear something to my detriment,' Mr Asquith said. 'And he would have done too. This is as much my fault as it is yours, Colonel. I ought to have taken better care of Miss de Bourgh.'

Unlike Will, Mr Asquith was not actually free to touch his beloved, but that did not prevent him from fixing her with a look of such total adoration that no one in the room could have failed to interpret its true meaning.

'We should not waste time apportioning blame,' Will said. 'Instead we must decide what to do about Sheffield.'

'He could be put on a ship back to Jamaica,' Anne suggested. 'That is where he planned to go once he extracted money for my release.'

'We could,' Will agreed. 'But that would hardly be punishment, and what is to stop him from returning to England and trying something even more desperate?'

'Surely he could be prosecuted for trying to steal Mrs Sheffield's estate,' Lizzy said. 'That would not implicate anyone.'

'Yes, that might be the best thing to do,' Will agreed. 'If he starts making accusations about Anne, no one will believe him because no one but those of us in this room knows about it. My servants will not say a word. You had best warn Mrs Sheffield and obtain her agreement first, Fitzwilliam.'

The colonel nodded. 'Very well. I shall speak to her this evening when they come to dinner.'

'What about Sheffield's accomplice?' Lizzy pointed out. 'Do we know who it was?'

'Oh yes, we had a frank discussion about that,' the colonel replied, flexing his grazed knuckles. Lizzy was sure there were fresh cuts on them. Asquith reflectively did something similar with his own fist and Lizzy noticed that his too was cut. 'A groom was dismissed by your steward for pilfering, Darcy, and he bears a grudge. Sheffield heard him grumbling about Pemberley while in the taproom and fell into conversation with him. Makes you wonder if he was planning something along these lines even before you exposed him for a liar and a fraud. Anyway, he knew where the man lived, looked him up as soon as he got back to Lambton. He only went five miles out of the village, by the way, had the coach stop on some pretence, and made his way directly back.'

'So he had been here longer than we realised,' Mr Asquith remarked.

'Exactly.'

'What is this accomplice's name?' Will asked. The colonel provided it. 'Right, I shall make sure he says nothing about his part in all of this. It will be the worse for him if he does.'

'Good,' the colonel replied. 'Then we are agreed on our course of action.'

Everyone confirmed that to be the case.

'We can now put the matter behind us and look forward to the play this evening,' Anne said.

'Are you sure you should participate, Anne?' Will asked. 'You have had a considerable shock.'

'But I am none the worse for the experience, and I would not think of letting the others down. Besides, if I do not take my part, we shall have to cancel and explain why. Mama would then know.'

'Well, if you are absolutely sure.'

'Perfectly so.'

Before the matter could be discussed further, the door opened and Lady Catherine sailed through it, an unknown gentleman beside her. Unknown to everyone in the room except Mr Asquith, it appeared.

'Sir Marius,' he said, looking astounded.

* * *

So that is where Mama has been all day, Anne thought incredulously. She had received a reply to her letter to Sir Marius and had gone to meet him somewhere in private. How extraordinary. Mama looked different too. Animated, younger, less disapproving. Anne studied Sir Marius as she waited her turn to be introduced, intrigued by Pierce's mentor. He was perhaps fifty years old, with thick grey hair and whiskers, a deeply tanned face etched with lines and a tall, upright stance. He must have once been very handsome. He was still elegant and commanded one's attention.

She watched as he greeted Pierce by clasping his shoulder and shaking his hand for a prolonged time.

'It is a pleasure to see you again, my boy,' Sir Marius said.

'As it is you, sir. I trust I find you well.'

'Fit as a flea,' Sir Marius replied cheerfully.

Anne breathed an inaudible sigh of relief. Mama would have lost no time in confronting Sir Marius with the accusations Mr Collins had brought to Pemberley. If there was any truth in them, Sir Marius and Pierce would not be on such congenial terms.

'Ah, so you are Miss de Bourgh,' Sir Marius said when Anne made her curtsey. 'I have heard a great deal about you and it is a pleasure to make your acquaintance.'

When everyone was seated and refreshments had been served, it was Sir Marius who broke the silence.

'I dare say you all wonder what brought me here uninvited, and where Lady Catherine and I have been all day.'

'You are very welcome here, sir,' Lizzy said.

'Thank you, Mrs Darcy. I would not have dreamed of intruding had I not received Lady Catherine's letter. When I heard of the accusations my daughter levelled against Asquith, I knew a visit in person was necessary to set the record straight. I assume you all know of these accusations.'

Everyone nodded, probably feeling as uncomfortable as Anne felt about having the subject discussed so openly, but at the same time curious, or in Anne's case anxious, to know the answer.

'I came to England because I plan to return here permanently. My wife died a year ago during some rioting by dissatisfied slaves from an adjoining plantation, so there's nothing left in Jamaica for me.'

'I am sure we are all very sorry for your loss,' Mr Darcy said.

'Thank you. I appreciate that.' Sir Marius rubbed the back of his neck. 'Now, where was I? Ah, yes, I was explaining about Jamaica. The place isn't what it once was. I have seen the best of it, made my fortune, and I want to end my days on British soil. All of my children are either married or at school over here. Miranda is the only one still living beneath my roof and there's a reason for that.' This time he rubbed his bristled jaw and took a sip of his tea. Anne surmised that rubbing certain parts of his person was a nervous habit and wondered what it was he was about to reveal that so upset him. 'She's a charming chit, but not quite right in the head. We all knew it the moment she came into the world. Asquith here took especial care with her schooling, showing devilish patience because she was slow, you see. She mistook Asquith's patience as something more and got quite fixated on him.'

'Ah,' Colonel Fitzwilliam said softly.

'Quite so,' Sir Marius replied. 'That was one of the reasons why I suggested he return to England. I thought she would get over him soon enough. Her memory isn't all that good, and she was bound to forget. But the moment we got here she found out where he was, waited until I was out of the way, and took off after him.' Sir Marius shook his head. 'I never would have credited her with that much guile. Anyway, Asquith is blameless in the entire affair.'

'And yet you kept silent when accused in order to protect the lady's reputation,' Lizzy said. 'I applaud your conduct, Mr Asquith.'

Pierce inclined his head. 'Thank you. I am just grateful that Lady Catherine did not accept Mr Collins's account at face value.'

'I was acquainted with Sir Marius when I was a girl,' she replied. 'I knew he would not recommend a man unworthy of his endorsement.'

'Well, Sir Marius, I do hope you will stay tonight and watch the play Mr Asquith is putting on for our entertainment,' Mrs Darcy said.

'Are you taking part in it, Miss de Bourgh?'

'Yes, sir, indeed I am.'

'Then I shall stay with pleasure. Thank you very much.' He turned towards Pierce. 'Dolores, Daphne and... er—'

'That is the one, sir. I had no notice to prepare anything else.'

Sir Marius laughed. 'Asquith wrote that himself. Don't suppose he told you that.'

'No,' Anne replied. 'He did not.'

'Wrote it and put it on in Jamaica with half my brood participating in it. Best entertainment we had in years.'

'Well then,' Mrs Darcy replied. 'Speaking personally, I now have an even greater desire to see it.'

Simpson was summoned to show Sir Marius to his chamber and Anne took the opportunity to escape to hers and rest before changing for dinner. She had had a very full day and it was far from over. She had no wish to see the doctor because there was absolutely nothing wrong with her, although she was very glad he had been called to attend Lizzy. She would never forgive herself if anything happened to the baby.

* * *

Joshua slid his arms into the coat Cox held out for him. He was nervous and on edge. The Briars and Celia would be arriving any moment. When the play was over he would be seated at table with her and knew it would be a living hell. He wanted her more than ever. The passion that burned inside of him each time he thought of her could not be suppressed, and so he must endure it with fortitude.

Celia was at her loveliest that evening. She wore a shimmering turquoise gown with delicate lace bows running from bosom to hem, its small capped sleeves trimmed with similar lace, drawing one's attention to her fine figure. Her eyes sought out Joshua the moment she entered the drawing room and he was powerless to look away from her. She appeared different somehow, almost carefree, as well she might. Her life was now hers to live as she saw fit.

There was no time for them to converse in private before they were ushered into the music room in preparation for the play. The gentlemen helped the ladies into chairs and took the ones behind them. Joshua did his damnedest not to sit behind Celia, but somehow that was how it turned out, and he was tortured by the sight of her lovely profile for the entire production. Her laughter rang in his ears, and every so often she looked back to share her pleasure with him. Ye gods, this was purgatory!

The play itself was light-hearted, funny in places and surprisingly well acted given the limited amount of time they had had to prepare. The girls threw themselves wholeheartedly into their parts and Captain Turner did not once stutter over his lines. The scenery the girls had agonised over appeared natural enough with the lights lowered, but even if it had not, no one was of a mind to criticise all the hard work that had kept the young people occupied for an entire week.

Joshua noticed Lady Catherine and Sir Marius sitting together, slightly apart from the rest of the audience. His aunt appeared to enjoy herself and actually laughed aloud in places. Joshua was astonished. He could not recall ever hearing her laughing without inhibition before. She considered such conduct unladylike. She had been heard to mutter disapproving comments all week about the play itself. Had anyone but Asquith suggested it, Joshua was sure Anne would not have been permitted to participate. He was filled with curiosity regarding her tolerance for Asquith, which obviously had something to do with Sir Marius. That gentleman certainly had a beneficial effect upon her temperament, and Joshua wondered about the nature of their previous acquaintance.

When the play came to an end, the applause was loud and prolonged. The players, flushed with success, mingled with the audience to accept individual congratulation – his cousin Anne included. He was probably not the only person to notice she never strayed far from Asquith's side, or the long probing glances they shared.

Joshua had the pleasure of escorting Celia into dinner, which was a rowdy affair and presented no opportunity for them to speak in private. And speak in private they must since Joshua had been charged with securing her agreement to prosecute Sheffield.

The gentlemen did not linger over their port, and Joshua knew he must now find an opportunity to see her alone. If he did not, he would have to go to Briar Hall in the morning for that purpose, and he couldn't take the risk. His resolve was not that strong. No, he would obtain her consent now and never see her again after tonight.

He was the last to leave the dining room. He followed the other gentlemen towards the drawing room but was waylaid by the touch of a small feminine hand reaching out to rest on his arm. He did not need to look down to know who owned that hand.

'If I did not know better,' said the melodic voice that haunted his dreams, 'I would say you were avoiding me, Colonel.'

Joshua sent her a raffish grin – he simply couldn't help himself – and steered her into the vacant small sitting room. 'We have been in one another's company the entire evening.'

'But there has been no opportunity for me to thank you for your kindness.'

'No thanks are necessary. It was entirely my pleasure.'

'I did not know quite what to think when the will and Percival's written recantation regarding his claim to my property arrived and you did not accompany them.'

'There was no need for me to push myself upon you,' he said, looking everywhere except at her. His words were hurtful, deliberately so. Perhaps that way she would understand she was under no obligation to him.

'Has it occurred to you that I might have been anxious to be pushed upon, as you so charmingly put it?'

'Celia, don't.' He turned away from her. 'I rejoin my regiment in a few days' time, and I dare say you are anxious to return to Buckinghamshire.'

'That is a miserable excuse for your neglect.' Still turned away from her, he heard the condemnation in her tone. 'I thought we knew one another better.'

Dear lord, she was not making this easy for him. 'Something happened today that you need to be aware of,' he replied in a deliberate change of subject.

Succinctly, he outlined the events of the day. Celia clapped a hand over her mouth, rightly appalled, her eyes luminous with shock.

'This is my fault. I should never have involved you. When I think what could have happened to Miss de Bourgh, and to Mrs Darcy as well.'

'Everyone involved is anxious to take the blame but in actual fact the only person culpable is Sheffield.'

'Perhaps, but I don't see it that way.'

'Mrs Darcy has been seen by the doctor and suffered no harm to herself or her baby.'

'Thank goodness.'

Joshua smiled. 'Precisely. Darcy would have ripped me apart with his bare hands had it been otherwise.'

'I am glad that proved unnecessary,' she replied with the ghost of a smile.

Joshua gave a theatrical shudder. 'As am I.'

'What have you done with Percival?'

'He is secured in the cellars here. We cannot charge him with abduction without Lady Catherine discovering what happened. We would much prefer it if she remained in ignorance.'

'I understand.'

'We hoped you would agree for him to be charged with attempted fraud, otherwise he will escape punishment.'

'We cannot allow that to happen. Certainly you may charge him with wrongfully claiming my property, forging a will, and anything else you think might help.'

'Thank you. Darcy will be pleased to hear it.'

'And so, Joshua,' she said after several tension-filled seconds of silence between them, 'we come to the real reason why you are avoiding me.'

'I am not avoiding you, Celia.'

'Liar!'

Joshua's body jerked. He was not accustomed to being addressed in such a fashion, even if it happened to be true. 'I do not have the pleasure of understanding you.'

'Was I wrong to assume you admire me?' she asked, looking down at her hands.

'How could any man fail to admire you?'

'That is not precisely the answer I was hoping for. I had not taken you for a prevaricator.'

The wounded look in her lovely eyes crushed Joshua's resolve. She deserved the truth. He owed her at least that much.

'I do admire you, Celia. More than that, so very much more, but I have nothing to offer you.'

Her clouded expression cleared. 'Oh, is that all? Your silly pride stands in the way. I ought to have foreseen as much.'

'It is not pride but plain economic fact. I live on a colonel's pay and very little else. You have not long been widowed and have had to battle to obtain your rightful inheritance. You do not need me complicating matters. You require time to adjust to your freedom and independence.'

'You treat me like a green girl rather than a woman of experience.' She sent him a smouldering look. 'I was attracted to you the first moment I saw you, as I believe you were to me. We were drawn together in a way I had long since stopped believing existed. It was as though we had been waiting to find one another our entire adult lives.' She placed her hands on her hips and glared at him. 'Deny it if you can.'

Joshua shook his head. He could lie to her but she would see through his falsehoods immediately. 'In all conscience, I cannot.'

Her smile was triumphant. 'Then be a gentleman and propose to me rather than leaving the matter to me.'

He pulled her into his arms, unable to resist a moment longer. 'Are you absolutely sure, Celia? I would not have the world think I married you for your money.'

'What do I care for the world's opinion? Besides, men marry for money all the time. Your aunt certainly expected you to do so, and the fact that you turned down those riches when they would have seen you comfortably settled for life is to your credit. I suspect few men in your situation would have done so, especially as you appear to be very comfortable in your cousin's company.'

'She is a very different person nowadays, for which Asquith must take full credit. I only hope she will not allow Lady Catherine to crush her spirit.'

'Let us all hope that.' Celia smiled up at him. 'You will be far less wealthy with me. My property is very modest, as is my fortune.'

'I disagree, my love. What you offer me is beyond price.'

He kissed her then because the urge to do so was all encompassing, too powerful to resist; he pulled her closer until their bodies collided. Her arms wound their way around his neck as though it was the most natural thing in the world. Her lips tasted sweeter than vintage wine, while the pressure of her body against his sent his mind spiralling in all sorts of inappropriate directions.

'I love you, Celia,' he said softly, whispering the words against her moist lips. 'Please say you will be my wife.'

'That depends,' she replied playfully.

'Upon what?' He kissed the end of her nose.

'Upon whether you know anything about managing estates.'

'A very great deal. And what I do not know, I can learn.'

'Very well then, Colonel Fitzwilliam. It sounds as if you could be very useful to me.'

He growled in her ear. 'You have absolutely no idea just how useful I can make myself.'

'But I have every expectation of finding out.'

This was all happening the wrong way round, he thought as he claimed another kiss. He still had to inform his aunt that he didn't intend to marry Anne and weather the fall-out from that decision. He should have done that first, but it didn't matter. Nothing mattered. He was the happiest man on God's earth. And the most privileged. He would spend the rest of his life proving it to his beloved Celia.

21

'Oh, have you been summoned too, Colonel?' Anne asked as she met her cousin outside the sitting room her mother occupied.

'No, I was planning to break the news,' he replied. 'I assume Lady Catherine has asked to see you.'

'Yes.'

'Then I shall come back later.'

'No, as you are here, we might as well tell her together.'

'I don't want you to have to shoulder any blame. Let me tell her alone and allow her to vent her anger on me first.'

Anne laughed. 'No, that is very gallant of you, but I insist. Come along, Colonel. I am sure you have faced worse situations during the course of your career.'

'Possibly, but at this precise moment I cannot think of a single one.'

He opened the door and stood back to allow Anne to pass through it in front of him. Anne blinked back her surprise when she discovered Sir Marius was also there. They really would have to delay telling Mama now. It was not something that could be achieved in front of a relative stranger.

'I beg your pardon, Aunt,' the colonel said politely. 'I did not realise you had company. I have no wish to intrude.'

'No, Fitzwilliam, close the door and sit down. What we have to discuss can be said in front of Sir Marius.'

Joshua flexed his brows. 'It can?'

'Certainly.' Mama straightened her spine, even though it wouldn't dare to be anything other than rigidly upright. Subconsciously, Anne found herself sitting a little straighter too, fingers laced together in nervous anticipation of the storm to come. 'I assume all those long afternoon drives have given the two of you ample opportunity to reach a decision.'

'Indeed we have, ma'am.' Colonel Fitzwilliam cleared his throat. 'I am very sorry to disappoint you, but the plain fact of the matter is that Anne and I have decided we will not suit.'

Anne's anxiety increased when Mama frowned, pursed her lips, but did not immediately respond. She had expected loud objections, insults, a diatribe about undutiful relations, or downright insistence that she do as she was told. Instead, the stillness was absolute.

'I thought as much,' she said, having drawn out the silence to its lengthiest extreme. 'I already told Sir Marius you would not do the sensible thing.'

Anne was confounded. 'You anticipated this, Mama, but do not mind?'

'Of course I mind, but what do you expect me to do about it? If it was only you being foolish it would be one thing, but I believe Fitzwilliam has fixed his interest elsewhere. It's as plain as a pikestaff.' Mama scowled at her nephew. 'Why the male members of this family will insist upon marrying for love is beyond my comprehension.'

'Now, Catherine,' Sir Marius chided.

Catherine? Anne and the colonel exchanged a glance. Neither of them had ever heard her addressed so informally before.

'Well then, miss, I suppose I had better find someone else for you.'

Anne took a deep breath. She had not intended to say anything about Pierce just yet, not until Mama had recovered from her disappointment. But with Sir Marius in the room, a gentleman who appeared to wield some influence with Mama and who had Pierce's best interests at heart, she might never have a better opportunity.

'Mama,' she said, lifting her head and finding the courage to meet her mother's gaze. 'I have already decided upon my future husband.'

'You have what?'

Colonel Fitzwilliam stood. 'Perhaps I should leave you to discuss this matter in private.'

'Stay, Fitzwilliam,' Mama commanded. 'I feel persuaded that someone will need to talk some sense into my silly daughter. I blame you for this,' she added, turning to Sir Marius.

'Me? What have I done?'

'I took on Mr Asquith on your recommendation, regardless of the fact the decision caused many raised eyebrows. Now see where it has landed us.'

'You have fixed your interest upon Asquith?' Sir Marius asked Anne in a kindly voice.

'Yes.' Anne elevated her chin another notch. 'He has proposed and I have accepted him.'

'You are not of age,' Mama said.

'No, but I soon will be.'

'Asquith has no money. He could never support you in the style to which you are accustomed, and I will not have him at Rosings.'

'He knows that. He does not want me for my money.'

'That's what he has told you, I have no doubt, but it cannot possibly be so.'

'Mama!'

'Be sensible, Anne. You know nothing of the ways of the world, or men like Asquith. Of course he says he is not interested in your wealth, but that cannot possibly be the case.'

'You are quite wrong. He will get another teaching position and I will go wherever he is.'

Mama snorted. 'You would not last a month. It is easy to say you do not care about living in luxury when you have never experienced anything else. When you face reality you will soon adopt a different view.'

'Since you asked me to remain, Lady Catherine, presumably I am permitted to express my view,' Colonel Fitzwilliam said.

'By all means, especially if you think you can talk some sense into her. The first attractive young man she meets and he has quite turned her head.' Mama shuddered. 'I must have been out of my senses, agreeing to take him on. At first, I thought it was a good thing he had brought Anne out of herself. I can see now he has done rather too good a job of it.'

'Actually, ma'am,' the colonel said, 'I wanted to enquire what your objections are to Asquith.'

'What they are?' Mama's glower was shared equally between the colonel and Anne. 'How can you be so obtuse? The man is a fortune hunter, the son of a Jamaican plantation manager looking to feather his own nest. He is intelligent and personable, I'll grant you that. But he is still a fortune hunter. Would you see Rosings reduced to being owned by such a man? A man of no family and no consequence? It would make us a laughingstock. Well, I won't have it. Do you hear me, miss?' Mama fixed Anne with the determined gaze that had always reduced her to silence on the few previous occasions when she had dared to disagree with her. This time it would not work because Anne was equally determined to have her way. 'If you insist upon this foolish action, I cannot prevent it once you reach your majority. But hear this, and hear it well: I shall disinherit you, and there's an end to the matter.'

'I know that, Mama, and so does Mr Asquith,' Anne said, fighting to retain her dignity, determined not to cry. 'It grieves me that we shall be estranged, but there is no help for that.'

'When he discovers I am serious, I think you will find his desire to marry you will wither on the vine. He will give you some charming excuse for breaking off the engagement and move on to another vulnerable young lady of fortune.'

Sir Marius, who had listened to this exchange without speaking, did so now. 'Before you absolutely refuse your consent, Catherine, perhaps you ought to know a little more about Asquith's history.'

'You also?' Mama turned to Sir Marius, but her expression softened. 'Does everyone think I enjoy denying my daughter her heart's desire? It is only that I know what is best for her, and she will thank me in years to come.'

'I take no sides, Catherine. I only ask you to hear me out. And since what I am about to tell you will come as news to Asquith as well, perhaps he ought to be present to hear it.'

'Very well.'

Anne could see that Mama's interest was piqued every bit as much as her own was.

'Ring the bell, Fitzwilliam. We will settle this matter now, this morning, once and for all.'

The footman who answered the bell was despatched to find Pierce. No one spoke while they waited for him to respond, but mercifully the wait was a short one. The moment Pierce walked into the room, bowed to Mama and Sir Marius then treated Anne to one of the slow, curling smiles she was persuaded he reserved exclusively for her, all her doubts and all her concerns about disappointing Mama evaporated. With Pierce beside her, she could achieve anything she set her mind to. Anything at all.

'Asquith, my daughter has just told me some preposterous story about the two of you marrying. Quite apart from the fact that you ought to have had the good manners to speak to me on the matter first, you must realise it is impossible. However, Sir Marius has something to say on the subject and wanted you to be here while he says it.' Mama transferred her attention to Sir Marius. 'We are all ears, Marius.'

Pierce took a seat beside Anne, curiosity forming the bedrock of his expression. They were not kept in ignorance of Sir Marius's news for long.

'I went to Jamaica as a young man.' Sir Marius's voice was firm and controlled, almost as though he had rehearsed what he planned to say. 'I had acceded to the baronetcy upon my father's death and also assumed his debts, which were substantial. Ergo, I had little other than my title, a few pounds in my pocket and a great disappointment to put behind me.' He stared at Mama as he said those final words, only increasing Anne's curiosity about their history, especially when Mama's face coloured and she looked away from him. 'I will admit I was reckless, and Jamaica was the right place for a young man to be reckless in those days. The more risks one was willing to take, the greater the rewards on offer. I also... Pardon me for mentioning such delicate matters, but I did not behave well. Or perhaps I should say, I behaved as many a young man would, once let loose to make his own way in the world and with a grudge to bear against it. Looking back, I regret some of the things I did – the corners I cut to make a start. But I hope I have atoned for those mistakes since growing older and wiser.'

'Speaking as one well acquainted with your plantation, sir,' Pierce replied, 'I think you certainly achieved that ambition.'

'Thank you, Pierce, but you do not know it all yet. When you do, you might not think so well of me. I will not offend your ears, ladies, by going into the particulars. Suffice it to say I sowed my wild oats.' He paused to rub his whiskered chin, looking embarrassed as he faced Pierce and spoke directly to him. 'The result of one such liaison is you.'

Anne's gasp was the only sound to break though the stultifying silence this admittance engendered.

'I... You are my father?'

'I have that honour, and it is one of the reasons why I have taken such an interest in you.'

Mama fanned herself rather violently but didn't look nearly as surprised as Anne felt, nor did she express her outrage. Instead, she looked thoughtful.

'There is so much I don't understand,' Pierce replied, shaking his head. 'How could I not have known? Why did you not say before now? Were you ashamed of me?'

'If you think I did not take you into my house for that reason, then you are quite wrong. I wished to do so the moment you were born. As Lady Catherine will tell you, I have never been one to shirk my responsibilities, but your mama would not hear of it. She wanted to keep you with her, and I could hardly refuse.'

'My father – I mean, the man I always thought was my father – was married to my mother when you... er—'

'Quite so. It was not my finest hour but I cannot regret I have you to remind me of it. I had sent him to England to act for me on plantation business, arranging markets for our sugar, and so forth. He was gone for a year.' Sir Marius cleared his throat. 'There is no doubt whatsoever about your being my son.'

'And my father, when he returned, just accepted what had happened?' Pierce widened his eyes. 'He did not care?'

'Oh, he cared. He loved your mother very much, just as he

loved you. It was your mama's most ardent wish to have a child and... well, he was unable to—'

'We understand, Marius,' Mama said briskly, with a significant glance in Anne's direction. 'We do not require to hear all the particulars.'

That is a great pity, Anne thought. She would very much like to know what the unfortunate man was unable to achieve. No matter, she would make Pierce tell her when they were next alone.

'Quite so.' Sir Marius took a sip of water. 'When the man you thought was your father died, you were just three years old. Your mama needed you more than ever, since she had no other children. But at least she then allowed me to take more of an active interest in your welfare, which is why you spent so much time with my children and why—'

'And why I enjoyed such a fine education. Thank you at least for that.'

'I never told you the truth because I promised your mother I would not. It took me a long time to establish my fortune, and she did not wish you to think yourself a gentleman's son and have expectations I was not in a position to fulfil. Now she is gone, and so is my own dear wife, which means I can publicly acknowledge you as mine and see you financially secure.'

Anne could see it was too much for Pierce to take in. She longed to reach for his hand and reassure him this was good news, but she dare not do so with her mother in the room.

'Are you against me too, Marius?' Mama asked, but Anne was astonished to see tears in her eyes.

'They are in love, Catherine,' Sir Marius replied softly. 'Any fool can see that.'

'Love, bah!'

'That is not what you once thought.'

'What is it, Mama?' Anne asked, unable to contain her curiosity. 'Were you once in love with Sir Marius?'

When Mama, who appeared to be lost in the past, made no response, it was Sir Marius's deep voice that intruded upon the silence. 'That, Catherine, is a very good question. I wonder what answer you will give.'

'Don't do this, Marius,' she snapped.

'You might as well tell us, Mama,' Anne said gently. 'Otherwise we will make up our own minds.'

'Oh, very well. If you must know, when I was younger than you are now, I met Sir Marius and Sir Lewis at a ball. They were childhood friends, and... Oh botheration, this is so difficult to talk about.'

'I flatter myself that Lady Catherine preferred me, but I was penniless, whereas Sir Lewis was not. Pressure was brought upon Catherine to do the sensible thing, which she did. To this day I have no idea if she regrets that decision.'

'And you cannot possibly expect me to tell you,' Mama replied with asperity and a slight smile.

'That is why you went to Jamaica and Mama was your great disappointment,' Anne said, her soft heart melting in sympathy.

'Quite right, my dear.' He turned to look at Mama. 'Well, Catherine, will you force history to repeat itself?'

Mama looked up at him. 'For history to repeat itself, I would have had to have been in love with you, much as you claim my daughter loves your son.'

'Were you?'

Sir Marius fixed Mama with a steady gaze she failed to meet, which was an answer in itself. Mama in love. Who would have thought it? Colonel Fitzwilliam sent Anne a probing glance. No wonder Mama was such a stickler for duty if she had been forced to give up the man she loved for its sake.

'I am not giving my permission for this marriage,' Mama said, almost reluctantly. 'But I will not dismiss Mr Asquith either. He may return to Rosings with us and we will see how matters progress.'

Anne's heart swelled. This was more than she had dared to expect, even in her wildest dreams. She felt Pierce smiling through his confusion and could easily imagine how his head must be reeling after Sir Marius's extraordinary revelations. He and that gentleman were now shaking hands, talking quietly together. Anne assumed they would need to talk for many hours more before Pierce learned everything he wished to know. She felt his glance repeatedly returning to her and knew he was desperate to hold her in his arms and celebrate their good fortune.

But it could wait. They had the rest of their lives to love one another.

22

Lizzy and Will were alone in the drawing room, enjoying the peace and solitude of Pemberley after the vicissitudes of the past few days. Jane and Bingley had left first thing that morning. Kitty and Georgiana had taken themselves off somewhere to get over the loss of Major Halstead and Captain Turner, who had returned to their regiment. And now Will and Lizzy had just waved off Lady Catherine and her entourage including, thankfully, Mr Collins.

'You are to be congratulated, Mrs Darcy,' Will said, stroking his wife's hair. 'Your guests were here for less than two weeks, but in that time you have managed to engineer two betrothals and keep Lady Catherine happy.'

'Just one betrothal,' Lizzy replied. 'Lady Catherine has not agreed to Anne's marriage.'

'No, but she will. There is little she will not do for Sir Marius, I think.'

'Yes, isn't it remarkable? I could scarce believe it when Colonel Fitzwilliam told me the particulars of their history. Perhaps it explains why Lady Catherine has always seemed so severe. She was disappointed in love and never recovered from that disappointment.'

'She seems quite rejuvenated now that Sir Marius is back in England.'

'Apparently he intends to purchase a small estate close to Rosings,' Lizzy replied mischievously.

'I know that smile, Mrs Darcy. Surely you do not expect my aunt to conduct herself with anything other than the utmost propriety?'

'I would like to imagine her behaving irresponsibly but even I am not that much of an optimist. Still, I am glad Sir Marius's company pleases her so much. He can make her laugh and I thought that was an achievement beyond anybody.'

'Well, I am glad Sir Marius has acknowledged Asquith as his own. I like the young man tremendously and he is very good for Anne. I have never seen anyone so altered.'

'Never underestimate the power of love, Mr Darcy.'

'I, of all people, ought to respect its potency,' he replied, placing a protective hand on the swell of Lizzy's belly. 'But I fear it has all been too much for you.'

'Nonsense, I greatly enjoyed playing the part of matchmaker. Not that there was much for me to do, other than listen to the afflicted parties singing the praises of their loved ones.'

'You speak of Fitzwilliam.'

'And Anne, too. Your cousin is at Briar Hall, making arrangements with his Mrs Sheffield to bring charges against her former brother-in-law.'

'Is that what they are calling it this week?'

Lizzy laughed. 'Well, at least Sheffield is no longer in our cellar but safely locked up in Newcastle gaol. For that I am very grateful.'

'Fitzwilliam is to sell his commission, you know, and settle down to being a man of property the moment he and Mrs Sheffield are married, which is to be as soon as the arrangements can be made, apparently.'

'I am very pleased to hear it. The colonel deserves to be happy, and Mrs Sheffield will make him so. I like her very much.'

'Mr Collins has a great deal of ground to make up with Asquith. He made no attempt to hide his disdain for him and now, if things turn out the way we expect them to, Asquith will eventually be the owner of Rosings, with Collins's fate in his hands.'

'If anyone can grovel his way out of a hole he has dug for himself, it is Mr Collins. However, Mr Asquith will suffer no interference from him, nor will he put up with false flattery.'

'Then life at Rosings will be very interesting.' Will massaged Lizzy's shoulders, causing her to moan and close her eyes. 'Where are the girls?'

'I have no idea. In one of their rooms I expect, discussing their paramours.'

Will frowned. 'Don't say that.'

Lizzy examined Will's face. 'You don't like Major Halstead very much, do you?'

'I don't think he is right for Georgiana, if that is what you are asking me.' Will removed one hand from her shoulders and waved it about. 'I know you think I am overprotective and that no one will be good enough for my sister, but there is just something about him that worries me. Don't ask me what it is because I couldn't tell you.' He shrugged. 'It is just an impression, I suppose.'

'If it puts your mind at rest, Kitty seems as keen as ever on Captain Turner, but I think Georgiana's interest in the major is on the wane.'

'Why do you say that?'

'I can't give you a reason, but I have noticed she no longer actively seeks his company.' Lizzy touched his face. 'You can stop worrying. Georgie has a great deal more sense than you give her credit for.'

'Then I shall take your advice, stop worrying about my sister and concentrate my concerns on you instead. You do too much, Lizzy. But from now until your confinement you will not move a muscle unnecessarily, or you will have me to answer to.'

Lizzy slid onto her husband's knee and wrapped her arms around his neck. 'For the sake of your sanity, my dear, I will do as you ask.'

Will grunted. 'Excuse me if I do not believe you.'

Lizzy laughed as she lowered her head in anticipation of his kiss. She counted her blessings, well aware how fortunate she was, even if her mother was still threatening to come north for Jane's confinement and remain for Lizzy's.

'You should believe me,' Lizzy said breathlessly when Will stopped kissing her. 'Because you are my life, my love, my entire reason for being, and I would never knowingly do anything to cause you anxiety.'

ABOUT THE AUTHOR

Eliza Austin is the Regency romance pen name of prolific, bestselling author Wendy Soliman. Wendy has written historical romance, revenge thrillers and cosy crime.

Sign up to Eliza Austin's mailing list for news, competitions and updates on future books.

Follow Eliza on social media here:

- facebook.com/wendy.soliman.author
- x.com/wendyswriter
- bookbub.com/authors/wendy-soliman

ALSO BY ELIZA AUSTIN

Pemberley Presents

Miss Bingley's Revenge

Lady Catherine's Demands

The Daring Miss Darcy

Kitty Bennet's Ruin

www.ingramcontent.com/pod-product-compliance
Ingram Content Group UK Ltd.
Pitfield, Milton Keynes, MK11 3LW, UK
UKHW012250290726
14090UKWH00016B/574